MW01031527

Tea With A Minotaur

Copyright

Copyright © 2023 Adrienne Hiatt

All rights reserved. No part of this book may be reproduced in any form or by any electronic or mechanical means, including information storage and retrieval systems, or be used in any way, including with or for AI, without permission in writing from the author. Reviewers may quote brief passages in a review.

Illustrator: Kaylee Becknell
Email: kayleebecknell.art@gmail.com

Editor: Crab Editing
Email: crabediting@gmail.com

Tea With A Minotaur

Adrienne Hiatt

Author's Note:

I use the word "minotaur" as both singular and plural, like "deer".

Some of the tea recipes contained in this book are real, while others have a bit of magic and fantasy to them. **<u>Please research each ingredient before recreating any of the recipes for yourself!</u>**

Much love and magic,
Adrienne

To the family we wish for,
The family we got,
And the family we choose.

To everyone who is still searching for their found family:
May you find what you are looking for.

And to all my neurodivergent and neurospicy readers:
May you feel seen, heard, accepted, and understood here,
between these pages.

ANCIENT RUINS

SUMMER CLAN CAMP

AZAR'S TUNNELS

CINNTIRE

OBELISK

MINOTAUR CLAN LANDS

KEKOROA CAMP

WINTER CLAN CAMP

ALINORK

WINDING WAY INN

MARKET

OSREALACH

THORIA

FAIRY LANDS

PUKA LANDS

Chapter 1

Minotaur are not meant to drink tea or daydream. Mahkai's father loved to remind him of this. Minotaur are proud and noble warriors, he insisted, often on a daily basis.

That was easy for the chief of the Makanui Clan to say. Corded, perfectly honed muscles covered every inch of his hulking four-meter frame. He was a bull among bulls, a beast among beasts. Quite the contrast to Mahkai's diminutive form. But he hadn't snuck into Aunti Lani's hut at the crack of dawn to think about his father.

Mahkai inhaled the sweet floral aroma wafting out of the stone cup Aunti Lani set before him. He grasped the cup with both of his small hands as memories of gathering honeysuckle blooms danced in his mind.

"Careful, dear, blow on it gently until it cools. It is much too hot to drink. It will burn your tongue, and then you won't be able to taste the sweet bread we spent all morning making." Aunti Lani winked. Her warm, brown eyes followed him as he carried his mug back to his stool situated in the corner of her humble kitchen.

"Yes, Aunti." He closed his eyes and inhaled deeply again. The warm stoneware between his hands grounded and comforted him, especially on a day like today, when icy rain drummed steadily outside and the fire did not quite chase the bone-deep chill out of their mud huts.

It was almost time to migrate to the winter pastures. Throughout every solarcycle, the minotaur clans migrated with their herds between their rainy and dry season huts. Mahkai didn't mind the migration so much, but most of the time it felt like a lot of "hurry up and wait."

He sighed and carefully sipped his tea as he watched Aunti Lani shuffle around the room, her honey brown shoulders stooped with age. She hummed a familiar tune as she prepared food for the clan dinner later that night. The packed dirt floor was worn smooth from decades of her hooves traveling back and forth from her worktable to the cookfire.

She danced and twirled across the room, stopping dramatically before him and offering her hand. He giggled as he set down his mug and let her pull him off his stool to dance with her. As her song reached its crescendo, Mahkai's eldest brother, Maleek, crashed through the door.

"There you are, Mahkai! I've been looking all over for you. Father is angry and sent me to come find you. You are late for training." Rivulets of water ran down his arms and legs, making puddles on the floor. His black fur, now a glossy obsidian, was plastered to his skin from the rain.

Mahkai huffed and shivered at the idea of going outside in this weather. "But I don't want to," he whined.

Maleek stomped over to him and grabbed his arm, hauling him to the door. "Father said not to return without you. I don't have time for your nonsense. The warriors are sparring with us today and I want to watch. Maybe they'll pick me to train with them next."

He peered around the kitchen and retrieved Mahkai's practice axe from where it rested, propped in the corner. The weapon looked small in his brother's hands—he was already large for his age. But it dwarfed Mahkai. The handle was longer than he was tall and weighed almost as much.

Maleek shoved it roughly into his hands. Mahkai balked, dropping it in the puddle his brother was making on the hut floor. Maleek gave Mahkai a look of exasperation. He scooped up the axe in one hand and grabbed Mahkai's arm with the other, dragging them out the door and into the pouring rain. "Hurry up, let's go." Maleek shoved the axe into Mahkai's arms again and stalked through camp toward the training grounds. His tail thrashed behind him in irritation.

Mahkai hunched his shoulders against the cold and squinted through the rain. He hated this. Why couldn't they just leave him alone and let him stay with Aunti Lani, inside, where it was dry and he could have all the tea and yummy snacks he wanted?

With a grumble under his breath, he trudged after his brother. Might as well get this over with. If their father sent Maleek rather than one of his other seven siblings, he was meant to be fetched sooner than later. Sometimes, Mahkai could divert his siblings long enough that they forgot about him, or at least long enough for him to make an escape. But not with Maleek.

Maleek was driven, focused, and never deterred from whatever he put his mind to. That was why he was to be the next clan chief after their father, not just because he was the oldest. Mahkai shivered again, but not from the rain. Being clan chief—or leading in general—was not something he aspired to.

The rain had slowed to a drizzle by the time they reached the training grounds, but Mahkai was no less miserable. His father raised an eyebrow at him, then frowned, his brow creasing between his wide-set dark eyes. Mahkai had given up trying to carry the heavy weapon and ended up dragging it behind him. He looked down at the muddy mess of it, then back up at his father towering over him.

"I will deal with you in a moment." His glare pinned Mahkai to the spot before he turned his attention to his eldest son. He pulled Maleek aside. Apprehension overrode Mahkai's misery from the cold and rain.

Mahkai could not hear his father's words, but his tone and

the rigid set of his dark brown shoulders said enough. Father was angry. But Father was always angry about something, it seemed. Maleek angrily huffed away to join some of the other sparring minotaur who were his age.

The rain poured harder, falling in giant, chilling drops. Mahkai wiped away the water dripping from his brow into his eyes, huffing at the futility of his actions. The steam from his breath curled in front of him, punctured by the fat drops. Mahkai huffed again, entranced by the beautiful yet fleeting patterns. He wondered what else he could do with the mist.

"I don't like you spending so much time with Aunti Lani." Father's deep voice rumbled as he turned his intense and weighty gaze back to Mahkai.

"Why?" Mahkai asked, dragging his attention to his father—or as much as he could manage at the moment. It wouldn't do to be caught not paying attention when Father was in this mood.

"Because she is teaching you very un-minotaur-like habits. Minotaur don't drink tea. We don't pick flowers. And we definitely don't frolic. We are warriors"—he pounded his fist on his chest—"and you need to start acting like it. Get your head out of the clouds and focus on what is important. From now on, you will train with me every day." He placed a giant hand on Mahkai's slim shoulder and his face softened a fraction. "Do you understand?"

"Yes, Father." Mahkai hunched his shoulders and shrank away from him.

"Good. Now go clean your weapon. I don't want to see it in that state again."

Mahkai hefted his oversized weapon as best he could and trudged dejectedly toward the tent covering the weapons racks on the other side of the training field.

Tranquili-Tea

Lavender
Feverfew
Nettle
Rosemary
Sage
White Willow Bark

Reduces headaches and sore muscles.
Use this tea after war games and sparring. Can be
brewed the night before and consumed cold if needed.

-Lani

Chapter 2

Minotaur are not meant to drink tea and daydream of frolicking in the forest. Well, that was exactly what Mahkai planned to do—what he wished he were doing right now, in fact—for the rest of the day after this. His heart pounded loudly in his ears as he crouched behind the boulder on the edge of the field. He wiped his sweaty palms on his leather war kilt. Not a lot of good it did, though. What he would give to be wearing his soft linen pants and loose shirt instead of this stifling leather armor.

He re-adjusted his grip on his double-headed battle axe and risked a peek around the edge of his cover. They hadn't found him yet.

Good. He was getting better at hiding, though they always found him in the end and forced him to fight them—if you could call it a fight.

He scoffed, then sniffed. *What is that delicious aroma?* He inhaled deeply but still could not place it. Mahkai glanced around, and seeing no one in the immediate vicinity, he crept toward the tantalizing scent. The soft grass underfoot was cool and damp in the early morning; the sun had not yet burned off the morning dew. He hesitated at the edge of the forest. It was easier to hide in here but also easier to be caught unaware.

He knew he should stay by his boulder where he could see his intended assailants' approach. Indecision warred inside him, rooting him to the spot. His teammates were counting on him. He should stay, but that scent was so interesting—sharp yet sweet, like crushed pine needles and nectar. It called to him. He needed to know what it was.

"There!" a deep bass voice boomed across the field.

His shoulders tensed with dread and disappointment. They had found him sooner than expected. He turned to face the owner of the voice lumbering toward him: a hulking beast with the broad head of a bull and the torso of a man. His twisted horns glinted savagely in the morning light, his dark, wide-set eyes locked on him.

Mahkai swallowed nervously and hefted his heavy weapon into a defensive stance. He knew how this would end. A bead of sweat rolled down his forehead and continued its way down the side of his nose. It tickled. He wiped at it with his wrist, drawing his attention away from the quickly approaching figure.

His assailant chose that moment to lower their head and charge, quickly covering the final distance between them. Mahkai snapped his attention back to the oncoming threat and barely raised his axe in defense before they crashed together.

Faster than Mahkai's brain could register, he was pinned to the ground under the weight of his much larger opponent. His axe went flying, but all Mahkai could focus on was breathing. His lungs had forgotten their purpose. He thrashed in panic, blinking to clear his vision, which was rapidly going dark on the edges, but it did not help.

Suddenly, the pressure on his chest lifted. He could breathe again. Mahkai wheezed and coughed, and his brother's face gradually came back into focus.

"Oh, Mahkai. I didn't mean to hit you quite that hard. I forgot how much smaller you are." Maleek rose and planted a fist on his hip, leaning casually against his own axe. Something like guilt or concern flickered across his face, but Mahkai wasn't entirely sure, as it was gone as quickly as it appeared.

Mahkai attempted to sit up but groaned as his body voiced

its disapproval. He contemplated a retort, but his lungs were still too busy relearning how to function. He settled for waving his hand instead. It was for the best. His retorts never came out as witty as they sounded in his head.

Maleek took the hint and grasped Mahkai's forearm, hauling him to his feet. "You know, you really shouldn't let yourself get so easily distracted." He smacked Mahkai on the back a few times. "What if I had been an actual enemy, like a bloodthirsty puka or a fairy?"

Mahkai glanced at him out of the corner of his eye as he brushed grass and leaves from his armor. "I thought Father and the other clan leaders were in peace talks? Did they fall through again?"

"You know how the fairies are. They dangle peace in front of everyone but go back on it when they don't get their way. I say we storm—"

"Maleek!" Mahkai interrupted. "Don't say things like that."

"Why? The others are saying it." He looked around and leaned in. Satisfied there was no one in hearing distance, he dropped his voice to barely above a whisper.

"There are many of us across all five clans who are unsettled. Demanding that we do more than just talk. They—we—are tired of the fairies and puka controlling Thoria." Maleek's eyes glittered dangerously. "They are intentionally keeping minotaur and other fae out of the revealing ceremonies. Intentionally keeping us from having magic. Limiting our powers!"

"But—" Mahkai tried to interject. This was quickly getting out of hand.

"When was the last time you heard of a minotaur gaining strong magical abilities? They are limiting us, I tell you." Maleek stamped the handle of his axe on the ground to punctuate his statement. His declaration sliced through the relative silence, making his words seem louder.

"That isn't how it works," Mahkai challenged his eldest brother.

Maleek lowered his voice again. "Are you sure? What if they are? We don't actually know how it works."

"Does anyone?" Mahkai muttered, digging his hoofed toe into the grass. He struggled to meet his eldest brother's eyes, the intensity of his gaze making Mahkai want to shrink away from the controversial topic.

"I bet they do. I bet they are keeping all the power to themselves in order to control us. We won't stand for it. I say we storm Thoria and take what is rightfully ours!" His voice took on a similar tone to the one their father used when trying to convince the clan leaders of the validity of one of his ideas.

"Aren't the clan leaders meeting with the rest of the fae to work that out?" Mahkai asked. "I thought that was what they left for."

"That's all they ever do—talk. No, it's time for us to do something. Take action," Maleek snorted.

"This isn't what Father would want." Mahkai tried a different approach, pleading with his eyes that Maleek would heed him.

"This is exactly what Father would want. He's always pushing us to take action, initiate, preempt. Just think of it like the war games we play. What is Father always saying about that?" The cunning light shining in his brother's eyes reminded Mahkai of a fox laying in wait for its unsuspecting prey. Mahkai shivered.

"The side that makes the first move and outmaneuvers the other, wins," Mahkai parroted with a sigh.

"Exactly. Don't worry, little brother. I got this. When we come back with all the glory and power we deserve, they will sing songs about us 'til the end of time. They will carve our deeds into the very foundations of the mountains, telling of how the minotaur are the mightiest of the fae. And then you can write about our triumphs in those books of yours, too."

Mahkai frowned. He had a bad feeling about this, but like always, his brother was not inclined to listen.

Right-as-Rain

Calendula Flowers
Dandelion Leaf
Hawthorn Berry
Lavender
Lemongrass
Marshmallow Root

Will keep a runny nose and chills at bay. Soothing and warming tea for snuggling up after you've been out in the rain—like how you feel looking up into the sky as warm rain falls onto your fur—or soothing and calming when you are cuddled up at home listening to rain on the roof.

-Lani

Chapter 3

Mahkai squinted at his hastily scribbled notes in his tiny grass hut, one of many huts dotting the hillside in orderly rows on the edge of the forest. He sat hunched over a small wooden table, notebooks full of sketches and daydreams spread around him. Steam curled gently upwards from the cup of tea at his elbow.

He was copying his notes from the clan leaders' meeting earlier that day. His father had invited him to listen, saying it would be good for him to hear what went into leading the clans—under the condition he did not interrupt or pester anyone with his incessant questions.

Mahkai couldn't help himself. He wanted to know and document everything; he *needed* to. He liked the way reading made him feel—seen, heard, and sometimes even understood—and loved learning new things. Relying on the history keepers to revisit particular details was tenuous at best. They tended to get annoyed with him when asked to show the same segment repeatedly while he took copious notes.

Mahkai did not understand why. Using their magic to re-play scenes from past events was not all that taxing, was it? They made it look so easy. But, in any case, he liked writing and sketching in his books made from thick tree-bark or leather with pages of pressed wood pulp.

He was running low on paper and would need to ask his cousin Kamea for more when she came back from her travels. She patrolled the western beaches of Osrealach and always found some of the most wonderful things. He gazed fondly at the row of oddities she had brought him. Bits of strangely twisted driftwood, a piece of coral, small rocks that sparkled in the sunlight, and translucent shards of glass in varying colors.

The rest of the clan gave her a hard time for humoring him, but she paid them no mind. He was her favorite. Unlike the others, she didn't mind his questions. She patiently told him all about what she saw, heard, smelled, and even tasted on her travels. She said it kept her sharp—more aware of her surroundings.

The whistle on his tea pot shattered the comfortable silence, and he rose to remove it from the fire. Another present she had brought him. She said it washed up on the shore among the driftwood.

He downed his first cup of tea, now at the perfect temperature to drink, enjoying the way the liquid seemed to warm him from the inside. Dropping a thistle flower and tea leaves into his now empty cup, he poured the steaming water over it and spooned a heaping scoop of honey from its small clay jar into his brew. This was his favorite honey he'd found so far. Nevermind it was a three-day round trip to get to the beehive from the clan's summer pastures.

The bees gathered nectar from the flowers that grew on the slopes of the far training grounds. He had to build a fire and smoke the bees so they would not sting him. The stings did not bother him so much, but he was afraid of hurting them if he swatted them by accident.

Mahkai inhaled the delicious aroma beginning to waft out of his cup and hmmed in pleasure. The steady drumming of the rain pouring outside felt cathartic and tranquil. Rainy days were the best for curling up in his favorite chair with a book or his sketchbook and sipping tea from his favorite mug.

He had just returned to his notes when his front door slammed open.

"Mahkai! There you are!" Mort, another of Mahkai's brothers, charged in. "What are you doing here? You should be outside with the rest of the family. We are playing war games!" Chocolate brown eyes glimmered with almost giddy excitement at the coming competition. His dark brown fur was sopping wet, and his grass-stained leather war kilt was splattered with mud—possibly even blood. He shifted from hoof to hoof, practically vibrating with energy.

Mahkai shivered just thinking of going outside in this weather.

"Not now, Mort! I'm busy." The wind blew through the open door, sending papers flying everywhere. "Oh dear!" Mahkai jumped up to collect them before they could blow outside—or worse, into his fireplace.

A page landed on the floor in front of Mort. Unaware, he stepped forward onto the sheet of paper as he continued. "Busy with what? What could you possibly want to do that would be more fun or important than war games?"

Mort, like so many of his family members, didn't understand or appreciate Mahkai's preference for other interests outside of the never-ending rounds of pointless competition.

An exasperated cry escaped Mahkai's lips as muddy water soaked into the page. He glanced up at his middle brother towering over him from his crouched position on the floor. "You know, it is considered polite to announce one's self before barging into someone's home. Besides, no one wants me on their team, anyway." He stuffed the stack of stray papers into the nearest bag and made a mental note to sort them out later.

"Aye. I've tried that and you don't answer, so I'll stick with this, thanks." Mort shrugged. "Besides, it doesn't matter. Family stuff is most important; you should be there. What do you need all this stuff for, anyway?" He gestured to all of Mahkai's books and tea paraphernalia scattered around the small room. "Where are all your weapons?"

Mahkai pointed to the corner, where his long-handled mace was currently acting as a cloak rack. His battle axes served occasionally as laundry drying racks, but at the moment they were weights for several newly bound book covers, a hobby he'd been experimenting with.

Mort gasped. "Don't let Father see that. He'd be furious." He shook his head incredulously.

"As opposed to his normal angry self?" Mahkai muttered under his breath. His older brother didn't seem to hear. He was too busy preening himself in the reflection glass Mahkai had hanging on the wall near the door. Mort flicked his ears, flared his nostrils, and glared at his reflection. He thought it made him look more intimidating. Mahkai thought it made him look ridiculous but refrained from telling him as much.

"Yes, fine. I'll be there shortly." Mahkai sighed in resignation and rubbed the space between his ear and the base of his horn. He could feel a headache building just thinking about it. He turned to put away the rest of his books wrapped in oilcloth in his chest on the dirt floor.

Mort brightened. "Excellent." He turned to leave, but paused for a moment, turning back to face him. "Don't wear that, though." He pointed to Mahkai's outfit, then turned and swiftly strode out, not bothering to close the door.

Mahkai grumbled under his breath, then closed the door behind him. He leaned his back against it and sighed. He hated war games. They were sweaty and bloody and tended to be very messy.

He looked down at his garments and frowned. He was rather fond of his attire; he wore his favorite forest green, sleeveless vest over a cream-colored tunic from which the top lacing had come loose again. At some point, he had rolled the sleeves up to keep from getting charcoal or ink on them.

He wore his most comfortable pants, but they looked nice due to the silver buttons he had added to the closure on the outside of his hocks to keep them in place. Earlier, he had removed his crimson scarf he normally wore wrapped around his waist. It now hung from the rafters, cradling a handful of drying flower petals.

He was not against getting dirty for the right reasons—like kneeling in the dirt to sketch a new flower or climbing a tree to watch the way a bird catches different drafts of air.

Unlike the rest of his kin, he did not like rolling around in the mud, pretending to try to kill each other just to say they could. But his family insisted he participate, even though they were always disappointed in his less-than-stellar performance.

It was not as if he did not try, but he just never got the hang of it. How could he be expected to focus on fighting one of his brothers while a kaleidoscope of butterflies fluttered over a sunny field? Besides, what was the point of war games? It was a useless waste of energy, in his opinion.

The games began with a ceremonial war dance, full of shouting, stomping, and slapping themselves. Mahkai always thought it was ridiculous, until his clan faced off against another clan and performed the dances. It was intense and quite moving.

After the war dance, they would partake in a series of challenges, each more difficult than the last, meant to push their bodies and test their minds. There were challenges for teams and individual challenges, everything from one-on-one combat to a complicated version of capture-the-flag.

Huffing to release the stress building in his chest and shoulders, he picked up the ruined papers off the floor. He could just make out the last line, but the rest of the page was a muddy hoof print in the middle of swirls of smudged ink. It was actually kind of beautiful in its own way. He tilted his head and blinked a couple of times.

That gave him an idea! He wondered if he could replicate the image, only with other colors. Could he intentionally make ink run where he wanted to and make other patterns? What kind of tool or brush could he use? Out of the corner of his eye, he caught a glimpse of the end of his tail and thought about the shape of brushes.

Stuffing the sheet into his nearby bag, he noticed the remnant of a stain from one of his paints that had leaked. He had spent days trying to get the stain out of his clothes and bag, but the fabric had readily soaked up the liquid and held it there.

That gave him another idea. Could he dehydrate pigments and only have to carry around little vials of powder to add to water or oil whenever needed? It would be far preferable to worrying about inks spilling in his pack. For that very reason, he had taken to mostly carrying sticks and nubs of charcoal. They were prone to crumbling if he was too careless with slinging his bags around, but they didn't stain nearly as badly. The drive to test his ideas burned in his chest as he thought about all the possibilities.

He grabbed his cloak and his favorite bags and stuffed them with some of his favorite notebooks and a handful of charcoal nubs and sticks. He strapped his knife belt to his hip and stuffed more items in another bag, making mental lists of the flowers and roots he would need to test his ideas.

Something nagged at the back of his mind. Wasn't he meant to be doing something? Going somewhere? He shook his head. He would remember what that was later. This idea and the possible implications were too important. This could be revolutionary for written communication, not to mention the many other uses it might have.

Exuberance buzzed through him as he slipped out the door and trotted toward the forest. He loved this. No one seemed to understand his love of learning new things. But he could not help himself; it was exhilarating. They ridiculed him for all the time he spent taking notes and documenting things. They did not see the point when they had historians who could magically recall anything from their history.

Mahkai wished he had received history magic rather than what he had gotten: air magic, and very weak air magic at that. Other Aerophyte could move whole carts or pallets of things from one place to another. They could create impenetrable barriers for shields in combat. The strongest could even change the weather. All he could manage were little eddies of wind that refused to behave and only caused him grief—and almost never on purpose.

Mahkai pushed his frustration away, choosing to focus on his mounting excitement. He could not wait to see all the things he could do with this. He hurried down the well-worn path through the trees and waved to a couple of calves—minotaur children—sending tiny boats made of leaves and sticks down the creek.

"Where are you going today, Mahkai?" A little girl with bright lavender eyes and glossy ebony horns poking out of dark, curly brown hair waved to him as he shuffled by.

"Oh hello, Molly." He paused to watch their boats float downstream. "I'm going to find more flowers to make colors to draw with."

"Oh, that sounds interesting."

"It is! I'm unsure as to what I will find, but it will be an adventure nonetheless." He took a few steps away, then turned back. "Oh, might I suggest you add a small sail to your boat next time? It will catch the air and propel it faster. And choose a more glossy leaf as your primary hull."

"Thank you, Mahkai! I'll try that." She grinned up at him and raced off.

He smiled back at her, then hurried on his own way.

Once fully in the cover of the trees, he lowered the hood on his cloak, gently lifting the holes cut out for his horns over the points, and loosened his grip on the part of his cloak covering his satchel. He probably made an odd silhouette for anyone who didn't know what he was. Would humans tell stories of the great deformed monster with horns deep in the forest? He chuckled to himself at the thought.

The occasional raindrop found its way through the thick treetops far above, but otherwise, it was quite pleasant. His mind was full of possibilities as he trotted down the path. Could he make colors with berry juice? What about flower petals? What gave flowers their color? Why those colors rather than another? He paused to take out his notes and charcoal to jot down his thoughts when a loud crash interrupted his musings.

Quickly, he tucked his notes into his satchel. "Hello?" His question was met with silence.

Hesitantly, he took a few steps toward the sound, unsure if he should pursue it or keep going on his way. He had gone much further than he intended, and he was unfamiliar with this part of the Cinntire Wood.

The forest was quiet. He inhaled deeply, enjoying the scent of damp earth and the peculiar smell he found only in the forest. There was a minty undertone to the fragrant pine and cedar that rose around him from the needles underfoot.

He knelt to gather some on a whim. Would they taste as good as they smell? What about in tea? He knew some of his kin used the sap to help hold things together. What else could it be used for? He pulled out one of the empty clay pots from his bag and used a stick to coax some of the sap from a nearby tree into it.

Mahkai placed everything back into his bag. He hummed a little melody under his breath. Kamea sang it the other night over the fire. Now it was stuck on repeat in his mind and would not leave. Not that he really objected. There were worse things to be stuck on.

A soft, distressed *toot* interrupted the next line of his song. It sounded again, a little louder this time, followed by a high-pitched trill. He'd never heard this particular bird call before. He guessed it might be an owl, but he wanted to see for himself to be sure. What was it doing awake at this time of day? Weren't owls nocturnal? Would it let him sketch it?

Ducking under low-hanging vines and branches, he followed the hoots to a small sinkhole in the middle of a clearing. Moss-covered roots grew twisted and gnarled across the opening. The bird call sounded like it was coming from the edge of the hole.

"Begging your pardon, were you calling to me? Where are you?" he asked, feeling silly all of a sudden. It was probably just calling for its family.

It trilled again, sounding almost excited. Mahkai climbed over a few larger roots as he attempted to move closer to the edge. He took extra care to watch where he stepped, the mossy ground and rocks being slick under his hooves from the rain.

Maybe it was a puka. They were supposed to be able to shift into bird shapes, among other things. He hoped that was not the case. Puka and minotaur were not on the most peaceful terms as of late, even though he would be thrilled to meet one any other time than when he was alone, deep in the forest. He had an abundance of questions he wished to ask.

Taking hold of the closest root that looked sturdy enough to hold him, he leaned over the edge. Caught in a tangle of roots was the smallest owl he had ever seen, peering up at him with large, soulful eyes.

Vitali-Tea

Cardamom
Cinnamon
Fennel
Ginger
Lemongrass
Licorice
Rosebuds
Saffron
Sencha Leaves
Tulsi

Energizing and stimulating to increase blood
flow, circulation and vitality.
                    -Mahkai

Chapter 4

"Well hello there," Mahkai greeted the little owl. "I don't want to intrude, but do you require assistance?"

Goldenrod eyes, surrounded by white-speckled dark brown feathers, blinked up at him. If owls were like other birds, he guessed this was a she-owl based on its camouflaging spots and the dark brown stripes on its head and chest. If she hadn't been calling out, or if the light hadn't reflected in her eyes, he might have overlooked her entirely.

Little tufts of feathers raised on the side of her head at a slight rustle of leaves behind him. The wind shifted, and he caught the scent of a cat. Slowly, he got to his feet, eyes scanning the area around him as his hand reached for the knife on his belt. A long black tail disappeared into the undergrowth. The fur along his neck prickled as his ears swiveled, listening for any indication of the predator's approach.

He'd never seen a forest cat before, but his clan warned about cats large enough to take down a lone minotaur. The fact that *he* was a lone minotaur in an unfamiliar part of the forest was not lost on him.

Another rustle sounded behind him, and he whipped around to face it. Or he would have, except his foot caught on a root and sent him crashing to the ground. A lithe, black body sailed over him and into the undergrowth, narrowly missing him as he lay sprawled out among the roots, heart pounding loudly in his chest.

Bright emerald eyes appeared in the shadows before him

as he sat up. An enormous black panther prowled towards him. Mahkai scrambled backwards, putting as much distance between himself and the giant cat as possible.

His hand slipped on the mossy root and he fell backwards, headfirst into the hole. He hit a few roots on the way down and then landed heavily on his back. He stared dazedly at the trees above him. The panther snarled down at him and paced back and forth around the opening of the hole ten meters above him but made no move to follow. He must have gotten turned around. He thought the hole was further away.

Mahkai's side ached where he'd landed on a particularly bumpy root. Sitting up slowly, he attempted to wipe the mud, moss, and grime from his hands and trousers, but only succeeded in smearing it around. He sighed, then chuckled as the realization hit him. He was worried over the state of his clothes when he had just narrowly escaped a panther attack.

He chided himself, hearing his father's voice in his head, telling him he was being careless—reckless even. Shaking his head, he assessed himself for injuries. He checked his satchel as well. The front cover of one of his books was damaged. He would need to replace it when he got home. Everything seemed to be okay otherwise. A few of his charcoals had crumbled, but they were still usable for shading in his sketches.

He looked up at the panther still prowling the mouth of the sinkhole. "Would you mind if I sketched you? You see, you are magnificent, and I would very much like to remember what you looked like for my journal."

The large black cat continued to prowl but made no indication it understood him. No matter. He was not going anywhere anytime soon, it seemed.

He watched the panther pace, drawing as many details as he could while it was in sight. At some point, the panther disappeared. Thankfully, he had the important bits done and only needed to do the shading and minor details. Mahkai worked quickly, worried there might be another way into the pit.

A quiet hoot beside him startled him out of his drawing. "Oh my. Hello. My pardon, I had quite forgotten you were here. How did you get down here?" he asked the owl.

She hopped toward him and hooted softly again, tilting her head as she stared at his sketch of the panther in his lap. She held one of her wings at an odd angle.

"Oh dear, are you injured?" Slowly, he reached out to touch her wing.

She trilled in alarm and hopped out of reach.

"My apologies. That was rude of me. I only meant to explore what might be wrong, but only if you will allow it." He placed his sketch in his book, wrapped it all in the oilcloth, and replaced it in his satchel.

He looked up. "Well, I suppose it is time to climb out and see if the cat is still stalking us."

The little owl hooted at him, then turned and hopped a little ways away, then turned back and trilled. Mahkai stood and stretched his limbs. They were stiff from sitting still for so long on the ground. He combed leaves out of the tuft of hair at the end of his tail, its color a reddish chestnut like the rest of him. She hopped closer, blinked at him once, then turned back and hopped a meter away.

"Do you wish me to follow you?" he asked.

She continued away from him, but with two strides he caught up to her. She darted through a space between roots and hooted at him. He peered through the tangled green and brown mass before him. "Is that a tunnel? Splendid, simply splendid." He clasped his hands in delight. "I was not keen on climbing up the slippery roots and branches." He pulled back some roots, ducking under others. After a few minutes of struggling, he was through the barrier and inside the tunnel. His fur was now slick with sweat mixed with mud and grime.

"Let's find out where it leads, shall we?"

The owl hopped forward a few steps, then hopped back to him and hooted expectantly. He crouched next to her. "I don't...erm...speak owl, unfortunately," he said sheepishly. She hopped next to him and butted his leg with her beak and flapped her wings.

"I...don't understand," he said, perplexed.

She ruffled her feathers and nudged him again with her beak. He reached toward her, and this time she did not run away; instead, she stepped into his palm. Startled, he almost dropped her, but her tiny talons gripped his finger.

"Well, I am to carry you, it seems." With a pleased smile, he rose slowly so as to not dislodge her and began following the tunnel. He was curious, awestruck. How did it get here? Was it naturally formed, or did someone put it here? Where did it lead? Were there more tunnels throughout the forest? Did his clan know about them?

He ducked around a few roots in the dimly lit tunnel and searched the floor for dead branches or something he could use as a torch. So far, enough light filtered in through holes in the ceiling to guide his path, but he would need a light source if it got much darker. His horn snagged on a root above him and he stumbled. "Perhaps I should slow down to avoid more potential hangups," he mused aloud to his new companion. She trilled softly in agreement.

Breathing a sigh of relief, he paused to inspect the walls of the tunnel in a particularly bright spot and noticed faint designs carved into the stones. They seemed old, like they had been carved long ago and had gradually worn away. He had not noticed them at first, because they merely seemed like pitting in the weathered stone. As he looked closer, a particular section resembled familiar constellations interspersed with swirls and shapes.

He transferred the little owl to his shoulder and pulled out a fresh page and a stick of charcoal. He attempted to make a rubbing, but the carvings were too faint, so he ended up drawing them individually. Further on, he found depictions of animals, fae, and even minotaur.

Exhilaration bubbled in his chest. He had no idea what they meant, but it was all very fascinating. He blinked in the quickly dwindling light. The sun was setting. *Have I really been here that long?* He was no stranger to losing track of time.

"Well,"—he tilted his head to look at the tiny bird on his shoulder—"shall we continue on or stay here?"

She did not answer; she had fallen asleep somewhere along their journey.

Gently, so not to wake her, he scooped her from his shoulder and tucked her into the top of his satchel. He removed his scarf and arranged it around her like a nest so she would be comfortable.

Apprehension, restless tension grew steadily in his chest the longer he trudged on in the growing darkness. *Is there an end to the tunnel? Should I turn back and try to climb out of the pit? Is the panther still there?* His pulse pounded in his ears until he was seeing shapes in every shadow.

He snorted and shook his head to clear the images and started reciting various types of trees and what they looked like, starting with his favorites. By the time he had gotten halfway through his favorite broadleaf types, his heartbeat was calm, his breathing had steadied, and he no longer wanted to jump out of his skin at every turn.

He continued to follow the tunnel until he could no longer see. "Well, I supposed I should find a place to rest for the night," he muttered to himself through a yawn as he felt along the wall of the tunnel. The stone here was warmer than where he had been previously. He yawned again. He was sure it was important, or at the very least, interesting, but he would write it down tomorrow.

A warm breeze caressed his face, and he braced his back against the wall and slid to the floor, happy to be off his feet. He scolded himself for not taking a break sooner. Like always, he had gotten so caught up in the excitement of it all, he had forgotten to take care of himself.

☕ ☕ ☕

The next morning, he awoke to little bird feet hopping up and down his arm, talons gently prickling his skin. He blinked repeatedly to clear the sleep from his eyes. His mouth tasted stale and his breath was probably not much better.

Rummaging through his pack, he found his horn of tea and opened it. The delicate minty flavor greeted him and he hummed his pleasure as he drank deeply, straight from the horn, not bothering with his cup.

A little chirrup broke into his thoughts. "Oh, begging your pardon, would you like some? It never occurred to me that an owl might drink tea. Do you? Drink tea, that is…" He trailed off as he pulled out his cup, filled it, and held it toward her. She hopped down his arm and stepped lightly onto the rim with her tiny claws.

Mahkai watched in wonder as the little owl delicately dipped her beak into the tea repeatedly. When they had both drunk their fill, he stood and brushed off the leaves clinging to his clothes. He surveyed the surrounding tunnel. Light filtered through the cracks around the gnarled, twisting roots that had forced their way through the stone and dirt. The roots continued down the sides of the stone walls and along the floor, but could not penetrate the smooth stone floor. That was interesting. The mass of roots completely covered the walls in some places.

Mahkai inhaled the sweet, earthy morning air and twisted his head and shoulders until his neck and back gave a series of satisfying pops.

Something was nagging at the back of his mind. He had the distinct impression he was meant to be somewhere.

He gasped. *The war games.* It had completely slipped his mind with the excitement of coming to the forest. He groaned. Mort would never let him hear the end of this. He trotted down the tunnel, looking for anything resembling a way out. If he could locate a way out of the tunnels, he could get his bearings and find his way home.

There. A large part of the ceiling had collapsed and looked wide enough for him to squeeze through. He thanked the stars he was not as large as his siblings, otherwise he would not fit. He scrambled through the hole, but his satchel caught on a protruding root and ripped. Some of his books dropped back down to the tunnel floor. Thankfully, their protective oilcloth stayed wrapped around them.

He wished he could use his wind magic to lift the books through the hole back up to him. It couldn't hurt to try, could it? Mahkai narrowed his eyes in concentration and reached out his hand, visualizing what he wanted, just like he'd been instructed all his life. He reached inside himself, feeling for the "something" within that would let him access his magic.

He waited…and waited. He blew out a breath of frustration. It did not matter how many times he did this exercise, he simply could not summon his magic—on purpose, at least.

It seemed at the least opportune moments his magic popped up and got him into trouble, unlike everyone else who had mastered at least the basics of their magic within a year of their Revealing Ceremony. He grumbled a very un-bull-like sound and gave up, then began shimmying back through the gap. The rocks and roots snagged and scraped his fur as he lowered himself gently.

Or, he would have, if he hadn't misjudged how much further to the tunnel floor he still had to go. His hooves hit the stone and slipped on the damp leaves, landing painfully on his tail. He groaned, rolled over on his side, and picked himself and his books off the floor.

The little owl hooted, peering down at him with her large golden eyes that made up more than half her face. He inspected his satchel. It was ripped down the seam on the side, but he thought he might be able to mend it well enough to get home. He stuffed everything back into it and wrapped it up, then tossed it through the hole to the ground above.

He took his time climbing out. His body ached from his fall. Once out, he sat on the edge, catching his breath and taking stock of his injuries. Other than a bruised tail and pride, he seemed to be no worse for the wear.

The little owl hopped up his arm and onto his shoulder and made a satisfied little chirp. With a grunt, he lurched to his hooves and retrieved his belongings. He leaned against a lovely birch tree while he sketched a diagram of the hole. He wanted to remember every detail so he might return with better provisions and continue where he left off.

After he finished, he wrapped his cloak around the torn bag and tucked it under his arm. He turned in circles for a few moments, attempting to find his bearings. He was pretty sure he needed to travel south. Preferably, he would find the path he had taken to get here, but would fight through the undergrowth if he had to.

Luckily, he did not have to. A few minutes of shuffling among the trees, following every deer and rabbit trail later, he found evidence of a lightly used path. Memories of the close encounter with the panther flashed in his mind and he hurried his steps as fast as he dared.

His mind whirled with all the things he had seen in the tunnels, trying to puzzle them out as he trotted home in the morning light. Every once in a while, the little owl repositioned herself on his shoulder, but was otherwise content. He wondered briefly why she did not fly away now that they were out of the tunnels, but he was too happy for her company to question it overly much.

Sunrise Tea

Butterfly Blue Pea Flower
Anise
Licorice
Fennel
Currant
Rosehip
Hibiscus
Star Anise
Nettle
Jasmine

For fun and alternate flavor, add citron and watch it change from purple to fuschia. Mul-tea-colored tea, if you will.
                                        -Mahkai

Chapter 5

Several hours later, just after Fiera had passed the highest point and began her descent toward the far horizon, minotaur and owl companions reached the end of the forest. Familiar rolling green hills dotted with clusters of huts greeted them.

Mahkai set his cloak-wrapped bundle in a tree hollow and shifted the sleeping owl from his shoulder, nestling her into his other pack alongside the first.

He tensed as several figures approached. He caught sight of Mort and attempted to make eye contact, but Mort avoided his gaze. Confusion and disappointment flashed across his face for a moment, then was gone. He turned away from Mahkai and hurried into the main hut.

Guilt tinged with shame warred in Mahkai's chest and burned in his cheeks. He hadn't meant to break his promise, but now his brother was mad at him.

"Where have you been?" Mahkai's father bellowed across the remaining distance between them. Even from this far, Mahkai saw his nostrils flare repeatedly, clenching and unclenching his jaw, as he thundered toward Mahkai. The fur on the back of his neck stood on end.

Mahkai cringed. He felt aflame and chilled all at once under his father's stern, bloodshot gaze.

"We were about to send the search parties out for you. Follow me." He stomped away toward the center of the cluster of huts, his tail thrashing back and forth in displeasure, not waiting to see if Mahkai followed.

Mahkai did indeed follow his father into his hut. He took a deep breath, bracing himself for the encounter before entering the spacious enclosure.

A stone table covered with maps and other important scrolls and books occupied the center of the room. Several stone chairs and wooden stools stood scattered around the table for the frequent elders' meetings.

Mahkai only spent time here when he was in trouble, so he was not terribly surprised that his stomach felt like he had been eating rocks when, in fact, he had yet to eat anything at all. For once, he was glad about that. He would have been further embarrassed by losing what breakfast he'd had.

Father stood at the fireplace on the far side of the room, glaring at the flames like they had personally offended him. Mahkai paused behind his father's overly large chair, instinctively keeping as many barriers between them as he could.

"Where were you? What excuse do you have for me this time, Mahkai?" Father demanded of the fire, refusing to look at Mahkai. His voice rumbled like thunder. Mahkai was sure that anyone nearby in the camp could hear him clearly.

"I...I...I mean...um..." Mahkai stammered. His words abandoned him in the onslaught of his father's fury.

"I did not think so." His words were clipped and harsh. "Are you seeing someone and keeping it from me? Is that what this is about?" Finally, he turned, leveling the full intensity of his glare on Mahkai, his eyebrows pinched together. The reflection of the firelight in his eyes made them glow menacingly. "Well?" he goaded.

"What? No, I... I mean..." Mahkai's mind raced with unspoken words, but he could not seem to make his mouth work. He took a deep breath to calm down, but under his father's scrutiny, his heart only raced faster and he became even more tongue tied.

His father's accusatory stare bore into him—assessing, judging, intimidating. Mahkai braced his feet and fidgeted with the hem of his tunic. He was uncomfortably aware of his grimy state from his climb through the tunnels last night and his journey through the forest this morning.

All he wanted to do was hide. He wished he were an Arboreal, a wielder of earth magic, so he could call the ground to open at his feet and swallow him. Or a stronger Aerophyte, to call a gale to sweep him away. What would that feel like—to be weightless, carried along by nothing but the wind? Not for the first time today did he wish he could control his magic.

"Mahkai! Are you even listening to me?" his father demanded, slamming his hands down on the stone table between them.

Mahkai flinched. He had not, in fact, been listening. Father was known to throw things when he was especially angry. Mahkai tried to make himself as small as possible, retreating around the table as his father advanced to sit down in the chair Mahkai had been practically hiding behind.

The Makanui clan chief sat down heavily, as though the weight of Osrealach rested on his shoulders. His eyes studied the textures of the table as Mahkai watched him warily. When his father made no further movement, Mahkai relaxed a fraction.

The fire was overly warm, or at least, it felt so to him. He had grown accustomed to his much smaller fireplace in his hut. He studied the ornately carved stones that made up his father's mantlepiece.

A pair of bronze bulls sat above it on the ledge. He'd seen the pair before. They had been Aunti Lani's. He picked one up and inspected it.

"Mahkai, what am I to do with you?" His father's voice broke into his thoughts. His tone softened with a tired sigh.

"There are certain expectations to uphold as my son. I know you hate training…and weapons practice…and this family…" Mahkai spun to face him fully and dropped the statue onto the table with a thud. "I do NOT hate this family," he stated vehemently. "How could you say that?" Hurt and anger pooled in his gut like a cold stone. How dare his father accuse him of this?

Father pulled out his knife and began cleaning his nails like they weren't in the middle of a heated argument. "You do, or you would be here,"—he punctuated his words by rapping the hilt of his dagger on the table—"happily attending all family and clan obligations." Another rap. "You would participate in all the contests with enthusiasm, like your siblings do." This time he slammed the hilt so hard Mahkai wondered if it would crack or chip the table from the force of it. "You would also take proper care of your weapons. Don't think I don't know about your 'cloak rack.'" He looked pointedly at Mahkai before returning his attention to his knife and nails.

"I have overlooked your embarrassing clothing choices thus far, but, Mahkai…" He glanced up. "How will you ever find a partner dressed like that? You certainly can't fight in them." His voice grew quieter, more resigned. Was it possible his father's eyes softened a fraction?

"I have no intention of finding a partner. *And* I like my garments. They are comfortable and I don't need to fight in them. I don't want to." Mahkai could almost hear the echoes of this same conversation reverberating in his head.

He retrieved the fallen bronze bull and bit his lip to keep from saying anything he might regret, prolonging the argument. As far as he was concerned, this conversation was pointless, just like the hundreds before it.

Nothing would change in the end. His father would spout some nonsense about him needing to be more like whichever of his elder siblings was his favorite at the moment, make him attend more weapons practices for a while, then eventually things would go back to the way they always were: Mahkai being the outcast, the white bull of the family, the one no one understood if they even remembered him at all.

His father sighed loudly and mumbled something about the youngest calves being overly coddled.

Mahkai ignored him, inspecting a hairline crack in the statue's base more closely. It did not look like a crack from damage. Maybe it was supposed to come apart.

First, he tried pulling it open. Then he twisted, tugged, and turned with no results. Eventually, when he pressed it together first, then twisted, something shifted. After a series of twists back and forth, he noticed small hatch marks of varying lengths on the base. He initially thought they were decorative, but what if they were a pattern—perhaps indicators of how far to turn it?

He tried turning to the longest one first, then incrementally shorter, but to no avail. When he started with the smallest and spun it to the incrementally larger ones, it sprung open.

The bottom piece had small lines etched into it. The top part was hollow, as if it were supposed to hold something, but it was empty. Disappointed but intrigued, Mahkai reached for the other one, curious if it too held a secret compartment inside.

This one opened much the same as the first, except in reverse. The second base also had a series of squiggles on it, in addition to something that looked akin to the sacred mountain monument. He held both bottom portions closer to the firelight. Some lines looked like they might connect. He held the pieces together. Sure enough, they created a crude map, the path therein ending at the monument.

Aunti Lani had taken him there a number of times when he was little. All he remembered of it was a long, steep climb, but the best view. He had tried to find the path again over the years but never could recall where it started.

He traced the path with his fingers and repeated, *left, left, right, left, right, straight, right,* in his head so he would not forget it before he could write it down. He needed his satchel, which he had left... Where had he left it?

Oh, that was right. He'd left it in the ash tree hollow on the edge of the grove near his hut so the little owl would not be disturbed. The owl! He had completely forgotten about her. She must be wondering where he went. He brought her all this way, only to abandon her.

He reconnected the bulls with their corresponding bases and replaced them on the mantle. *Left, left, right, left, right, straight, right.*

He turned around, prepared to make some excuse about needing to go relieve himself, only to find the hut empty. When had Father left?

Thanking the stars, he hurried through camp toward the ash tree, pointedly ignoring anyone he passed, shuffling to the beat of the mantra in his head. *Left, left, right, left, right, straight, right.*

He arrived at the ash tree, relieved to see his cloak and satchel undisturbed. At his approach, the little owl poked her head out and hooted quietly at him in greeting. She seemed pleased to see him.

"Hello again. My apologies for leaving you so suddenly. My father wished to speak with me." A shiver ran through him that had nothing to do with the cold. He paused, shaking his head as if to dislodge the memory of his father's heated stare.

"Oh, but while I was there, I found a map to a trail that leads to the best view of the valley. One moment." He withdrew a notebook and scribbled down the directions he'd been repeating in his head and as much of the map as he could remember.

"There. I was concerned I might forget them in my haste to come back to you."

The little owl looked down at his notes, then back at him, and blinked.

"I know it doesn't look like a map, but it was all I could manage. I found it quite by accident, though." He leaned closer and dropped his voice. "It was hidden in a secret compartment in the bottom of two ornamental statues Aunti Lani had. It has to mean something, doesn't it?" He rubbed the pendant she gave him with his thumb as he thought of her. He had taken to touching it every time he missed her.

"Now, I was thinking, do you not have a family somewhere looking for you?" He blanched. "Not that I resent your company," he said hurriedly. "I didn't mean to take you away from them…if I did, in fact…take you away, that is. Though, I suppose you could have left any time along the way if you did not want to be here. So I suppose you do want to be here." The words came out in a rush. "I do so hope you want to be here, but only if you actually want to be here." He paused, his eyes pleading with her and his heart in his throat. He did not like feeling vulnerable, but there it was.

"Do you…want to be here?" he asked quietly. His heart beat wildly, terrified of her rejection. If he was being honest with himself, he had gotten used to her presence. It simply felt right in a way he could not explain.

She stared at him unblinkingly. He got the feeling she was giving him a look that meant something like "don't be ridiculous." She hopped toward him and ruffled her feathers.

He let out his breath in a *whoosh*. "Well, you are welcome to stay for as long as you like." He placed his hand over his heart, then held it out to her. "Well then, allow me to show you to my humble home."

She hopped onto his outstretched hand and tucked her wings

close to her body. He made his way to his little hut with his owl companion in one hand and his cloak-wrapped satchel tucked under the opposite arm.

🍵 🍵 🍵

Mahkai and the little owl arrived at his hut to find books strewn everywhere. Papers fluttered in the breeze from the open door. His chest was upturned, its contents scattered across the floor.

"What happened here?" he wondered aloud.

"Hey, little brother! Where ya been?" Malena leaned against the doorway with a hand on her hip and a sly smile on her face.

Mahkai sucked in a breath and braced himself, instantly wary. Malena never visited him unless she had an agenda. And based on the look on her face, he wasn't going to like it.

"Hello, Malena." He turned to tidy up and put his things in their place with a quiet sigh.

"Who is this?" She gestured to his owl friend perched on his shoulder and laughed. "Get it? *Whooo*. Because, you know, owls say *hooo*."

Mahkai gave her his best "not amused" face.

"So, where were you yesterday?" She ignored his look. "We missed you. Well, we missed beating you, yet again," she taunted. "You know, maybe it was for the best you didn't come. Maleek and his band were in rare form and dominated the entire field. It was impressive. Everyone was fawning all over him after…"

Mahkai tuned her out as she gave a play-by-play of the entire games and everyone's reactions. He made tea instead and didn't bother offering her some. Last time he did, she made fun of him for a week. It was best he pretended he was listening until she got to her point. She would eventually.

"So, Mahkai."

There it was.

"I noticed Hannah from the Kekoroa clan also wasn't at the war games." She wagged her eyebrows at him.

Was she serious? He rolled his eyes and set the little owl on the table as he selected leaves and flowers from his stash. He couldn't make up his mind between orange blossom or mulled orange. The owl hopped over in front of him and looked at both of them for a moment, so he offered each of them to her to choose. She pecked at the small clay jar of mulled orange tea. He smiled at her in thanks.

"What about it?" he asked Malena after what he deemed an appropriate amount of time. He dared not protest too quickly and confirm her unfounded hypothesis that he was, in fact, having a dalliance with this Hannah from Kekoroa. He wasn't sure he knew her from all the rest of Kekoroa, to be honest.

"Were you?"

"Was I what?" he quipped, annoyed and wanting this uncomfortable conversation over with already.

"You were, weren't you?" She grinned. "Ha! Mort owes me a week of chores."

"Malena, I said no such thing." Exasperation and panic laced his tone. This could quickly get out of hand. "I was in the forest collecting things for tea and I ran into a panther and fell into a hole, which turned out to be a tunnel system that I stayed the night in and climbed out this morning. Oh, and I made a friend along the way." He gestured to the little bird.

"Mahkai." Malena took on a patronizing, condescending tone. "You don't have to lie about it. You shouldn't be embarrassed about wanting to see her and spend time with her. We all know war games aren't your thing." She turned to go and gave him a wink over her shoulder. "Don't worry, little brother, I'll keep your secret. But next time, if you are going to lie, pick something believable. Not panthers and secret tunnels." She smirked and closed the door behind her with a bang, and he was left in blessed silence.

He snorted then chuckled, shaking his head. "She thinks I was sneaking out to see a girl," he said to the little owl. She ruffled her feathers and let out a soft hoot that sounded like a snicker.

"Sometimes, I feel that when my family looks at me, they see what they envision me to be rather than the real me—all the time actually," he explained, his shoulders dropping in dejection.

He pulled out a tiny cloth sachet with a drawstring at the top and spooned a couple helpings into it, tied it shut, then dropped it into his teapot. Today felt like a more-than-one-cup-of-tea kind of day. A whole pot should be sufficient to get him through at least a few pages of his current book.

"Have you ever felt that way?" he asked the little owl before him. "Not right. Not good enough, like you are letting them down by just existing?" He sighed and ran a hand over his face. "Don't suppose you would. Look at you. You are magnificent. Perfect. How could anyone find fault with you?" He had a lot of mixed feelings and needed to sort them out. But not right now. He was tired. He would most certainly do it later.

The little owl made a mournful sound. She hopped closer to him and rubbed the side of her face against his hand like she was attempting to comfort him. He gently stroked the top of her head. Her feathers were silky smooth and incredibly soft.

"Thank you. I appreciate it." He smiled tiredly at her, then poured the tea into two cups, blowing on hers to cool it down before giving it to her.

She chirruped her thanks and began dipping her beak into the spiced dark amber liquid. His smile broadened into a grin as he lifted his own mug to his lips. He would have never guessed owls liked tea.

Mind Your Teas

Lemongrass
Peppermint
Chamomile
Rosehip
Spearmint
Valerian Root
Hibiscus
Cornflower Petals

A tea to help clear your mind and settle your nerves and stomach.
I debated on calling this one Min-tea but that seemed ridiculous, though maybe just as ridiculous as what I chose to call it in the end.

-Lani

Chapter 6

Mahkai stumbled up the rocky slope toward the summit. Anticipation buzzed through him, making his skin tingle. It had taken him several days before he had the free time to attempt the journey up the mountain.

His father and siblings were especially insistent on his participation in their activities. They were preparing to move to the cold season camp, so everything needed cleaning, packing, and organizing. But finally, he was here.

His aunt had a map to this location for a reason. His father's voice nagged in the back of his mind that there was nothing here. But what if there was a secret spot with who-knows-what hidden inside, like the space in the bull statues? It did not matter. She had meant for him to find it and follow it here. He just knew it.

He was mad at himself for not finding it sooner. How long had it been there? She had passed away and joined the ancestors in the night sky twenty solarcycles ago. But he still felt her absence every day. No one else had understood him like she had.

He leaned against the obelisk-shaped summit as he caught his breath from his climb. He remembered coming here with his aunt when he was younger. He always assumed she wanted a vigorous walk with a nice view.

The view was spectacular. It looked out on the wide open rolling hills of the valley to the south and the forest of Cinntire to the north. On really clear days you could even see the Kailua sea to the east.

When his breath steadied, he wandered around the spire, looking for anything that might be what she wanted him to find—what she had left behind for him. Twice, thrice, four times around, and still he had yet to find anything other than weather-worn stone. In his pocket, he rubbed the pendant Aunti Lani had given him with his thumb, as was his habit when he was thinking over a particularly perplexing question.

His other hand brushed along the rough pink and black speckled granite spire. She told him this was a monument to the dragons of old. It depicted a great battle between groups of fae long extinct. Strange winged creatures fought half cat-half fae fought half deer creatures. It also depicted a strange light dispersing between the combatants.

Some of the carvings had been worn smooth. What had that side shown? Moss covered parts of the images in several places and almost an entire side of the six-sided monument. He contemplated the stone, then sighed. He surmised he might need to clear the moss but was loath to do so.

He sat on the ground with his back to the monument, facing the setting sun, and pulled out his pendant. He wished he had thought to bring tea. Tea made everything better. Holding the cord, he watched the spiral-shaped rock sway in the wind. He always thought it looked like the symbol for air and wind, or a fishhook. He was not sure it would be very useful as a fishhook, as it spiraled too tightly in the center.

She gave it to him years before his revealing ceremony when his air magic was unveiled. She could not have known all those years before what his magic would be, could she? No one could see the future… Could they? He shook his head. Maybe she just thought it was pretty and he would fancy it. Which he did, very much. From the moment he had laid eyes on it, he loved it, and not just because she had given it to him.

He blinked. She could not have known what magic he had. But what if it was more than just a pretty carved rock? She had hidden the map to this place in the base of her bull statues. Why couldn't this be something more, too?

But what?

Mahkai sighed and set the pendant on the ground next to him. He closed his eyes and leaned his head back against the granite. Ideas and questions roared through his mind. Possibilities. Questions that led to more questions. More questions without answers.

He let his mind wander, enjoying the wind buffeting him from one direction, then another. He imagined his thoughts floating like clouds on the breeze. Not trying to hold on to one thought too tightly, he let his mind sort things out.

His aunt's voice played in his head from the innumerable times she had told him, "Inspiration and insight, like tea, need time—need to steep before they are fully ready. And like ideas, different teas need differing amounts of time to steep."

They would spend the minutes between tea steeping or the hours waiting for their dough to rise sitting on the floor doing breathing exercises. Other times, they would dance until their feet hurt and they were out of breath. One of her other favorite sayings was, "Breath is life. Be mindful of your breathing, Mahkai."

Mahkai took a slow, deep breath in and out, counting his heartbeats in each breath. Four in, four hold, four out. Repeat. He found this helped him relax. It was also the only thing that subdued his unruly magic when it acted up.

He hated that he could not control it, but he was learning to accept it. He hated that not only the clans, but all the fae measured their social standing and worth by the strength of something they did not get to choose and could not control.

His jaw ached. He clenched and released it to relax his face muscles. He rubbed the spot between his horn and his ear. The beginning of a headache prickled there. He opened his eyes and was letting them wander when he caught sight of a familiar repeating pattern to the stones he was sitting on.

Jumping to his feet, he tilted his head and shifted so his shadow would not darken the stones before him. The sunlight sparkled on a vein running through the ground and the obelisk, lighting it up. He squinted at the almost-invisible line and ran his finger along the vein so he would not lose it. He ran into a patch of moss and pulled his little knife out of his belt. Gently at first, then more quickly, he scraped some of the moss away, revealing the continuing vein of quartz running through the granite. It looked natural from afar, but it was too precise, too specific to be unengineered. No, someone had altered this rock beyond just the carvings.

He continued clearing away the moss until the entire rock face was revealed. The quickly-fading light painted the rock in brilliant colors of the sunset. He peered at the place where the vein stopped abruptly. There was a gap, a hole. A piece was missing. It must have worn or chipped away with the wind and weather over time.

Depressed, he let his shoulders slump. His excitement from his discovery dwindled. He shuffled back to look at the whole obelisk. Something skittered across the ground. He looked down and saw his pendent laying a little ways away where he'd accidentally kicked it. He bent to pick it up. As he straightened, the sunlight caught the stone. It sparkled like the vein in the obelisk.

His breath hitched. His pendant was about the same size as the hole. Tentatively, Mahkai placed it in the spot, no more than a small divot. He held his breath and waited. And waited. Nothing happened. His breath released in a disappointed *whoosh.* He chastised himself for getting his hopes up.

If there was anything here at all, it probably needed magic to activate it. He sighed in frustration. Feelings of falling short of expectations threatened to overwhelm him. He reached to take his funny-looking hook from the stone. As his fingers brushed the pendant, it shifted and rotated a fraction.

A *click* and stone grinding on stone joined the howling of the wind on the mountain top. Mahkai's heart raced as a small portion of the stone sank and slid sideways, creating a small opening in the previously unblemished rock face. Gently at first, then with increasing pressure, Mahkai pushed aside the loose rock.

It opened into a small alcove carved from the interior. Inside lay a small, flat object wrapped in oilcloth. Tentatively, he removed it. He unwrapped the covering to reveal a leather-bound book with a brass latch. He attempted to open it. It was locked, but there was no keyhole. He inspected it more closely, turning it this way and that, squinting in the dim light. Giving up, he put it in his satchel to inspect more closely later.

The sun had set, and dusk was quickly fading into darkness. The moon had not yet risen, but if he remembered correctly, it would not be long before it breached the horizon. He felt around in the alcove, curious if there was something else in the little hidden hole in the rock, on the top of the mountain with the forgotten path to the summit, whose map was hidden in halves in secret compartments in the base of two sculptures his aunt had left for him when she passed away, which his father had been keeping for him… Why wouldn't there be something else?

He laughed out loud at his own thoughts. He loved his aunt and knew she was different, but this was a whole other level of different. Brilliant, actually. What other secrets did she have? He was meant to find this. Why else would she leave him clues? What else was he missing?

Mahkai withdrew his hand and pulled his pendant from its place, no more than a chip in the rock face. He expected the rock to move back into place once he removed it. Surprisingly, it did not. He stepped back to observe the monument and caught sight of the stars. Without the light of the sun or moon, they seemed to wrap themselves around him like a familiar cloak or blanket.

He enjoyed watching the stars as he waited for the moon to rise so he could write in his notes. They were familiar old friends. He used to lie in the grass at night during the hot season, outside the hut he shared with his family, when it was unbearable to be cooped up with so many bodies. He used to make up his own stories about the characters, pictures he saw in the stars, until Aunti Lani let him sit in the corner of her hut and listen to the story weavers.

The story weavers weren't the same as the fairy and puka history keepers who could replay actual events from the past for all to see.

No, these were different. These were myths and legends of the time before. When magic was wild and unpredictable. Before even the dragons came to this land.

Dragons. A thrill ran down his back. He did not know why, but the gigantic, magnificent, winged beasts had always fascinated him.

Mahkai traced the stars, making up the great huntress and her twin brother, the weaver. Their story was his favorite. As the story goes, there once was a pair of stars: Gemini. Twins, but opposites in most everything. In a time before day and night, the sky was both light and dark without end. Then they fell from the sky, or were cast down, depending on who was telling the story. He grinned as he remembered Aunti Lani getting in a heated argument with one of her friends over it every time that particular story was told.

The tale went that the twins made everything. They split the light and dark, the day and night, the land and water, they even created the different elements and the elemental keepers. Mahkai traced their stars, too. Chantara was given charge of water, Kynthelic, land, Vesuviius, fire. There were three others, supposedly, but their names were lost over time.

He inhaled the cooling night air. It smelled old. He could not explain why, but the air around him felt ancient. It was not a decaying old, but of a deep thoughtful age brimming with secrets and long-lost wisdom.

As he breathed slowly in the ever shifting wind, he mentally cataloged the various scents it brought him. The trees and grasses of the forest, the deer and moose and other wildlife, fresh clear mountain air, the moss and stone cooling from the day's heat, his own musky, floral scent, and the one he did not know. He tried to follow the fragrance, but it was so faint he kept losing it.

The wind shifted, taking a biting edge to it. He needed to head down the mountain and take shelter for the night. He tightened his hold on his cloak and tucked his muzzle beneath the folds to keep his nose warm.

The moon, Nocturne, finally breached the horizon, painting everything in its silvery light. It was whole in its patrol tonight, giving them its full attention. In the coming weeks it would turn away a little each night, patrolling elsewhere, then gradually return to them. The protector of the dark, he had been taught. And Fiera, the protector of the day.

He always wondered what they were protecting against, but when he asked his instructors, he only received lashes for speaking out of turn. Even his Aunti could not—or would not—give him an answer. She only smiled at him, her eyes twinkling, and asked him what he thought.

Lightning flashed in the distance, followed by the rumble of thunder soon after. A storm was blowing in, and he definitely did not want to be on the mountain when it did. He paused for one more look into the small alcove, grateful it was on the side that faced the moon. The veins of quartz continued through the rock in the carved hole as well.

Mahkai squinted in the dim light. If he did not know better, the quartz looked like it depicted something, but that couldn't be right. Could it? He was just about to reach for his candle to see it better, but lightning flashed and thunder rumbled much closer now. He needed to go. Now.

Hastily, he withdrew his arm from the hole and bumped the rock that had receded from the opening. It groaned with stone scraping stone and moved back into its original position like it had always been there.

He half ran, half stumbled down the moonlit path toward the trees below. He needed to reach the treeline before the storm covered the moon, obscuring his light. Also, he did not want to be struck by the lightning because he was the tallest out here. The ground already buzzed as if in anticipation of the coming storm.

Mahkai tripped and tumbled the last short distance to the trees. He found himself mostly upside-down, with his head and shoulders at the base of a large fir tree and his legs and tail leaning against the trunk further up.

Relief burst in his chest. He had made it. Chuckling at his inverted position, he righted himself. He wished he could see himself; he was quite sure it was rather comical.

Lightning lit up the sky in a breathtaking display of raw power, striking the obelisk he had just been standing next to. The thunder almost sounded like a growl this close. He shook

his head to alleviate the pressure in his ears and brushed himself off. The air was thick with pine, fir, evergreen, and rain.
The clouds burst and let loose torrential rain that swept toward
his safe-haven from the lightning.

Mahkai retreated further into the trees, looking for a place
he could rest for the night and a dry-ish place to write down his
thoughts.

Sleepless Nights Tea

Chamomile
Passionflower
Skullcap
Oatstraw
Lavender
Rose Petals
Valerian Root

A tea to help lull you to sleep on nights when your mind is too busy and your body too restless.

-Mahkai

Chapter 7

Mahkai had just sat down to a nice cup of tea and was still stirring in his honey when he remembered his aunt's book he'd found in the obelisk. Hurriedly, he got up and retrieved it from his bag. The torn seam he had mended was coming undone again. He needed to ask the clan weaver to help him mend it more securely.

He sipped from his mug with one hand and held the book with the other, turning it over to inspect it. The latch was not a single piece of metal like he had thought before, but was made up of several interlocking pieces. He wondered if they moved.

Aunti Lani loved her puzzles. She had come up with quite a few for him to play with to keep his hands busy during very long, very boring clan meetings as a calf.

Mahkai pushed and pulled gently until one piece moved. It only slid a fraction, but emitted a little *click* and did not retreat to its previous position. Piece after piece, Mahkai slid, twisted, and turned the tiny lock until it emitted a final, louder *click* and fell open.

He laughed and shook his head. When unlocked correctly, the latch formed the letter 'M'. Mahkai ran his fingers along the stiff leather and inhaled deeply. The book smelled of leather, stone, and a faint hint of the old smell from the mountain. He reverently opened the cover and was greeted with his aunt's flowing handwriting and the comforting aroma of her favorite tea, honeysuckle and jasmine. She had titled it *Minotaur Musings*. He read a few lines.

Friendships are like tea. They grow stronger in the steeping.

Hot water reveals the true nature of many things. Tea and people alike.

Mahkai flipped through pages full of sketches, thoughts, musings, wisdom she had gleaned throughout her three hundred years of life, and dried leaves and flowers pressed between the pages. He stopped on a page simply titled "Tea." He gasped quietly.

Aunti Lani *had* written them down. For the last twenty years, he had been faithfully practicing making the teas she had shown him. Well, those he could remember. He had forgotten ingredients or steps in the brewing process for many of them. Others, he forgot what they were intended for.

He'd tried taking notes, but those were some of the pages destroyed when his siblings had gotten a little too overzealous in their endeavors to get him to participate in their antics. They knocked his tea all over his papers. Other pages had gotten wet when the wind blew rain through his open window.

Tea to ease an upset stomach, tea to warm you up on a cold day, tea to clear a headache, tea to help you focus, tea to lift a bad mood, tea to comfort, tea for good sleep… he flipped to the next page. A small scrap of paper folded between the pages read,

Mahkai, my dear. Do be careful with these recipes. Some of them are meant for harm and not to heal. I have written them down, so should you need them, you know them and know what to avoid.

Remember, not all knowledge should be shared with everyone.

And some knowledge is best never written at all. I believe you have the wisdom to know the difference. I am so proud of you. Have fun finding the others.

—Aunti Lani

P..S. Be gentle with your father. He is a product of his circumstance.

Mahkai read the note several times before replacing it between the pages and closing the book. Her comment about his father made him uneasy, especially after the last lecture he had given him. He sighed, tucked the book back into his bag, and leaned his back against the wall to finish his tea. He would pour over every word written in her journal later.

So she *had* meant for him to find it…and there were others! He felt torn—he wanted to go back and explore the tunnels where he had found the little owl, but he also wanted to search the obelisk alcove more thoroughly. He also wanted to talk to the historians to see if they had anything they could show him about both.

He gulped the last of his tea and washed his cup and teapot. Tomorrow he would go see the historians. Tonight was the harvest solstice celebration. His family claimed to want him there, but they never liked his contribution—until the last harvest, that is.

Quickly, he changed into the family kilt and gathered his contribution to the feast. He made the drink of fermented honey and berries he'd brought last year. It had been quite by accident, but his family loved it and begged him to keep making it.

He did not actually like it. It made his head feel fluffy and his thoughts jumbled. Last time he drank it, he had woken in the middle of the training field covered in a mountain of fallen leaves with a very sore throat, not remembering how he had gotten there.

Everyone said he had been singing at the top of his lungs, then decided he was a dryad and wanted to become a leaf. They still teased him about it. He let out a harrumph, then banked the fire and strode out to face his clan.

🍵 🍵 🍵

The next afternoon, Mahkai set out for the historian. He was in a foul mood and his head ached like there were tiny drummers in his skull. He only drank tea and water last night, but everyone stayed up way too late and insisted he stay up with them when all he wanted to do was sit in bed and read his aunt's journal, drink tea, and go to sleep.

It wasn't that he resented spending time with his family and the clan, but they had such differing opinions of how to spend their time. He preferred exploration and contemplation. They preferred activities more…physical in nature, followed by the retelling stories of said activities, each telling getting further and further from the truth. He sometimes wondered if they preferred the boasting even more than the fighting.

Maleek's favorite saying was, "Never let the truth get in the way of a good story."

Mahkai sighed and rubbed his temples and forehead in hopes of alleviating some of his headache. When he woke up that afternoon, the little owl was gone. He wondered if she was off hunting or if she was gone for good. A strange feeling coiled in his chest. Like bees trapped, demanding to be released. Would she come back? Had he done something wrong? Had she tired of him already? He hoped she would come back, but he supposed he should be prepared if she did not.

Mahkai sighed again.

The historian's hut was located near the outskirts of the Kekoroa clan camp. From the outside, it looked like every other hut except for a small stump resting near the tent flap with the phases of the moon burned into it. Other minotaur waved to him as he approached. He waved back and hoped they wouldn't approach him, since he couldn't remember their names.

"Hello." He called out to announce his presence and waited for permission to enter the historian's hut.

The Makanui clan did not have someone possessing history's magic, so he often had to travel to one of the other clans. They were all in the middle of the season's migration, so locating them had been a bit of an endeavor.

"Enter," a soft, lilting voice called back.

Mahkai straightened and smoothed his clothes, doing one last check to ensure he did not have a stray bit of grass or leaves clinging to him. Not that anyone else would particularly care, but he cared. He entered and blinked to let his eyes get accustomed to the dim light.

He wondered if all historians preferred the dark. He resolved to ask her after his other questions.

The room was cozy. A small table with stools sat against the wall of the tent. A hammock filled with blankets hung out of the way across from him but could easily be brought out to sleep in. He noted several hooks at varying distances around the room and puzzled over them for a moment until he realized they were likely either for multiple hammocks or to adjust how close or far away from the fire one was. That was brilliant. He reached for his notes to write it down. He wanted to remember it for later and try it out himself.

Kali, the historian, cleared her throat, bringing him back to the reason he was here.

"Good afternoon, Historian Kali. My family sends their

well wishes and the last of the season's spiced apples." He set a wax-sealed jar of stewed apples before her.

"Good afternoon, Mahkai." She sounded annoyed or bored. Or both. Mahkai decided on both.

He took a deep breath. He needed to talk fast and hope she would hear him out. "I've come to ask for your assistance and insight into a couple matters," he began unsteadily.

"Only two?" She raised her eyebrows and pursed her lips. She was still salty over their last interaction. Not good.

"I was wondering if you knew anything about the old, overgrown tunnels in Cinntire Wood? And also the obelisk at the top of the mountain? There are carvings up there I found interesting, but they are worn away in places. What do they mean? What is missing? Where do the tunnels lead? Why are they overgrown and abandoned? Who made them? What are they for?" Mahkai ran out of breath and gasped, prepared to continue asking his questions, but Kali interrupted him.

"Mahkai. Choose one."

"So you'll show me?"

She gave him a look of long suffering. "I will try. Not much is known about either of them, I'm afraid."

Mahkai clasped his hands and shifted from hoof-to-hoof as his tail thrashed excitedly, knocking over one of the stools. His mind raced and his heart beat wildly in his chest. More questions flooded his thoughts and fought for preeminence. She held up her hand.

"It is best not to get your hopes up. Sit." She closed her eyes and held out her hands in front of her, palms facing each other. "Now, which do you want me to look for?"

"Oh, um…" He paused and chewed his lip. Which was more important to him? He didn't know. He wanted to know more about both. "I suppose…"

"Choose or I will choose for you." She sounded more annoyed.

"The obelisk," he blurted out.

"As you say." She nodded. Eyes still closed, she took a deep breath.

"How does it work? Your magic, do you see every second of everything in rev—"

"Mahkai, I need to concentrate. And your incessant questions are distracting." She peeked open an eye to look at him pointedly.

"My apologies." He laced his fingers together and attempted to be still.

He only managed a brief time before he started twitching and shifting on his stool. He looked around the room as he waited and cataloged what he could see in her hut. It wasn't much. Then he took out his book to take notes, but in the low light, he could barely make out what he had written previously. He put it back in his bag and clasped his hands in his lap again.

He did not remember falling asleep, but he was startled awake when he felt a hand on his shoulder. He was embarrassed to find he had drooled a little down his chin. "What did you learn?" he asked when he found his voice.

She shook her head tiredly. "Nothing."

"Nothing? As in nothing, nothing?"

She shrugged. "I am not strong enough to see back that far or that clearly. Maybe one of the other historians will be, but I am sorry, I cannot help you." She ushered him to the door.

Clearly dismissed, he thanked her again and dejectedly trudged out of her hut.

The sun was setting, and the rest of the clan was preparing for their evening meal. Several minotaur he vaguely recognized as sparring partners with his siblings offered to let him join their campfire, but Mahkai was preoccupied.

How long ago was the obelisk created? Why couldn't she tell him anything? Was there another reason? He shook his head at the thought. She wouldn't tell him that to get rid of him, would she?

He wasn't watching where he was going apparently, because he ran face first into a tree. He rubbed his stinging nose and forehead. His hopes of no one seeing his blunder were dashed when giggling rang out nearby. Embarrassment burned in his chest and his already warm face.

He ducked his head and turned away, only to trip on a root in his haste in the growing shadows. His frustration and embarrassment deepened as their giggles grew into full laughs. He knew word would spread like fire in dry grass. Soon everyone in camp would be laughing at his blunder.

The air warmed and little eddies and dust devils sprang into being around him. To his further embarrassment, they didn't stay close by. They spread out and multiplied, kicking up dirt and leaves into the air. Campfires roared and crackled in the wind. Leaves caught fire and rose into the sky, carried on invisible air currents.

Was he doing this? *Oh, no!* He couldn't stop it. He had not brought any of his calming teas either. He tried closing his eyes and doing breathing exercises, but it didn't help, judging from the chaos ensuing around him.

A yelp caused him to snap his eyes open. One of the cyclones of air had grown and tore through several tents, causing the roofs to cave in or collapse entirely.

"Stop this!" a rust-colored female minotaur demanded, shaking a fist in his face. The Ardere, fire wielders, were keeping the fire contained. The Aerophyte, like him—if he could even call himself that—called wind of their own to stop his out-of-control currents. The Arboreals, tree and ground magics, smothered any flames before they reached the trees. If the fire had reached the forest, it could have caused significant damage.

One of the Aerophyte made dirt devils of his own, swirling in reverse, systematically stopping each of Mahkai's errant magical outbursts. When the last one had died down, Mahkai slumped to the ground, exhausted mentally, emotionally, and physically.

A crowd formed a little ways off, angrily demanding to know who started it. They were pointing fingers at each other. It was only a matter of moments before they turned to him. "Who did this? Why? Did one of the children lose control of their magic? Why are they unsupervised?"

"You need to go," the rust-colored minotaur snapped at him.

He nodded wordlessly and fled. He didn't stop until he got to his hut in his own camp sometime later. Mindlessly, he managed to hang his hammock before collapsing into it, exhausted. Only, the anchors in the walls crumbled and fell, dumping him unceremoniously on the ground. He groaned and stayed on the cold, hard-packed dirt floor, too spent to get up. This day couldn't end fast enough.

It was only a matter of time before his clan heard what happened. He couldn't face them. They already thought he was a waste of space, a burden. Perhaps being gone for a few days would be good. It would let the heat of their ire die down and maybe they wouldn't make him do latrine duty for the rest of his life—or worse, guard duty.

He shuddered. They wouldn't exile him for this, would they? He was already considered too different and problematic, so why would they not? There were some things even his father couldn't protect him from. He replayed today's events over and over in his head, tearing himself down further with each pass. Some of the things he called himself might surpass even the most scathing of comments others had whispered about him behind his back. That was the trick he had learned early on—their comments didn't hurt nearly as bad when he called himself worse things in his head.

He would collect his things and go on a journey. But where? He thought for a bit, then decided on his favorite bee hive.

But in the morning. He was too exhausted to do anything other than throw his cloak over himself and roll over on his side, his bag serving as a pillow.

Spill-the-Tea

Peppermint

Cinnamon Chips

Ginger

Licorice Root

Clove

Léargas Leaf

The drinker tells the truth and cannot lie for a day.
Steep for 100 measured breaths while concentrating—no
more, no less, otherwise it has no effect.

-Lani

Chapter 8

Mahkai climbed out of his well-used camping hammock into the crisp morning air and stretched. He still had half a day's walk ahead of him to his favorite beehives, but he was already a little sore from the journey the day before. He'd intended to come a little earlier in the season, before it got so cold. Normally, he would have come a full moon cycle earlier, but one family obligation after another had delayed him. He would need to make sure he left enough for the bees to have plenty of honey to get them through the cold season.

The little owl hooted a good morning to him from a nearby tree branch. At least he assumed she was saying hello. He couldn't quite tell, though sometimes it was very obvious.

Carefully, he picked a few spear thistles growing near his camp and placed them in a pile where his fire was burning low. He should have just enough time to heat water for tea and breakfast before it went out.

He retrieved a small sack of dried oats, placed a handful in his little wooden bowl, and waited for the water in his kettle to boil. He wished he had thought to bring goat's milk with him. That would have been lovely. A bit of honey and bark from the cinnamon tree. He licked his lips and huffed a little puff of mist into the cool morning air.

When he was younger, he would pretend he was one of the great dragons, huffing and puffing out billows of smoke and steam. His father had caught him once and didn't manage to hold back his smile at Mahkai's antics before he chastised him, saying he better hope he never ran into a dragon, as "They're likely to eat us first and ask questions later." That didn't stop Mahkai. He just made sure no one was around when he pretended to be a dragon after that.

Mahkai smiled at the memory and poured the steaming water into his bowl of oats and his cup for tea. He dropped a few thistles into his mug and squeezed out the last drops of honey from last year's supply. The owl hopped over to him and chirped happily when he offered her some oats and tea.

After they finished breakfast, he drained the last of his tea. He packed up his little campsite and continued on the trail, notebook and charcoal in hand, taking notes on the trees, and leaves, and any wildlife he saw. The owl perched in her customary place on his shoulder, watching everything around them with wide eyes.

At some point, the owl moved to nest in his bag and was fast asleep. He wondered if she slept at night or during the day—or, like cats, whenever she pleased.

The morning passed quickly, and soon he was topping the ridge near the hives. Several bees were buzzing around the flowers and thistles still in bloom.

The first time he stumbled upon this place, it had been completely by accident. He had spent hours following the bees from flower to flower until they showed him to their hive. It had not been pretty. He didn't know to wear protective clothing or to not just reach in and attempt to take part of the comb. His entire left side had been swollen for days.

"And what do you think you are doing here, bothering my bees?" A sharp, elderly voice cut into his musings, jarring him from his thoughts.

"I… I beg your pardon. But did you say *your* bees?" Mahkai sputtered. He didn't know anyone could own bees. They did what they wanted, where they wanted, and very few things could tell them otherwise.

"Yes. My bees, and you are disturbing them," she said sharply. Grouchily.

"I'm not… That is to say… I was not…"

"What, did a bee sting your tongue? Spit it out." She paused. "It would serve you right if it did, though," she added as an afterthought.

Mahkai looked at the tiny hunched woman with silver, curly hair before him. He wasn't sure what she was. If he were asked to describe her, he might guess she was a fairy, a puka, or something else entirely. "I have no intention of disturbing or harming them. I came, as I do every year, to see if they might have a surplus of honey to share," he said indignantly.

"AH HA! So you're the one who's been stealing my honey. Well, I've caught you now, and you won't be allowed to continue." She pointed a crooked finger at him. He had no doubt she would have poked him in the chest with it if they were the same height.

Mahkai blanked. "But who are you to claim them as yours? I always leave plenty. They are a thriving hive. Surely both of us may partake of their golden treasure and still leave more than enough for them." Mahkai was not sure where this confidence and sass were coming from. He would never talk to one of the clan elders this way.

She harrumphed and padded wordlessly over to a large rock where her bag, almost as large as she was, rested. She practically crawled in and pulled out several frames made of sticks. They were tied together with string criss-crossed between them to make corners. He watched as she made a small fire and added green branches to make lots of smoke. She then blew it toward the hive with a large fan made of braided leaves.

She pulled aside the smaller rock that served as the cover

for the hive opening and reached in to remove several large pieces of the comb. She replaced them with her frames. She glanced over her shoulder at him and seemed to consider him for a moment. "What do you think, ladies? Do you want to give him some, too?"

Mahkai blinked in surprise. This granny talked to the bees. No wonder she thought they were hers. Did the bees answer her in their own way, and could she really understand them?

"Yes, alright, that seems very fair." She turned to look at him. "They said they will happily let you have some of their honey like they do every year if you've brought the jasmine blooms they so adore."

He smiled broadly and pulled out the assortment of flowers he had brought for them. "I brought jasmine, orange and apple blossoms, some fresh apples and berries, and some of these flowers, which I don't know the name of." Mahkai pointed to the flowers with cone-shaped centers and long, thin purple petals, which he'd stumbled upon that morning.

"Oh, no wonder they like you. You spoil them," she tutted at him. "And those are echinacea and aster flowers. They taste nice and their leaves make a lovely tea."

He felt like he had passed some sort of test. "Well, I just assumed if they were sharing with me, it is only fair that I bring something for them in return."

She considered him for a moment, then nodded and motioned for him to hold his honeycomb box out for her. She placed a piece much larger than he normally took inside.

"I don't need quite this much, but thank you."

"Mmmm…best not argue with the bees. They said for you to have this much. Said you would need it. Hmmm? They have a sense about these things, you know."

"I did not, but that is very interesting." He placed the lid on his box and pulled out his notebook and charcoal to write down his latest insights. The little owl blinked sleepily at him from her place, snuggled up in one of his scarves, then tucked her head under her wing.

"What's that you got there?" she asked as she closed the hive up and replaced the rock across the opening.

"Ah, these are my notes." He held his book where she could see it.

"Notes on what?" She had an inquisitive and thoughtful look on her face.

"On everything, of course."

"Why do you need that?" One of her eyebrows shot up and the other furrowed. Mahkai was not sure he could make his eyebrows do that no matter how hard he tried.

"It helps me to remember, I suppose. And it makes it easier to share with others," he said thoughtfully.

"What does it say?"

"About what?" Admittedly, he was still somewhat distracted trying to figure out how to make one eyebrow go up while the other went down.

"Oh, anything. Tell me something you have learned and written in that book of yours." She looked genuinely interested and not at all judgmental like he'd grown to expect from others.

"Well..." He flipped a few pages back and considered various things he could say. Many of them seemed to be rather obvious, and he wanted to share something special. "Did you know honey helps soothe itchiness and pain from a sting or bite?"

She looked thoughtful and rested her chin on her fist for a moment, then let out a *hmmm.* "What else you got?"

So he shared a few more things he found particularly interesting. She sat down next to the fire with her back to the boulder. "Would you care for some tea?" she asked him.

"Why yes, that would be splendid! What is your favorite?"

He was delighted. She was the first person he'd met, other than Aunti Lani and her friends, who knew of tea, let alone drank it regularly enough to have it with her on a trip to get honey.

"The name's Bree. Bree of the bees. But not of the cheese variety. No, that is my twin sister. She is the cheesemaker."

He hid his chuckle with a cough and cleared his throat. "Pleased to meet you, Bree. Mahkai of the Makanui clan."

"Hmmm, and so much more, I expect."

"I beg your pardon?"

"I told you." She waved her hand at him. "The bees tell me many things because they have a way of seeing and knowing things. And they see you—very clearly, in fact."

Mahkai was baffled by her words. What did they mean, and what was he to do with them?

She looked up at him and patted the ground next to her. "You are a big one. Don't make an old lady crane her neck to look at you." Her words were sharp, but her eyes sparkled with humor, and their corners crinkled with lines that spoke of a preference for laughter.

"Now about that tea."

They spent the rest of the afternoon together, swapping stories and sharing tea. She named off her favorites, and he took notes of the ones he had never heard of. He offered up some of his favorites. She shared some of her blends and recipes, and he did as well. He even brought up one particularly troublesome recipe not explained in the journal. Together they puzzled through it.

As the sun began to set, they packed up their things. "May I help you carry your bag home?" he offered, marveling at how strong she was for her size.

"No, no. It's no bother. I can manage." She reached for the oversized bag, but Mahkai picked it up and swung it over his shoulder with ease.

"No, really, you have been so kind, I must insist. Please lead the way and I will follow." He gestured for her to go ahead of him.

She said her goodbyes to the bees and finally hummed her agreement. She hobbled her way along a narrow dirt path Mahkai had not noticed until then. She walked fairly slowly compared to Mahkai's naturally longer stride, but he did not mind strolling next to her, keeping her pace. He was in no hurry and had nowhere to be, especially since his hut lay in ruin back in the clan camp.

Mahkai frowned. Frustration at his inability to control his magic bubbled to the surface. His thoughts swirled in his head like a war chant before battle: *Not good enough, never good enough. Never strong enough. Weak.* Bree reached up and patted his hand but remained silent as she shuffled along the path. Something in his chest loosened and he felt better as the chanting in his head dispersed.

Possibili-Tea

Spearmint

Dandelion Leaf

Sage

Rosemary

Fennel

Wild Yam Root

Green Kukicha Twig

Aigne Root

Will open your mind to endless possibilities. Drink sparingly and infrequently, as it is easy to become dependent and lose touch on reality.

-Lani

Chapter 9

They traveled in companionable silence down the winding path until she stopped before a hill on the edge of a grove of trees. Along the hillside, golden light spilled out from evenly spaced hexagonal windows. A sign hung on a post at the end of the path that read, *Winding Way Inn.*

"Come in and rest a bit. Eat, stay the night, if you will." Bree patted his hand again and took his silence as agreement. She led him through the grand, ornate door built into the hillside. It swung open effortlessly without her even touching it. Like it was waiting to do her bidding.

"What is this place?" Mahkai asked in awe. He stepped into a large, open room with tiny lights like fireflies twinkling along the ceiling. In the room adjacent, tables with a handful of fae seated at them each held several candles, creating a warm and inviting ambiance.

Mahkai wiped his hooves on the mat in the entryway so he wouldn't track mud onto the gleaming stone floors. He hung his cloak on a peg next to several others on the wall. It seemed like the correct thing to do. He assumed someone would yell at him if he did something incorrectly.

"This is my inn. Judging by your reaction, you have never seen one before. This is a place where travelers can stop for a hot meal and a safe, dry place to sleep at night. Sometimes there is even a bath, depending on the recent rains." Her eyes twinkled with laughter as she hung up her own cloak on a peg lower on the wall. "I will warn you, this is a sanctuary for everyone.

There will be no fighting here. If you have a dispute with some-one, you'll have to take it outside and far enough away to not disturb the rest of us."

Mahkai reached into his bag for his notebook, but his hand brushed a tuft of soft feathers. The little owl poked her head out of his satchel and climbed her way onto his shoulder.

"Oh, and who might this be?" Bree asked.

"This is my little owl companion. We met in the forest and had a bit of a run in with a panther. She chose to stay with me ever since."

"Oh! That is exciting. What is her name?"

"Do you have a name?" Mahkai inquired sheepishly. He had not thought to ask before now. In his head he simply called her 'little owl' but that was not a proper name, was it? He could not very well call her that, could he?

She blinked at him and tilted her head. Mahkai furrowed his brow. Was that affirmative? "What should I call you?" he tried again.

She made a series of hoots and trills then looked at him ex-pectantly. When he did not immediately respond, she nudged his cheek with her beak and repeated the sounds.

He blushed. That was her name. "That is quite lovely. My deepest apologies, but…erm…I don't quite know how to make that sound."

She repeated her name again. Mahkai bit his lip in frus-tration. "Can I call you Hopper?" She screeched at him and flapped her wings. He winced. That was a very clear *no* if he'd ever heard one. Bree chuckled, watching the entire exchange with a delighted glint in her eyes.

The owl called her name again.

And again.

And again. Each time he listened, the sound became more impossible to replicate in his mind. He blew out a breath of frustration, his face burning with embarrassment. It sounded so simple, yet impossibly complex. His shoulders slumped in defeat, convinced he could not make that sound no matter how hard he tried.

"She says her name is Gwendolin, mate." A voice croaked into his spiraling storm of thoughts. The voice, inexplicably, came from a raven sitting on the windowsill nearby. How had he not noticed it until now?

The raven shifted into a male with sun-kissed golden skin, long, glossy ebony hair that framed the high cheekbones, and the most piercing eyes Mahkai had ever seen. He pulled all of his hair back and braided it over his shoulder, then tied it with a cord he produced from his pocket.

"P-pardon?" Mahkai asked, startled. He had never seen a puka shift. It was a little unnerving, but amazing and awe-inspiring as well.

"Your little owl companion. You asked her what she is called. The closest translation into our language is Gwendolin." He looked to her for confirmation.

Gwendolin trilled softly and blinked at him. Mahkai got the distinct impression they were having a silent conversation somehow.

"Not to be rude, but how do you know?"

"She told me."

Mahkai blinked repeatedly at him, as if with each blink he might suddenly understand. He was missing something, he had to be. He glanced at Bree for an answer, but she just grinned.

"I'm a puka. Some of us can talk with certain animals if we have the affinity for it. It takes a bit of practice, mind you, but it is doable." He reached his hand out toward the tiny owl and she hopped onto his finger.

"Can I do that, too?" Mahkai was blown away by this new insight.

"Sorry, mate. Not unless you have puka blood in you."
Mahkai's shoulders slumped a little.

"She is rather expressive though, so I wouldn't worry about it," he continued as he stroked her wings. Gwendolin leaned into his touch and made little happy noises. "After you spend more time with her, you should be able to understand the general feel of what she is saying. She said you rescued her. Something about a panther?" He inspected Mahkai like he was seeing him in a new light.

Mahkai blustered. "I don't know about that. All I really did was distract the panther by tripping and falling into a hole."

The puka and Bree laughed and Gwendolin hooted softly. "Well, Gwendolin, it is an honor and pleasure to meet you." Bree flourished and bobbed in a little dip.

Mahkai thought he remembered Kamea calling it a curtsy. It seemed a strange gesture, but who was he to judge? He made a note in his book.

"Cael, Mahkai." Bree introduced them. Cael dipped and tilted his head in greeting in a very bird-like fashion. "Will you be joining us for dinner, Cael? We were just about to eat."

"I'm afraid I have a few things to attend to first, but I'll be along later." He gave her a look of genuine regret and held Gwendolin close to Mahkai's shoulder so she could retake her perch.

"I'll have someone send something to your room if you like."

"That would be very kind of you. I appreciate it," Cael said, giving Gwen one last stroke on the head.

"Oh, pardon." Mahkai paused his note taking for a moment. Cael turned back to them. "Would you... I mean, if it isn't too much of a bother..." He stalled. His mouth had started talking before he had fully formed the question in his mind. He rushed on before he lost his nerve, "Would you be willing to answer some questions I have? You see, I have never met anyone like you and what I have been told seems wildly incorrect, so… I would very much like to learn about you from…well…you." Mahkai stumbled over his words as he rushed to finish. He was so used to being talked over or interrupted, he was actually a bit shocked they had let him get to the end of his thoughts.

Cael glanced at Bree, who nodded her head slightly. "I'm afraid I cannot tonight, but if you are available tomorrow, I believe I could," he offered a small smile. His eyes held Mahkai's with an intensity that made him uncomfortable. He felt seen, like Cael could see into his soul.

"Oh, thank you!" Mahkai grinned in surprise, not sure how else to respond. Cael had said yes.

"I really must be going, but I look forward to our chat tomorrow, Mahkai. Good to see you, Bree, as always." He shifted back into a raven and flew out the nearest window and into the night.

Mahkai scribbled notes about how big Cael's raven was, how fast he shifted, and his immediate questions like whether it hurt to shift or not. Clothes seemed to shift with him, but did personal effects and items? Bags? He didn't see him carrying anything, though.

"Follow me, dear." Bree waved at him to follow her into a doorway further along in the entryway room.

Mahkai hurried to follow so he wouldn't get left behind. The door swung open, also of its own volition, and Mahkai's mouth watered from the delicious scents wafting from what he guessed was the kitchen. Spicy and savory blended together with an underlying sweetness, causing his mouth to water in anticipation.

"You can set my bag over there in the corner and I'll have someone attend to it. Here. Sit." She gestured to a stool next to a small table on the side of the room near the fires. He had quite forgotten he still carried her sack of things.

The room buzzed with energy. Three fairies tended a half dozen pots, stirring, pouring, and beating in a flurry of activity. Other fairies retrieved plates and bowls of food and disappeared out the door, returning with empty ones in a steady flow in and out of the kitchen. Some carried giant jugs and pitchers of a sweet smelling liquid.

They peered curiously at him while they continued working while seeming to know what to do and where to be without even needing to speak. Mahkai had just begun to sketch the kitchen when Bree set a plate piled with round and triangular shaped pastries before him.

He closed his eyes and inhaled the buttery sweet aroma tickling his nose. A little drool escaped the corner of his mouth. Wiping it with his sleeve, he hoped Bree hadn't noticed. He let out a sigh of relief. She had already turned away to taste something in the largest pot.

He blinked when a tiny fairy child flitted unsteadily over to his table and set down a pot of honey and a plate of butter. Sheepishly, they pulled two blunted knives out of their pocket and set them down before him as well. He smiled warmly at them.

"Hello there. Thank you," he said, remembering his manners. They peered at him through wild, dark ringlets and bobbed in the air before zigzagging across the kitchen and out the door.

"That's Camron. He's a little shy around newcomers, but once he warms to you, you'll never have a moment of silence." Bree appeared behind him. Her sleeves were rolled up, and she was dusted with a white powdery substance he guessed was some sort of flour.

"Well, how do you like my scones, dear?"

"I haven't tried one yet."

"Well, hurry up! I need to know if I should add anything before I finish the next batch." Her eyes sparkled as she planted her hands on her hips. She never lost her air of authority, even covered in flour.

Even sitting on the ground, he still towered over her, but there was no mistaking who was in charge here. It was fine. He was used to taking orders and was more than happy to if it meant tasting whatever a scone was.

Gwendolin ate some of the crumbly bits that had fallen off and hooted her appreciation. Bree grinned. "Well, I'm glad you approve."

Mahkai selected one and bit into it. His eyes practically rolled in the back of his head as the crisp outer shell gave way to a soft, warm center. It was sweet and tasted like summer berries with a hint of something he couldn't quite name. He didn't remember finishing the rest of it, but when Bree chuckled, he opened his eyes to see her watching him.

"That good I take it?"

"Good? Good doesn't even begin to describe this masterpiece of deliciousness," Mahkai sputtered, wiping the stray crumbs off his chest.

Bree laughed again and returned to her work table. She called over her shoulder, "Try the next one with butter and honey."

He did exactly that. He ate one with butter, then honey, then both butter and honey. At some point, his plate disappeared and a new one appeared. These smelled different—more savory and filled with melty cheese. He devoured these too. A mug of warm spiced cider appeared before him at some point, to wash it all down with.

When he and Gwendolin couldn't eat anymore, Bree

directed them to follow her. She walked with him through another grand doorway. What lay on the other side took his breath away.

They stood in a courtyard rimmed with gorgeous trees. But not just any trees, these trees had been grown by Arboreal architects. Golden evening light highlighted ornate rooms and houses growing from the trees themselves. They were like nothing he'd ever seen. He wanted to draw them all.

Branches and vines wove and curled into intricate designs, patterns within patterns, each different but complementary to all the others. It was breathtaking; the minds that could come up with such little details. Mahkai was used to the efficient, pragmatic huts of his people—too easily destroyed to put much effort into decorating them. They were only meant to last for a season or two before being rebuilt. Except Aunti Lani's hut. He remembered with fondness how she had meticulously maintained her hut so it would last and insisted it be rebuilt in the same place when an especially harsh storm knocked it down.

"Oh my," he breathed, at a loss for words.

"I'm glad you like them! My nephew and granddaughter designed them. Do you want to see inside one?"

He looked at her full of hope and wonder. She cackled and patted his hand. "Here, you can stay in this one. I think it should be your size."

Mahkai saw what she meant as she gestured to one of the larger rooms available. He looked at her again with questions brimming in his eyes, unable to voice any of them.

"We have rooms of all sizes to accommodate most. Here." She handed him a large key. He followed her inside. The interior was spacious and well kept and reflected the same design as the outside. It was perfect.

"There is a hammock hanging in the corner, or there is a soft mat if you prefer sleeping on the floor. Wash room is in there. And before you ask, yes, it was magicked by Althenaea, the water master herself." She raised her chin proudly. "She seemed to fancy our little project here. Now I'll leave you to it. I've got a few things to attend to before I turn in for the night. Is there anything else you need?"

"Why?"

"Why what, dear?" Her silver eyebrows raised in concern.

"Why are you doing this? I have very little I can trade and no magic to speak of." He blurted out.

"Because the bees accepted you. You have a way about you. I've lived my entire life according to the bees. I'm not about to stop now," she said matter-of-factly.

Mahkai's throat constricted. He was at a loss for words, and even if he had any, he wouldn't trust his voice to work properly. She patted his arm, smiling affectionately, and left. The door closed behind her with a soft click, leaving him in peaceful silence. He breathed a sigh of relief, then remembered his tiny companion.

"Gwendolin, you have a fine name," he said, setting her to perch on the windowsill. She hooted at him sleepily. "May I call you Gwen?"

She blinked at him and hooted once. It sounded like her consent, but he was still getting a feeling for her mannerisms. He hoped the more time he spent with her, the more they would understand one another. He would figure this out. It wasn't like he was around puka all the time to ask them what she was saying.

Crickets and frogs chirped outside, announcing dusk and the coming night. Mahkai found a round cushion in the middle of the floor by a low table and made himself comfortable. He spread out his books, charcoal, and inks around him, placing them in rows by length and color.

He sketched and took notes of anything and everything—one

thought flowing into the next, until his hand cramped. He tried writing with his offhand, but it was much slower and he couldn't make any of his drawings look the way he wanted. He needed to practice more, so he could write for longer periods of time before stopping or maybe not have to stop at all. He could only imagine how much he would accomplish if he didn't have to take breaks all the time.

He rose from the floor and stretched slowly, letting his tired, aching muscles relax. It hurt at first, but after a few moments, he felt much better, as he always did after stretching. Gwendolin had disappeared from the window at some point, but he knew she would come back. He had learned that after his last panic. It still worried him when she disappeared randomly, but he was learning to trust that she wanted to be here and would come back.

He was curious what a washroom was. Now that he could no longer write for the time being, he was ready for his next mini adventure. He opened the door, narrow compared to the entry door, but still fairly large.

The first thing he noticed was the floor was entirely covered in soft, spongy green moss. A thick, fluffy fabric hung from a hook on the wall across from a delicate chain cord with a note attached to it. *Pull Me* it read, so he did. The clearest water he had ever seen poured from a hidden spout. He ran his hand under it for a moment, then drank deeply. It was sweet and lightly fragrant with the smell of roses.

He pulled the cord again, and the water stopped. There was an amber medallion resting on a tiny shelf next to the cord. It had two ornate overlapping W's with a little bee inscribed on it. He sniffed it; it smelled like honey. He tasted it and spat, instantly regretting his decision. It tasted like soap. He chuckled. Washroom indeed. A washing sounded delightful. He had only ever bathed in lakes and streams, so this would indeed be an adventure.

He removed his clothes, pulled the cord, and stepped under the stream. His skin tingled and trembled from the cold. After a few moments, the water became gradually warmer, as warm as a hot spring. When he was thoroughly wet, he pulled the cord to stop the water flow and lathered himself with the soap.

A song popped into his head, so he started humming as he washed. He pulled the cord and the warm water cascaded over him, washing away the soap and much of his aches. His fur had never been so soft and he felt very relaxed.

When he was completely clean, he pulled the cord a final time, cutting off the flow of water. He marveled at how the water running off him soaked into the moss and did not run into the outer room like he suspected it would.

Normally, after washing in a lake, he would shake himself to get rid of the excess water and then lay on the bank in the sun until he was dry, but that did not seem wise indoors. Also, the sun had fully set by now.

He picked up the fluffy fabric from its hook on the wall and pressed it to his face. It felt amazing and soaked up the water in his fur easily. He dried the rest of himself, then pulled out his change of clothes from his bag, glad he'd brought them at the last minute. He would have hated putting his dirty clothes back on now that he was clean.

The soft lights in his room twinkled at him every so often. Finally ready to sleep, he searched all over, trying to find a way to blow them out. First, he had tried simply blowing, but they did not work like a candle. He assumed they were magic, but simultaneously hoped they were not. How did one extinguish magic lights?

He yawned as he contemplated this and eventually gave up. He could sleep with light and was struggling to keep his eyes open anyway. In the end, he lay down in the hammock and pulled the blanket over his eyes. Soon, the pull of sleep beckoned him into its gentle embrace.

Totali-Tea

Spearmint
Dandelion
Red Clover
Rose Petals
Calendula
Echinacea
Aster

A cleansing tea. Drink daily for soft fur and strong, gleaming horns and hooves.
                    -Mahkai

Chapter 10

The next morning, Mahkai wandered back toward the kitchen with Gwendolin perched in his hand. A small pond speckled with purple and white lilies bubbled in the center of the garden. Little orange and white fish peered back at him. The trees seemed taller, grander, with their twisting vines and branches sparkling in the daylight.

The scent of fresh baked bread wafted around him as a dwarf lumbered out of the inn. His stomach rumbled in anticipation. Bree had said last night they were guests of the bees, so he wondered if that included breakfast. He very much hoped so.

Raucous noise greeted him as he entered the main room. A large group of dwarves, fairies, and even three minotaur sat scattered throughout the room at various-sized tables. Relief flooded through him when he didn't recognize any of the minotaur. They caught sight of him and raised their mugs in greeting.

"Come sit with us!" they boomed over the loud chatter of the room.

Mahkai shuffled over to their table, careful not to step on any tails, keeping his tucked tightly to him. "Good morning to you," he greeted them and pounded a fist to his chest, as was minotaur custom.

They mirrored the gesture and waved over one of the serving fairies buzzing by with a tray. Mahkai remembered him from the night before, but had completely forgotten his name.

"Say, you look familiar." One of them eyed Mahkai with special interest. "Aren't you the Makanui chief's youngest—the

one who destroyed half of the Kekoroa camp a few days back?"
He chuckled.

"I heard they were up all night rebuilding," another said.

"All I know is, it threw them off enough that we easily defeated them the next day in our friendly little competition." The third minotaur grinned with a malicious glint in his eyes. The others laughed and pounded each other's backs in congratulations.

Mahkai hunched his shoulders, instantly uncomfortable. *Are they laughing at me? Is that the only reason they called me over here?* His eyes darted around, looking for a way to slip out without offending them. He hoped they wouldn't notice the added color in his cheeks from his embarrassment.

The server headed to their table caught sight of Mahkai. He could have sworn the fairy glowed faintly as his wings beat faster. It couldn't be the sunlight glinting on his wings. It was the wrong color, more silvery than golden hues. What magic did he have that his body glowed with it? Did magic behave differently for different fae?

The fairy bowed deeply to Mahkai over his tray. "We have prepared a special meal for you, most honored guest. Would you prefer to take it out here, in your room, or somewhere else? I can even have it packed to take with you if you are in a hurry." He gestured to Mahkai's tablemates.

Gwendolin ruffled her feathers anxiously on his shoulder. Mahkai turned to them as well and noticed their tense posture and flared nostrils. Dread trickled like cold water down his spine. They saw the fairy's bow as a sign of aggression.

Mahkai held up a hand as one of the minotaur rose to his feet abruptly, his hand reaching for his weapons. Mahkai flinched and hastily interjected, "Wait, he didn't mean offense. Quite um…quite the opposite, actually. He was giving me respect… of the highest level. For what, I have no idea, but respect and deference nonetheless." He muttered the last bit, feeling apprehensive, embarrassed, and nervous all at once.

The minotaur looked suspiciously between Mahkai and the alarmed fairy, then shrugged, removing his hand from his axes and retaking his seat. The fairy advanced again after it had retreated. "My deepest apologies. I did not intend any offense." He started to bow his head again, but stopped himself.

"Thank y—" Mahkai began.

"That's just like a fairy to not be aware of our customs," one minotaur sneered to the others, as if the fairy could not hear them.

"Rude is what it is," the other agreed.

Mahkai gritted his teeth and turned his back to the minotaur, placing himself between them and the fairy. "Might we step away for a moment? I have a few questions for you," Mahkai said loud enough for the three minotaur to hear him. The fairy nodded in agreement and zipped toward the nearest exit. Mahkai followed without another word.

When they emerged outside, the fairy hovered before him, twisting his hands on the edge of the tray nervously. Gwendolin settled down and Mahkai let out a breath of pent-up air. He let his shoulders slump a little and smiled kindly at the fairy. "I am so sorry about them. Not all minotaur are like that, but any is too many."

The fairy straightened at his words and smiled back at him. "Queen said you were different. Now I understand." He nodded to himself.

"Queen?" Mahkai asked.

"Yes. She is Queen Bree of our hive. Some fairies choose to live in hives and colonies as opposed to the rest of the fae. Not unlike minotaur clans, though."

Mahkai smiled. So she was a fairy; how had he not seen that before? Maybe he didn't know as much about fairies as he thought he did. Queen seemed a fitting title for Bree. She had an air of command about her, and everyone seemed to follow her direction.

"Food?" the fairy prompted, interrupting his thoughts.

"Ah, yes. Wherever is fine. I don't mind. Just anywhere out of the way will do." He shrugged.

"Hmmm…" The fairy drummed his fingers on his chin. "I know just the place. Follow me!" He zipped down one of the many paths branching out from the Inn.

Mahkai wondered how he kept them all straight as he trailed behind the fairy, taking in the beautiful scenery. Where did they all lead? He let his imagination run wild with possibilities. More rooms and huts for the inn? A meeting hall, perhaps? Nooks for secret rendezvous for forbidden lovers? He smiled at the last one, inspired by a tale he'd heard not long ago.

The fairy stopped a little further down, next to a simple yet elegant open structure with no walls. A small stream trickled unhurriedly across a pebbled bed. Lilies, asters, carnations, and daisies, among other flowers he didn't recognize, grew along the bank, their long leaves dipping their tips in the water. Trees bloomed and shed their blossoms over everything, lending their fragrance to the peaceful charm of the area.

"How is this possible?" Mahkai turned to the fairy, but he was gone. Mahkai shrugged and sat down in the bank under the impossible tree. It was the harvest and soon would be the cold, dormant season. This tree simply should not be in bloom. He wished he had not forgotten his bag with his notebooks in his room in his haste to find food.

The wind was also unseasonably warm. He took a deep breath and tried to name all the things he could smell. The shuffle of feet alerted him to someone's approach. He turned to find Bree carrying a ginormous basket in her arms.

"Oh, let me help you with that!" He jumped to his feet to assist her.

"It is alright, I can manage. I carried it this far already." She shooed him away and set it down on a low table in the structure. "Do you like my tea house? Koby told me about what happened. That was kind of you and good thinking creatively. You know, you have a natural gift at alleviating conflict." She began unpacking the basket as she spoke.

She uncovered a plate full of scones and set butter, honey, and jam next to it. Next, she set out a bowl of berries and other fruit. There was another bowl with a white substance he didn't recognize, but it smelled delightful. She pulled out a plate with a variety of cheese wedges. Another bowl contained nuts and seeds.

Mahkai watched her silently, his mind still trying to wrap itself around her words. Gwen made an appreciative trill and spread her wings for balance as she hopped over to the table.

"Sit." She pointed to a cushion next to her. She shuffled over to a small cabinet and opened the ornate doors, pulling out a tray with several cups, a teapot, and three rows of small jars the color of dove feathers.

They were quiet for a long time, enjoying their breakfast and tea, when Bree finally broke the comfortable silence. "So, Mahkai, what are you doing?"

He froze and looked up at her with a mouth stuffed full of scone. He had no idea what she was referring to. Was he not meant to eat another scone?

Mirth wrinkled the corners of her eyes as she covered her smile with her tea mug, taking a sip. She set it down and buttered another scone for herself, adding berries and the mysterious white substance, which she'd informed him was cream.

He swallowed hastily and took a gulp of tea to wash it

down. When he could finally speak again, he asked, "What do you mean?"

"What are your plans? Where are you going from here? Where is home? You didn't look prepared for an overly long journey, but who am I to judge? You may not need much. I simply mean you have an air about you of someone untethered." She gazed at him intently.

"I don't actually know." He shifted uncomfortably on his cushion, suddenly unable to look her in the eye.

"Well, you are welcome to stay here as long as you like."

He looked up sharply, not daring to hope.

She held up her hand to halt his protests. "Before you say you have nothing to offer, I can think of a few things you can help with if you feel you need to balance the scales, so to speak. You have more to offer than you realize, you know?"

Mahkai held his breath. This was more than he could have hoped for. He needed time and space away from his clan, and this was much closer to the historians he wanted to meet with about Aunti Lani's journal and the obelisk. What would she ask of him, though? He hesitated. Fear of agreeing to something he didn't want prickled at the back of his neck. He shook his head quickly to remove those intrusive thoughts. She wouldn't do that.

"I am well aware this is only temporary, as you'll be needing a place for all your books and things. Unfortunately, I don't have anything that might fit what you need. Hmmm." She tapped a finger on her chin thoughtfully. "Tell you what, after we finish here, I need someone to run to the market to pick up a few things."

She chuckled at his look of glee. He always wanted to go to a market. He had heard wondrous things from Kamea and Maleek and the others when they were sent. Their clan was fairly self-sufficient and usually avoided interaction with the other fae, so there had never been a reason to send him. That, and they knew he would most likely get distracted and forget his purpose of going.

Mahkai cleared his throat. "I would be happy to do whatever you require of me. I am most grateful for your generosity." Tales of fae who could entrap the unwary came unbidden into his mind as he said those words, but he quickly dismissed them. They were just campfire stories used to teach calves to be mindful of the meaning of their words.

"My pleasure." She popped a berry into her mouth and closed her eyes and smiled, clearly relishing the taste of the delicious fruit.

Anxi-e-Tea

Lemongrass
Hawthorn Berry
Gingko
Ginger Root
Hibiscus
Corraithe Berry

Similar to a Blood Calming Tea. The only difference is steep time. If over-steeped, it will
induce anxiety and paranoia. May also bring
out nervous habits.

-Mahkai

Chapter 11

The market was a bustling, writhing mass—an overwhelming chaos of smells, sights, and sounds. Tents and stalls of all shapes, sizes, and colors were practically, and quite literally, stacked on top of each other. Fae zipped and flowed through the mass, seemingly not bumping into each other. How they managed it, Mahkai would never know. He did not fare so well. Everywhere he moved, he ran into someone or stepped on someone's tail.

"Pardon me. Excuse me. Oh dear." He ducked into the nearest mostly empty stall for a breather from the throng of a mob outside. There was a delicious aroma emanating from the various pots full of bubbling liquids inside. Sweet and savory with a hint of tangy… What was this food?

"Ah, hello there! What can I get for you, my young bull? Can I entice you with a tasty treat, delectable delight, or a magnificent morsel?"

"Oh, um, hello! I don't…" He hesitated, letting the scents linger in his nose and on his tongue. He wasn't hungry since breakfast with Bree wasn't that long ago, but this—whatever this is—was making him hungry. Was it magic? Or did it just smell so good it was naturally irresistible? He took a step closer, debating. Out of habit, he rubbed his thumb over the edge of his pendant around his neck. He had no idea how he would pay for it, though.

The magic glamoring the food and holding him captive shattered like tiny, glittering fragments of ice on the edge of his vision. The food that had smelled so good a moment before turned sour and rotten.

He watched in horror as the vibrant colors dulled to muddy browns and sickly greens. He shook his head and retreated toward the door. "Not today."

Out of the corner of his eye, the fairy furrowed his brow and planted his hands on his hips. Mahkai rushed out before he caused an altercation. He had a task to do. As much as he wanted to explore every inch of the market, he needed to pick up the items on Bree's list and return to her.

Eventually, after fighting through the crowd, getting run into on numerous occasions, and being knocked over by several dwarves carrying large crates and sacks, he found the first shop on the list and stepped inside. The shopkeeper was slim and wiry, dressed in a maroon and russet patchwork shirt tucked into dark brown pants with a matching dark brown vest trimmed in yellow embroidery. The hilt of a dagger just above his right hip peeked out of an orange sash tied around his waist. It took him a moment to realize he was staring. The shopkeeper stared at him, equally surprised.

Quickly, he informed the shopkeeper he was here to pick up Bree's order. He blinked at Mahkai in surprise. "You are not her normal delivery person," the fae remarked, appraising him with a narrow gaze.

"Ah, no, she sent me today."

"Hmmm. I can see that. What can you do?"

"Do?"

"Yes, as in what do you have to trade?" He pursed his lips and tilted his head expectantly.

Mahkai sputtered. "I'm not—I mean, I don't—Oh, dear. Has she not…"

The shopkeeper cracked a grin. "Relax, this is my debt to her we are clearing." He waved his hand.

Mahkai glanced around the bare shop. "And, erm… what is it you make or sell? If you don't mind my asking."

"Ah, nonsense. I don't mind at all. I procure hard-to-obtain items."

Mahkai eyed the orange sash around the man's waist, then down at his own crimson one.

"Would you care to trade?" The shopkeeper's eyes twinkled. "That is quite the lovely shade of red you wear, and I think it would match my ensemble better than this one."

"Where did you get it?"

"The human kingdom." He shrugged as if it were no big deal, but his face gave away his excitement—his smile, the way his eyes caught the light—his entire demeanor gave off energy.

Mahkai gasped. "Did you really travel to the human realm? What is it like?" Excitedly, he pulled out his notebook and scribbled down notes, then glanced up.

The trader's smile took on a slightly mischievous glint as he glanced at Mahkai's sash. "Tell you what, I'll trade you my orange sash for your crimson one. You show me how you tied it to get it to look like that, and I'll tell you stories about the humans. What do you say?"

Mahkai considered him for a moment. His excitement threatened to override his need to think it over. Nothing about this exchange seemed malicious or deceitful as far as he could see, so he nodded.

He set his book on the table and untied his sash, showing the trader each wrap, fold, and tuck as he went. They swapped cloth. The orange fabric was silky smooth, like water sliding through his fingers. He re-tied it around his waist, again showing the trader step by step and offering slight adjustments so it would lie correctly.

He had to adjust his a few times because it didn't want to stay the way he tied the other one. Eventually he gave up and just tucked in the loose ends and hoped it would stay. The shop-keeper nodded and brought out a couple of stools for them to sit on.

"Would you like anything to drink or eat?" he asked Mahkai.

"No thank you, I have my own." He pulled out his horn of tea. It was no longer warm, but it was still delicious. He had used the leftover berries from breakfast and a recipe from his aunt's journal. Its fruity fragrance wafted around them in the tent. The trader sat up straighter and watched him intently. "What is that?"

"It is my own special drink, made by steeping leaves and fruit in hot water. It is called tea."

"Interesting. The humans have something similar, but theirs is a dark brown liquid and can be quite bitter. They add cream and honey to it. Yours is quite a bit different. May I taste it?" He produced a tiny ceramic cup from his pocket.

"Most certainly." Mahkai filled the cup. He wondered at its small size. It held no more than a mouthful. Why would anyone want to drink out of a cup so small?

"Mmm." The trader sipped it slowly. "You should think about selling this. Fae would come from all over to drink it. What do you call this particular blend? Is it just for hydration, or are there other benefits?"

"Oh, erm, I call it berry tea."

The trader frowned. "No, that won't do. You need catchy names to hook your clients. What about Berry Good Tea? Hmmm, no." He rubbed his chin. "Ah, I have it. Frui-Tea." He chuckled.

Mahkai mulled it over. It did have a nice sound to it. "Alright." He jotted it down in his notebook. "So, about the humans?" Mahkai prompted. He did not want to be a pest, but humans were like dragons—everyone knew they existed, but no one got to see them or knew much about them. Not only had this trader seen humans, he had even interacted with them.

The trader leaned in conspiratorially. "They are strange creatures—like a small dwarf or a large fairy or puka, only with weirdly shaped, rounded ears and teeth. They also have a very odd sense of justice and trade. They trade in rocks."

"Rocks?" Mahkai blurted out in surprise. "Why would they do that? That is preposterous, deranged even!"

The trader nodded. "They even kill each other and fight wars over it. I've never seen it for myself, but customarily, they eat the heart of their enemies slain in battle."

Mahkai gasped and covered his chest with his hands before resuming his note-taking. "That's barbaric and disgusting."

"Like I said, I never saw it, but they do this whole weird ritual around it. Their death practices are quite fascinating really. Anyway, I digress. They—" he was cut off by the arrival of a small fairy, holding a small box, riding a gust of wind.

"Here you are, Uncle." He presented the box to the trader, who gestured to Mahkai. The fairy offered it to Mahkai, who accepted it.

"Well, it seems our business is concluded for now." He rose, his teacup disappearing into the folds of his clothes somewhere. "Thank you for the tea. Think on what I said about starting your own tea shop."

Mahkai rose from his stool as well and tucked his books away in his satchel and the box into the bottom of the large sack for Bree. "I will." With that, he shuffled out into the late-morning light in search of the other items for Bree.

☕ ☕ ☕

Over his shoulder, Mahkai hefted the last of the sacks with everything Bree had requested. His mind buzzed with everything he had seen, heard, smelled, tasted, and touched. At first, he'd tried taking notes, but there was so much, he had to relinquish his notes back to his bag and hope to remember everything, lest he miss something from staring down at his notes.

He was just turning to leave when a stall, tucked out of the way, caught his attention. Or, not the stall itself, but what it hawked.

Miniature trees with buildings grown into them, like the trees around the inn, sat in neat little rows on shelves and ledges and even dangled from the ceiling. Other shelves boasted different sorts of buildings. All were extremely fine, crafted with masterful skill. Mahkai had never seen something so intricate. It was beautiful, yet functional. They were perfect.

"What are you in the market for? Can I help you make your selection?" An elderly fae with thin lips and a slender face peered at him from over little frames of clear glass resting on his nose. He sat on a stool behind the high counter running across the stall. An ornate woven curtain covering a doorway leading to the back of the stall rustled gently in the slight breeze.

"Ah, no thank you. I was just admiring your craft." He straightened and shuffled back a step.

"Are you in the market for a new home?" The shopkeeper raised an eyebrow inquisitively. The sign on the stall read "Master Architect Arlo". He rose from his seat and came around the counter to stand by Mahkai's elbow. He was almost a meter shorter, but carried himself with a graceful regality that surprised Mahkai.

"Well, yes, but no. Not at the moment. I, erm, you see, I cannot…" Mahkai trailed off. Shame burned in his cheeks and neck. He wanted nothing more than to flee when the fae gently laid his hand on Mahkai's elbow.

"Say no more. I cannot help you, but…" Master Arlo paused, running a hand over his chin and short, graying beard.

"My apprentice needs more practice. Perhaps you both might benefit from a collaboration?" He gazed into Mahkai's eyes and a corner of his mouth quirked up. "Hartley? You have a potential project," he called over his shoulder to the back of their shop. Leaning in, he dropped his voice and spoke to Mahkai conspiratorially, glancing out of the corner of his eye. "She's a bit free-spirited. Best to just go with it." He winked at him, then straightened and stepped back.

"What?" Mahkai whispered, perplexed.

"Hey! You wanted to see me?" A fiery amber fairy with four semi-translucent wings, like a dragonfly, slid onto a stool. She pushed her wild, curly, burnt-orange hair out of her eyes and looked him up and down, then grinned.

Mahkai thought she looked a little frazzled and out of sorts, but who was he to judge? He probably didn't look much better. The wind shifted, and he caught the light fragrance of roasted almonds, vanilla flowers, and an earthy scent he couldn't place.

"He is looking for direction and input into a new home, and I thought it would be a wonderful exercise for you to tackle," the elderly fae said to his apprentice.

"On my own?" she squeaked, balling her fists in front of her face with excitement.

"If you think you can handle it?" he said with a twinkle in his eyes.

"Yes! This is awesome! This is... ahem. Thank you very much. I am honored you would put your trust in me for this significant task." She reined in her overabundant enthusiasm and bowed to each of them.

"I... Oh, erm... You are most welcome." Mahkai blinked at her abrupt change of demeanor. He liked her enthusiasm, though. He hoped he wouldn't end up messing everything up or letting her down somehow. "What, em... What do you need from me exactly?" He bit his lip.

"Oh, lots of things. I need to know your wants and needs. What are the essentials you simply must have and what are extra things you would like?" she explained. "What styles do you like? How big…" She rattled off a long list of requirements.

Mahkai blanked. He did not know there was so much that went into a new hut. "I… I need to be getting back with my supplies I said I would deliver…" Guilt from interrupting her made his stomach churn and his chest tighten.

"Where are you headed?" she asked, unbothered by the interruption.

"The Winding Way Inn?" he offered hesitantly.

"I can go with you!" she declared, then turned to her mentor. "Can I go with him?" she asked.

He chuckled. "I think you have the order mixed up, young apprentice. You are meant to ask first, before making promises."

"Why would I do that? If I asked first, then you might say no. This way I've already said yes, but you still get to give permission, so everyone is happy." She smiled with feigned innocence, looking up at her mentor through her golden eyelashes.

The shopkeeper took the wire and glass thing off his face and pinched the bridge of his nose with his forefingers. "You know what, yes. Please go. I don't know what to do with you sometimes. Maybe I'll actually get something done around here." He waved his hand dismissively at her, then winked at Mahkai.

"You know you love me." She grinned back.

"Don't hurry back," he teased affectionately.

"I wasn't planning on it," she shot back.

"Bring me back something, though?" He raised his eyebrows and tilted his head.

"You know I always do." Hurriedly, she threw a few things into a bag and slung it over one shoulder. "Ready!" she declared.

Her wings hummed quietly, moving so fast they were only a shimmery blur. She bolted out of the stall and zoomed through the center of the market, not waiting for Mahkai. She reminded him of a hummingbird zipping through a garden.

"I feel I should thank you again," Mahkai said to the shop-keeper.

The elderly fae laughed. "Don't thank me yet. But I'm sure it will be an interesting experience for you both. You are doing me a favor, honestly. I look forward to what you come up with together. She is a dreamer, that one. If you give her creative freedom, there is no telling what she will come up with. Now, don't you have a delivery to make?"

"Oh, yes!" Mahkai shifted the sacks on his shoulders and turned to follow the fairy as bright as a flame bobbing up and down through the sea of people ahead of him.

🍵 🍵 🍵

On their journey back to the inn, Hartley peppered him with questions. He was a little unnerved about several things. First, he was used to being the one with all the questions. Second, she listened to his thoughts and made comments and suggestions. Third, she flew at eye level with him most of the way. He was so used to looking down or up to others that he didn't realize he liked being at the same height until she landed on the dirt path before the inn.

Mahkai followed her into the inn's main entrance and was mildly surprised she knew where she was going until he re-membered her exchange with the Master Architect.

As he entered the bustling kitchen, several fairies immedi-ately relieved him of his burdens. A rainbow of fairies dashed and darted everywhere with steaming kettles and pots, trays, bowls, and plates with a variety of foods and liquids. Others were cutting, cooking, slicing, dicing, washing, and everything else imaginable that one might do in a kitchen.

Bree swept Hartley into a hug. "Hartley, what a nice surprise! I see you have met my newest guest, Mahkai. Good, good. I was hoping to introduce you, but it seems you have beaten me to it." She tucked one of Hartley's stray curls behind her ear. "It is good to see you, dear. Would you like some lunch?" She addressed both of them.

"Yes please! Arlo said to bring him back something as well." Hartley smiled triumphantly.

"Of course. I wouldn't dream of sending you back empty-handed. How long do you have? Do you need to head right back, or do you have a little while to catch up?"

"He said to take my time." Hartley's eyes sparkled mischievously. "I'm to help Mahkai design his new dwelling." She turned to him. "How do you feel about lofted tree-homes? As in a home made out of a tree, but rather than on the ground, it's suspended in the branches."

Mahkai blinked at her. "I do not know… I've never considered it. I am open to the idea, though," he said haltingly.

"Oh, good!" Hartley responded. "What are you used to living in? My Arboreal skills are in tree craft as opposed to stone or ground craft, but if you want those, I could talk to a few friends of mine."

"No, no. I'm happy to explore trees. Honestly, I think it is fascinating and would be delightful. I do love trees."

"Sit, sit." Bree ushered them to the small table on the side of the room and gestured for someone to bring another stool. Mahkai retrieved two of his notebooks and charcoal sticks and handed one of each to Hartley.

With wide eyes, she opened it and flipped through some of the already partially filled pages. She squinted, then reached up and pulled little wing-looking things with wires attached to them out of her mass of curls and placed them on her nose.

"What are those?" Mahkai blurted out. He had assumed they were purely for decoration.

"These?" She pointed to the thing on her face. "They are spectacles for seeing small things, so I don't squint so much. Here, try them." She took them off her face and balanced them on his nose.

He attempted to look through them, but they made his eyes cross with the effort. He looked at the book on the table in front of him and closed one eye. Suddenly, he could see everything in clear detail.

"How are they made? What are they made from? Why are they called spectacles? Are they magic? Where can I obtain a pair?" He sputtered as he handed them back to her, blown away by how much better he could see his books. She balanced them on her nose and hooked the side wires on top of her tiny pointed ears.

He muttered to himself. "I suppose I could try to make them, or something like them. These are amazing!"

"Oh! I could talk to my friend who makes them. She has them in a shop at the market. Although we might need to modify them for your face, as they are meant for a different shaped nose. But I'm sure that won't be a problem for her. She will be thrilled about a new commission to tinker with." She waved her hand at his face.

"What will she require in return?" he inquired, a little wary since he didn't have magic to barter with or secrets to speak of.

"Probably nothing, I expect. But either way, don't worry about it," Hartley dismissed.

"I… oh… That is…" Mahkai stammered. "I don't know what to say. I'm not accustomed to the generosity of others."

"It is nothing. Really. Here, what do you think of this?" She turned the book to face him.

He looked through her sketches and his jaw dropped. "These are amazing!"

"Excellent!" Hartley clapped her hands together. "Do you mind if I borrow this to continue sketching?"

"By all means, please do."

Bree set steaming plates and bowls piled high before them. Mahkai tucked his book of notes into his bag and inhaled deeply. His mouth watered from the delicious smells of the brightly colored food. He had no idea what half of them were, but he did not care. Anything that smelled this good was bound to taste amazing.

There was a bowl filled with a creamy golden broth with a variety of roots floating in it. Another one was red and had fruit and bits of meat, likely lamb by the smell. It had a tangy, spicy aroma. There were bowls of steaming grains and a plate piled high with flatbreads.

"Thank you, Gran. The curry smells amazing," Hartley said as she spooned some of everything into her bowl. She tore a piece of the flat bread and used it like a spoon to scoop up some of the grain and curry, stuffing it in her mouth.

Bree gave her a disapproving look, but she ignored it. "You'll have to excuse my granddaughter's lack of table manners," she said as she also used her flatbread to scoop a much smaller bite.

Mahkai let out a sigh and released the tension in his shoulders. She didn't disapprove of the eating with her hands, but rather the overlarge bite she had taken. He was adept at using a variety of utensils, but enjoyed using his hands as well. He followed their lead, savoring the burst of flavors and textures on his tongue.

Between bites, Hartley continued to pepper him with questions. "Do you like birch, pine, oak, ash, or maple?"

Mahkai swallowed a bite too quickly, sending him into a coughing fit. Bree handed him a cup of water. He accepted it gratefully. When he could finally speak again, he responded, "I'm afraid I will be of no help. I like the look of all of them but am unsure of the benefits, the pros and cons, if you will, of choosing one tree over another."

"Well, you are small for a minotaur but huge for a fairy, so I believe we should choose a hardwood that will support you naturally without making too many modifications. You see, we run into issues if you try to make too many changes from what the original wants."

"I don't understand."

"We can't change the essence of something. Like, we can't ask a softwood tree to be more rigid than it is naturally. More than a little, at least. Just like we can't convince grass to suddenly grow into a tree."

Mahkai nodded his understanding. "Well, what are the strongest trees able to withstand storms or…erm…a series of small cyclones that may accidentally arise?"

Hartley scrunched her nose in thought as she studied him. She tapped her fingers on her chin as she thought. "Ah, I know of an oak that will be perfect for you. There is an oak tree I am thinking of that is rather receptive to change. Are you ok with oak?" She peered up at him inquisitively.

"If you think it is good, I will defer to your judgment." He nodded, wide-eyed, as she sketched more things in his notebook.

Excitement bubbled in his chest. He was really doing this. He was going to live in a tree on his own, away from the clan. Apprehension quickly followed. What would his family say? Would he even be allowed? He snorted, startling Hartley.

"Is there something wrong?"

"No, no. I was just thinking. When can we go see it?"

Hartley glanced inquisitively at Bree, who nodded, then returned her attention back to Mahkai. "We can go tomorrow if that is ok with you. I need to do some preparations, gather supplies, and rest if I'll be performing big magics." Excitement danced in her eyes and her wings fluttered and buzzed.

"Let's see, I'll need..." She trailed off, lost in thought.

Bree began clearing away their lunch. "No rush, but when you are finished, I believe Cael is available for your chat."

"Oh yes! I had quite forgotten." He stood abruptly, knocking over his stool in his haste. "Please excuse me, Hartley. I will return a little while later." He hesitated when she didn't immediately respond.

"She'll be right here when you are finished, I suspect." Bree chuckled. "When her mind starts working on a project, she tends to forget the rest of us exist until she works out whatever it is she is thinking about."

Mahkai understood that very well. "My family says I do the same."

Bree grinned up at him and patted his knee. "I suspect you are more alike than either of you know. Yet also very different." She hummed as she finished wiping down their table and shuffled out the door.

Zippi-Tea

Peppermint
Eleuthero Root
Gingko Leaf
Ashwagandha
Eucalyptus
Rhodiola

Makes the drinker faster for half a day. Will make you sleep for a day and a half after. Do not drink more than 2 cups at a time and no more than twice a moon cycle.
                              -Mahkai

Chapter 12

Mahkai found Cael sitting under a tree with a book balanced on his knees. Nearby, children played with something like over-large darts or small odd-shaped arrows. Cael smiled and rose to his feet at Mahkai's approach.

"Hello there."

"Is this a good time to chat? If you are not busy, that is?" Mahkai stammered. The puka was several feet shorter and more lithely built than Mahkai. He had a stillness about him, radiating a quiet confidence Mahkai envied.

Cael nodded and gestured to the seat under the tree he had just vacated. Mahkai nodded his agreement, but was distracted by the children's shouts. One boy in particular was crowing in celebration and doing an odd sort of victory dance. He must be the victor of this strange game.

"Do you play?" Cael asked with a tilt of his head.

"I'm afraid I am unfamiliar with this activity." Mahkai's face warmed in embarrassment.

Cael smiled, his eyes softening with understanding and empathy. "Let's change that then." He led them to an empty spot in the green space and signaled to one of the fairy children watching from the perimeter.

Moments later they flew over and set down seven brightly colored arrows—three bright blue, three flaming orange, and one daffodil yellow with striped fletching.

"Alright, so we start by defining the space that is within bounds and what is out of bounds. For learning purposes, we'll use this open space here. We choose our color and divvy up the darts. One person throws the yellow dart somewhere in the designated area, then we take turns throwing our darts as close to the yellow one as possible. Whomever is closest when we have run out of darts wins. Loser throws the target next."

"Oh, splendid. That is similar to a game my clan plays, only with round, colored stones." He clapped his hands in delight.

"May I?" Cael held up the yellow dart.

Mahkai nodded. He tossed the dart into the air and it landed a short distance away, close enough Mahkai was fairly sure he could reach it with his darts, but not so close it would be too easy. Or at least that's what he hoped. His palms began to sweat as doubts crept into his mind. Could he do this? Would he just make a fool of himself in front of Cael?

"Would you like to be orange or blue?" Cael held all six remaining darts, three in each hand.

"Is there a difference?"

"There shouldn't be, other than color. Although I wouldn't put it past these rascals to weight their darts oddly for an advantage." Cael smirked.

Mahkai chose the blue ones. They were weighted predominantly on the tip and were surprisingly heavy for their size. The urge to jot down his thoughts and sketch the dart rather than play made him twitch, but he resisted. There would be time for that later he scolded himself.

Cael flourished his hand, gesturing for Mahkai to toss first. He attempted to throw it like a stone, but it landed in the grass a few meters in front of him. He flinched, waiting for the mockery he was sure to come from Cael. His face burned, his chest tightened, and his stomach clenched with embarrassment.

When he finally had the courage to look Cael in the eyes, he saw amusement mixed with pity looking back at him.

"You did better than my first go. Try it again to familiarize yourself with their balance," Cael instructed.

Mahkai glanced around as he retrieved his dart, but no one else was watching. He took a deep breath and tried an underhanded toss, like he had seen the fairy children do earlier. This time, the dart sailed through the air much further than the first. It was still a good distance away from the yellow target dart, but it was a vast improvement.

Cael nodded to him, then tossed one of his striped orange darts. It glided through the air in a perfect arc and landed less than a pace away from the yellow one. Mahkai groaned under his breath. "Oh, what's the point?" he muttered.

"You grew up with a family that pitted you against each other and then mocked or ridiculed you when you didn't perform perfectly the first time, didn't you?"

Mahkai's eyes widened in surprise.

"The point is to learn the game and compete with yourself, not me. Think of it simply as both of us trying to best our own together. You don't need to win against me or impress me with your skills. That is not the point of this exercise." Cael said gently.

"But…" Mahkai couldn't seem to form coherent thoughts.

"Here, ask me a question. Don't focus on trying to beat me, just try to do better on each throw." Cael jogged over to collect the orange and blue arrows. He left the yellow one where it rested with its nose buried in the grass and tail in the air. He handed Mahkai his two blue ones and gestured with the feathers of his dart.

"Oh… erm… I don't even know where to begin. I have so many questions," Mahkai stammered, trying to get his brain to re-engage. "If you don't mind my asking, what…magical affiliation are you?"

Cael smiled warmly and shook his head. Tendrils of his

long black hair slipped free of its tie, framing his angular face. "I don't mind at all, as long as we both share equally. Be prepared that any question you ask I will also ask in kind."

Mahkai nodded his agreement. That sounded reasonable.

"I am an Aqualite," Cael continued. "I specialize in mist, fog, and cloud manipulation." With a flourish of his hand, mist rose from the surrounding grass and drifted toward them. He released it with another flourish, just as easily.

"Oh, that is delightful!" Mahkai was impressed. He had seen other Aqualites manipulate water to varying degrees, but this was altogether new to him. "I am an Aerophyte. No specialty as of yet." His chest tightened, waiting for Cael to ask for a demonstration, but he was surprised yet again when Cael merely accepted him at his word and didn't press him for more when he didn't immediately offer.

"Where did you grow up?" Cael's turn to ask a question.

"The minotaur clan lands in the Makanui clan. What about you?"

"I was raised by my step-dad with my half brother not far from here actually." Cael shrugged.

Mahkai was delighted when Cael took out a similar leather wrapped set of pages to take notes on. They traded questions back and forth about puka and minotaur.

Cael asked about how the minotaur grew up. He was especially fascinated by their migration practices. Mahkai never thought it was noteworthy before, but to someone who lived in the same place their whole life, he supposed it would seem rather strange. Cael even asked about what they like to eat, and how they find it, and their magical abilities.

The longer they talked, the more Mahkai found he liked Cael. He'd never met someone who asked questions like this puka, other than himself, of course. Was this what Aunti Lani meant about kindred spirits?

By this point, their game of darts was long forgotten.

"Alright, your turn," Cael prompted, picking a handful of long grasses and twisting them between his deft fingers.

Mahkai thought for a few moments, then asked one of his burning questions. "What is it like?"

"What?" Cael glanced up at him.

"To talk to animals and understand them?"

"Oh, hmmm. It is like any other conversation, I suppose, except not. They don't use words and language like we do, but they use pictures and feelings. They hint around things when they don't know exactly how to communicate what they are trying to say."

"That is fascinating! What are some things Gwen has said to you?" Mahkai wished he could speak to animals too. Imagine what a red bird or deer might have to say.

"She likes your tea and sleeping in your satchel, and she finds your scribbles and sketches intriguing." He laughed good-naturedly and Mahkai joined him.

"Oh! Okay. How do you know what you can turn into? What can you turn into, actually? I know of your raven. Are there others?" He blurted out the next questions that came to mind.

"Puka can typically shift into three, though some can shift into more."

"How many more?"

"The strongest I know of currently is my half brother, Ronin. He has five that I have seen."

"Five? That is incredible. What are yours?" Mahkai wrote as fast as he could. He shook out his cramping hand as he changed charcoal sticks.

"The raven, you know of course, a fox, and a lynx."

"How did you know?"

"Know?" Cael glanced up at him again from whatever he was doing with the grass.

"What and when to shift? Does it hurt?" Mahkai found himself becoming increasingly curious about what Cael was doing. "I spent a long time just listening to me, the inner me. My true self. I had to block out all the voices and expectations—however well intended—and just listen until I knew myself best. Shifting takes more than just changing shape; the animals reflect a part of yourself. But you can also lose yourself in them if you are not careful. You must know yourself best to return to your true form.

"What happens if you don't know your true self, or you forget?"

"If you stay in one form too long, you can forget your true self. It's like wearing a mask or playing a role. If you pretend to be someone you are not for too long, you lose hold of who you are and become that role." He got a faraway look in his eyes. "Many puka have lost their way and could not or did not want to shift back."

Mahkai felt an ache deep in his chest. Did he know his true self? Did he know himself best? Or was he just trying to be what was expected of him, what everyone else wanted for him? Who was he? Who did he want to be?

"It isn't an immediate, overnight knowledge, Mahkai." Cael's gentle voice broke into his reflections. "It is a journey. Puka learn meditation from birth in preparation for our first shift. Most take many seasons or cycles of seasons. Some even take scores of cycles. But before you can become anything or anyone else, you must be yourself." He rose to his feet and dusted off stray bits of grass then put out a hand to help Mahkai up. Mahkai took it, marveling at its warmth.

"Thank you! I have much to ponder and consider," Mahkai said thoughtfully as he slipped his notebook back into his bag. "This has been most insightful."

"Same for me. I have learned a great deal. I hope we may

have more conversations like this in the future." He caught and held Mahkai's eyes.

"I would like that."

"I will take my leave, then. Thank you for the good company and stimulating conversation. I'd best be on my way. Until next time." Cael dipped his head.

Mahkai nodded. "Until next time." He watched Cael shift into a charcoal-grey fox and trot away until he was out of sight.

Mahkai stretched and settled himself into a comfortable position against the tree they just had vacated. He wanted to get to know himself like Cael had suggested. He glanced over to where Cael had been moments before. Resting on a small rock at the base of the tree was a tiny fox of woven grasses.

Subtle-Tea

Green Sencha	Ginger Root
Saffron	Orange Peel
Fennel	Clove
Cardamom	Cinnamon
Black Peppercorn	Safflower
Tulsi	Licorice Root

Steep for 160 measured heartbeats, concentrating.
Makes the drinker more eloquent and clever for a day.

Note: I almost named this one Nic-e-Tea, but tea is nice in general and while this tea makes you somewhat nicer,
it does so much more.

-Mahkai

Chapter 13

Mahkai met Hartley outside the Winding Way Inn the next morning. The cool harvest air made him shiver and rub his hands together for warmth. Hartley bobbed excitedly in the air, her wings beating so fast they were merely an amber blur around her. She greeted him warmly.

"How are you not cold?" he asked, forgetting his manners and blurting out the first question that came to mind. He covered his mouth with his hands and looked at her sheepishly. "My apologies. That was quite rude of me," he stammered. His words came out muffled through his fingers.

Hartley grinned. "I don't mind. Ask me anything you like. I do that too. I also tend to overshare. Bree says I'm an open book." She shrugged.

"How do you do that?" he asked, unable to keep his amazement from his voice.

"Do what?"

"Not care what others think of you?"

She tapped her chin with her finger thoughtfully. "Hmmm, I think I just got tired of being tired all the time from trying and failing to make everyone happy."

Mahkai looked at her in shock. "I don't… I mean, I'm not sure…" He sighed and tried again. "That is to say, I don't know how to even begin to do that."

She considered him as they walked down the path. Or well, he walked; she hovered above the frosted ground sparkling in the sunlight.

"Why don't we practice, then?"

"How do you mean?"

"Well, we are going to look at this oak tree, and I want you to focus solely on how you feel about it and what you think, not what anyone else might say. Can you do that?"

He mulled it over. What was it like to not care what everyone else thought? To not be constantly worried he might make them mad or displease them in some way? Could he do that? Could he make decisions solely based on what made him happy? He took a deep breath, letting it out slowly. He would like to try. He wrestled with it a while longer as they walked.

They made good time, soon stopping in a small clearing beneath the branches of the most magnificent oak tree Mahkai had ever laid eyes on. It was tall and broad as it should be. Its leaves were just starting to change.

"This one turns russet and crimson when in full color," Hartley said fondly.

"So, how does this work?" Mahkai took out his favorite notebook and watched her with interest.

Hartley tilted her head to the side as she considered the tree, consulting her notes and sketches. "We'll see what this tree has to work with. Stand back. Sometimes they react badly to change."

"When you say react badly, what do you mean exactly?" He arched an eyebrow and made a few notes about the possible temperament of trees.

"Trees have personalities of sorts, if that makes any sense. Some are more pliable and take direction better than others. And some are downright nasty." She made a face, her nose scrunching in distaste. "They are not sentient exactly, but they are more than just sticks and roots." She glanced at him over her shoulder.

He blinked at her, then scribbled hastily. He'd never thought of it before, but that made sense in a way. He stepped back a few paces when she made shooing motions at him.

She placed a hand on the trunk and slid down to the ground, going completely still. The wind chased leaves around him, swirling like dancers to inaudible music as he waited for whatever Hartley was going to do. It was entrancing.

She was so still that Mahkai was beginning to worry when she stepped back and turned to face him, grinning. "Just as I'd hoped. It is strong, but not unwilling. It will work with me!" she said triumphantly, rubbing her hands together in excitement.

"Now for the fun part. Come here." She gestured to him to join her at the base of the tree. "Place your hand here, like this." She showed him where to touch the bark of the tree. He felt a little silly, like he was a child petting one of the great rams his people tended for the first time.

"Good." She nodded. Her approval warmed his chest and alleviated some of his shyness. He could do this, whatever this was.

She placed her hand over his and placed her other hand beside it on the tree. "Now I want you to close your eyes and let your awareness go a little fuzzy. You know, like how you can let your eyes unfocus for a bit? Kinda like that." Her voice was calm and warm and soothing. He did as instructed.

He heard her take in a deep breath and release it, and he did the same. His hand tingled a little where it met hers. His fingertips felt a little numb. *Right, focus on not focusing.* And then suddenly, all the sounds around him went fuzzy, quieter. He felt different, more sturdy, more grounded.

He was falling, then something called to him. He watched as a little acorn sprouted and grew, emerging from the ground and into the sunlight. He was witnessing the tree's life story. He felt the seasons pass by all in a blur, yet every moment of it as if it stretched on forever. Everything was timeless.

He knew the feel of the other trees as they grew up around him. He knew the loss when a tree finally died and gave itself back to the ground and became a part of all the rest of them, nourishing them. He knew each animal that called his trunk and limbs home. He knew the tug and flavor of the curious little fairy the color of autumn. She called to him even now. Asking of him to be more, to change. He was so very fond of her. If she asked it of him, he would do anything for her.

Hartley.

Mahkai gasped and pulled away from the tree, coming back to himself. Had he really just experienced what the tree did? He reeled at the thought. Was this what arboreal magic was like? He fought back his own jealousy. To think, every tree and every plant was like this? He wished, not for the first time, that he had been given different magic.

She watched him, waiting. He nodded. "Yes, this one." His words barely above a whisper.

Hartley's eyes sparkled with anticipation as she turned once more to face the giant oak in the center of the clearing. She removed her boots, digging her toes into the soft ground, and sighed happily.

Mahkai moved so he could watch her face as well as the tree. He had never seen architects build anything and didn't want to miss even a moment. Hartley held her arms outstretched, palms facing down. He held his breath and waited. And waited. Nothing happened. He let his breath out with a whoosh. Was something supposed to be happening?

"There you are," she breathed, barely above a whisper. Raising her hands, she waved them in slow, sweeping movements, like a painter before a canvas or a weaver before their loom.

Mahkai started when he realized the tree was following her movements. As her hands dipped and swirled, pulled and pushed, branches repositioned themselves. New branches grew and braided themselves together into a railing. A hole that began as a tiny knothole halfway up the tree grew until it was easily as big as he was.

Hartley paused to consult her notes on the ground beside her, then continued her movements. The whole tree seemed to widen. The ground beneath his feet rumbled faintly, shifting as he assumed the roots grew and spread like the portion above ground.

Then, suddenly, it all stopped and Hartley sat abruptly on the ground. She giggled tiredly and gazed up at the tree with fondness in her eyes.

"Are you alright?" Mahkai asked, kneeling next to her in concern.

"Better than alright! That was amazing! Look at it. It's... it's..."

"Marvelous? Magnificent?" he offered.

She nodded. "That. And I did it all on my own. It's not finished, mind you. Not even close, but I've never done so much in one session before. And definitely not on my own."

Now that he knew she was not injured, he turned to fully take in her efforts. "Hartley, it is beautiful," he said around the sudden tightness constricting his throat.

It was almost unrecognizable from the tree that had stood in the center of the clearing moments before. It was still an oak tree, but that is where the similarities ended. It was many times broader and possibly even taller. Running all the way around its broad trunk was a walkway of intricately woven branches. Even from down here, he could see it was a masterpiece. She said it wasn't finished, but to Mahkai it was more than he'd ever had. More than he could have dreamed of—there was only one issue.

"Erm... not to complain, but... erm... well..." He hesitated, unsure how to tell her.

"Is there a problem?" she asked as she slid her feet into her boots.

He couldn't be sure, but she looked to be glowing less brilliantly than she normally did. Her golden, amber skin looked muted, dulled. Her wings lacked their normal luster and drooped behind her.

"Well…"

"Mahkai, spit it out."

"How am I meant to get up there? I cannot…"

"Fly?" She laughed openly.

Mahkai felt like he was missing something.

"I'll show you." She jumped to her feet and flew up to the walkway, disappearing into the arching hole he suspected was a doorway. She reappeared a moment later and dropped something over the side.

"Ok, you can come up and see how you like it now," she called down to him.

He shuffled quickly to the base of the tree, mindful of any exposed roots. Hanging from the tree was a ladder of sorts made from tough braided vines with hand and hoof-holds for climbing. He smiled delightedly and tucked his notebook into his bag, shifting it to his back so it wouldn't get in the way of his climbing.

As he climbed, he listened to Hartley hum and huff as she inspected her work up close. Anticipation raced through him and he climbed faster, eager to see it. He hesitated at the top, then peeked his head over the edge to get his first look of his new home.

His breath caught in his throat and he forced himself to haul his weight up onto the platform. He turned in a circle, eyes wide, and took in everything, not wanting to miss a thing. His throat tightened and his eyes stung. He blinked quickly. He was fine. He was. He was not overwhelmed. He was absolutely not about to cry in front of a perfect stranger.

"Mahkai? What's wrong? Do you not like it? I can change anything you want. Say something…" Hartley fluttered to him, gentle concern in her voice.

"I… It… erm… It's… I don't… There's…" He choked on the words.

"Oh, honey." She caught sight of his face and placed her hand gently on his shoulder.

"I seem to be leaking…" Mahkai offered lamely as a couple of tears escaped.

Hartley laughed and pulled a small square of fabric out of her pocket. She wiped his face and waited patiently for him to work through it. She didn't judge or ridicule him like one of his clan would have if they were here. He was very glad they weren't here. This was special, and for once, he didn't have to share it with anyone if he didn't want to. Guilt gnawed at him but he shoved it away.

He took a deep, shaky breath to calm himself down then offered her a watery smile. He hoped it conveyed his gratitude.

She smiled back at him and grabbed his hand, tugging playfully. "Here, let me give you the grand tour." He let her lead him into the first room. "This is the main room for your kitchen and fireplace and sleeping. Bree said you like to sleep in a hammock, so there are rings up there to suspend it from. Do you have one? Or do we need to get one when we go to the market next?"

"We?" Mahkai couldn't stop it from slipping out.

"Well, yes, of course. You don't think you are going to get rid of me that easily, are you? I'll help make sure you get the best of everything you need. And maybe things you don't, but trust me, you do." She smirked at him, her eyes twinkling.

"A fireplace in a tree? How will it not burn everything down?" Mahkai asked, bewildered.

Hartley's eyes sparkled with pride. "I thought of that, actually. I found this special fire moss that doesn't burn and lined the chimney with it."

"Look over here. Bree also said you were rather fond of your tea, so I made you a tea nook. These little hooks will hold your spoons and this shelf will hold your pot and cups. Although, given how big of a cup you need, it would probably be more like a bowl. Tea bowl!" She giggled at her own revelation. "And this shelf is for your different tea jars. The market has some of the prettiest clay jars by this Ardere I know who specializes in that sort of thing. Oh, look here." She pointed to an "M" in the design of the tea nook. "I saw you looking at your book with the M on it a lot and I thought it was cool, so I added it here. M for Mahkai the Minotaur. And then…"

Tears welled in Mahkai's eyes again and threatened to spill out all over again. "I'm sorry. I'm sorry," he blubbered, overwhelmed by how much she paid attention to the little things, however small they might seem to her, even though they had only just met a couple of days ago.

"There is nothing to be sorry for. Let it all out. Take as long as you need." She still held his hand. His giant hand dwarfed her tiny one, but she didn't seem to notice. When he had calmed down again, she continued their tour through the treehouse. She pointed out little things here and there, occasionally asking for his opinion on this detail or that.

"Do you want a big table or a little one? I had this idea that it could be suspended from the ceiling and you could raise or lower it. That way, you can have the extra space without having to put away all your books and papers. What do you think? I think you need a map. I saw one in one of the Council chambers and I think you need one, too." She rambled, not waiting for him to answer before she moved on to the next thing.

They both pulled out their notebooks and started scribbling furiously for a moment. Then they looked up, and when their eyes met they both burst out laughing.

"We really are two bees in a hive, as Bree says." She grinned at him from her precarious perch on the balcony railing. "Do you want a map on the table itself or on the wall? Although if you are going to add to it, maybe both…" She trailed off and wrote some more in her book.

"Oh!" She jumped into the air. "I forgot to show you the best part." She zipped over to a vine hanging from the roof and tugged sharply on it twice. A circular staircase descended from the ceiling.

She flew up the stairs, too giddy to notice Mahkai.

"Erm, Hartley."

"Yes? Hurry up!" She poked her head back down to stare at him inquisitively.

"I don't fit." The stairs were made for a much smaller person and were too narrow for his broad shoulders.

"Oh, ha!" She smacked a hand to her forehead. "I forgot to scale this up. One moment." Her brow furrowed as she concentrated. The stairs glowed green and silver, then pulsed and expanded wide enough to allow him to ascend comfortably.

When he reached the top, he gasped. There were no walls or ceiling up here, only open sky. They stood higher than most of the forest, allowing them to see all the way to the horizon. The forest sprawled out before him matched Hartley with its many colors—gold, amber, and orange, as well as crimson, purple, and scarlet mixed with the lingering greens. Clouds gathered over the Thorian Caldera Mountains looming in the distance to the west.

"I thought you might want a place to observe the sky and the stars. I love stargazing."

"Me too!" His chest warmed at the thoughtfulness.

A dark, winged shape swooped out of the clouds and dove straight for one of the far mountains. "Look, Hartley! Look there! Is that a...dragon?" They rushed to the edge. Mahkai, careful not to trip. It was a long way down.

"I have always wished to see one up close. Have you? Seen one, that is? What are they like?"

Hartley shook her head. "They don't interact with anyone from what I have seen. Since the Ardra left, according to what Master Corsen said. Supposedly, the only ones who can talk to them are all gone." She shrugged. Master Corsen was the Arboreal Master on The Council. "I'm not sure he is completely right because I think one of them works with the Fire Dwarf Twins in their forge. They are my heroes. You should see the things they make! They are so creative and talented and are constantly doing and trying things no one else has done before. Next time we are near there, I wonder if we could meet them? Would you come with me?" Suddenly she looked shy and unsure of herself.

"Of course, I would be delighted to come with you!" Mahkai beamed back at her.

"You can move your things in anytime you like now that I have the main parts of the home finished. If it is ok with you, I'd like to come back and make a few adjustments over the next couple days. I will have to go back to my normal duties for a bit too, but I promise I will finish it." She fluttered to the stairs leading down to the main part of the treehouse.

"I should go get Gwen. She will love this." Mahkai took one last look at his new home and felt a part of him settle at the thought of calling it home. Despite being in a tree, scores of meters above the forest floor, he felt grounded for the first time since Aunti Lani had passed. He hadn't known he was restless, but now the absence of it just made sense.

"Your family won't miss you?" Hartley asked quietly. He suspected she had been wondering about it for some time and only now felt comfortable voicing it.

He huffed out a breath. "They might. Then again, they might not. Some days, I think they forget I exist in all the chaos. Other days, I am painfully in the center of everyone's attention." He rubbed the back of his neck and let out another breath.

She made sympathetic noises. "Well, for what it's worth, I'm glad you are here and I hope you are, too."

"I am. Very much so."

They shared a look of understanding and a knowing smile before heading down to the ground. Hartley showed him how to raise and lower the rope ladder and how to disguise the vine to release it.

They made plans to finish it over the next few days. Then, just as they parted ways, Hartley zipped back over to him and collided with his chest, throwing her arms around his neck to hug him tightly.

He staggered in surprise, but then hugged her back, careful not to crush her. She pulled back and smiled warmly, then zipped away into the afternoon sunlight.

Immuni-Tea

Elderberry
Orange Peel
Licorice Root
Echinacea
Citron

A tea to help boost your health when the weather is turning cold and wet. Add honey as desired.

-Lani

Chapter 14

Several days later, a delicious aroma wafted from the fireplace. Mahkai salivated in anticipation. He had finally perfected it, this sweet bread Bree called scones. He chuckled. It sounded like stones, but they tasted nothing alike.

He took a deep breath and removed his latest concoction from the flames. He had mixed some wild blueberries he fancied into the dough just before putting it in the fire. He had learned on previous attempts that if he was too rough with the berries or mixed them in too early, they burst, giving him a blue-ish-purple bread, but the unique flavor of the berry was lost.

He cleaned his knife and sliced into his berry bread, making small triangular wedges from the round loaf. He blew gently on it until it cooled, then bit into it. The hot juice flowed over his tongue as one of the berries burst, mixing with the slightly sweet bread perfectly.

"Oh, my. I think I've done it this time, Gwendolin." Mahkai hurriedly made a note on his page.

She blinked at him from her perch above the door and ruffled her feathers, tilting and turning her head, as was her way. She preferred raw fruit or field mice but didn't protest tasting his culinary endeavors either. He loved that about her. She simply watched without judging him, happy to go along on any of his adventures.

He poured a mug of pine needle tea he had steeped overnight to go with his scones and sat on a cushion next to the low table Hartley had made for him. He inhaled the aromas wafting around his new home and sighed. Songbirds chirped their merry tune from nearby trees. Gwen seemed to like them too, judging by the way she watched them flit about from branch to branch.

He wondered, not for the first time, why she had yet to fly. It had been many days since their forest adventure. Surely she had healed by now, but she seemed mostly content to hop around where she wanted to go when she wasn't being carried.

Mahkai let his mind wander as he finished his mug of tea. He liked to sit and think of what was and what could be. What if... Those two wonderful, terrible words, full of so much potential. They got him into more trouble than he cared to admit and caused him much pain and suffering. But he could not help it. They buzzed in his mind all the time.

What if he cut a channel in the ground on the upper side of his mud hut to help funnel rain water around his hut rather than through it? What if he soaked different grasses and flowers in warm water or cold? Would that change the flavor or potency of the tea? What if the bees and butterflies followed a pattern to certain flowers or meadows and not others? What if he added berries to bread before baking?

He smiled at the last one as he finished his blueberry scone. "I think perhaps we should go explore the obelisk again or the tunnels," he said to Gwen as he set about filling several satchels with papers, books, scrolls, and empty vials. Just in case he needed them.

She hooted her assent and hopped closer. He gently placed several pieces of his still-warm bread in a cloth and placed them with his mug and pot, for tea of course. He could not very well go adventuring without tea, now could he?

He was just reaching for Gwendolin when his vision went a little blurry and he staggered. He blinked and shook his head to clear his vision, but it didn't help. The room tipped sideways. Nothing he did seemed to right it. What was happening to his treehome? As his shoulder collided with the floor, he realized rather belatedly that it was in fact he who had tipped sideways.

Gwen screeched and trilled at him, but he heard it distantly, as if he were underwater. That wasn't right, was it? His stomach roiled and protested, and the darkness creeping in the edges of his vision closed in on him. He tried to call out—to say anything at all, but his mouth wouldn't work. The last thing he recalled was the sound of Gwen's claws on the wooden floor hopping toward him.

☕ ☕ ☕

Mahkai's dreams were filled with a bizarre collection of nonsense, each situation he found himself in more ridiculous than the last. Ships that sailed in the skies, great dragons, winged humans that shone like the sun, and tea that drank him. His dreams shifted darker. His father found him and the little haven of his treehome, and forced him to leave this life he had made for himself. The despair and defeat ached deeper than anything he had felt before.

He shivered as he awoke to something cold pressed to his face and little feet hopping across his chest. The remnants of his dreams lingered in the space between dreaming and awake. He shuddered again. They were just dreams. His father was not here, and he was fine.

"There you are." Cael's smooth voice broke the silence, followed by a series of hoots and trills from Gwen.

Mahkai blinked against the bright morning light as he tried to ascertain where he was. Gwen stood on his chest, peering down at him with piercing goldenrod eyes. She bumped the tip of his nose with her beak and retreated. He tried to sit up, but his body refused to cooperate. His muscles trembled and quivered. Even holding his head up took more effort than it should have.

"I wouldn't do that yet, mate. You are still recovering." Cael's bronze, angular face appeared over him, concern etched in the corners of his eyes and the grim set of his mouth.

"W-what happened?" Mahkai stuttered. His tongue felt swollen in his mouth. His brain felt hazy trying to remember the events leading up to his blacking out.

"You were poisoned," Cael said grimly as he rested a hand on Mahkai's shoulder.

"Poisoned?"

"Aye, by your own hand too, by the looks of it, unless you let someone else handle your tea blends. I found yew mixed in with the pine." He shook his head slightly at Mahkai.

"Me?" Mahkai asked, bewildered. How could he have gotten hair in his tea, and why would it poison him?

Cael snorted. The worry on his face melted into a smirk. "No. Yew, as in the very poisonous tree or bush."

"Oh." His face burned with embarrassment. How could he be so stupid and careless? He chastised himself.

"You are lucky I was nearby, and Gwen called out to me. You were in a bad way when I got here."

Something in Mahkai's demeanor must have tipped Cael off because he quickly continued, "It is an easy enough mistake to make for sure. You are not the first person to accidentally poison themselves by eating, or in your case drinking, something you ought not to." The corner of his mouth quirked up in a slight smile.

Mahkai attempted to get up again, but Cael pressed on his shoulder firmly. "Rest, my friend. You will only hurt yourself further if you rise before you are well."

"I'll be ok."

Cael raised an eyebrow at him. Mahkai resisted a moment longer, then gave in with a sigh. "I can't just lay here. I need to be doing something."

"Why?"

Mahkai wrung his hands, afraid to answer. "Because I need to be doing something productive so no one thinks I'm lazy," he blurted out.

"Well then, why don't we chat. Do you mind if I ask you more questions? You may ask some of me as well if you like." Cael released his shoulder and held a cup to Mahkai's lips to sip.

Warm broth glided over his tongue and down his throat, warming him from the inside as it went down. When he had enough, Cael set it aside and looked at him expectantly.

"What would you like to know?" Mahkai rested his head back against the pillow and stared at the intricate designs of the ceiling Hartley had woven.

"How does minotaur hierarchy work and who is in charge of the clans and celebrations?"

Mahkai startled at the question, completely caught off guard. He didn't expect that. "Oh, erm… I will answer to the best of my ability, but the more we talk, the more I realize there is a lot about my people I don't know. I don't know how other clans work, but in the Makanui clan, we have the clan chief, the strongest and wisest of the clan. Then he has his elders and advisers. They help make the decisions, but ultimately, all the big decisions are up to him. He is grooming my eldest brother Maleek to be the next clan chief."

Mahkai thought over what questions he had, but many of them he wanted to take notes on, so he chose easier questions he thought he could remember. "What about your family? Do you have any siblings or cousins?" Mahkai turned his head to look where Cael was reclining with his feet propped up.

A gentle smile played on Cael's lips as he gazed out the window. "I have a half brother. We share a mother. She returned to the stars when I was very young, though. I never found out who my father is."

"Oh, I'm so sorry. My mother died too," Mahkai said softly. Cael met his eyes and held them for a moment. A look of understanding passed between them, as if their shared experience connected them somehow. "My brother is an arrogant ass, but I guess I would be too if I was as great as he is and could do all the things he can." Cael shrugged and resumed looking out the window.

Cael asked his next question after a brief pause. "What were you doing when you met Gwen? She mentioned a panther."

"Oh, yes. And we found some old tunnels as well."

"That is interesting. What was in them?" Cael looked visibly excited as he helped Mahkai drink more fluids.

Mahkai rambled on and on about the carvings and patterns in the tunnels and how some parts of the stone felt warmer than others.

"I heard rumors the old council seat used to be located somewhere up there," Cael mused as he helped Mahkai drink the last of this cup of tea. It tasted a little different than the rest.

Mahkai nodded. "I hope to go back and explore more. Maybe you could...we could..." His eyes grew heavy, then fluttered closed as his thoughts drifted like clouds. He was in the middle of saying something, but couldn't remember what.

When he woke again, he found Hartley curled up on a cushion in the middle of the room, reading one of his books. Immediately, she got up and brought him more of the tea Cael had given him. She alternated it with more of the delicious broth and even gave him a bite of soft bread.

"Thank you, Hartley. You are most kind," he said between sips. She smiled warmly back at him.

He looked around the room and gave a small sigh of disappointment when he realized Hartley was the only one here with him. He had hoped to speak with Cael a bit more.

"Cael said he had some urgent matters to attend to but hoped to check in on you later," Hartley offered, guessing the meaning of his wistful sigh.

His fingers played with the edge of the blanket draped over him—only it didn't feel like any of his blankets. He attempted to sit up to get a better look at it, but his body was still disinclined to cooperate.

Holding it up to his face, he realized it wasn't a blanket at all, but a finely made, dark forest-green cloak. It smelled of evergreens and dawn before the sun has burned away the morning mist. It smelled like Cael. He let his head rest back on the pillow and closed his eyes, inhaling deeply and letting out another, more comfortable, sigh.

"Can I read to you? I know you have already read it, but it is so good."

He nodded, too comfortable and content to get up. She read to him from the book until it was dark, then regaled him with stories of her family. He asked her similar questions Cael had asked him about their celebrations and of her exciting new project and getting to work on the new council seat until his eyes could stay open no longer.

An-Tea-dote

Peppermint
Nettle
Dandelion Leaf
Licorice Root
Ginger
Milk Thistle

Drink this tea when you have ingested something you shouldn't have. Again.

-Cael

Chapter 15

Several days later, finally well enough to do more than barely get out of bed, Mahkai decided to gather tea ingredients he was running low on. His conversation with Cael played on repeat in his mind, teasing and enticing his curiosity until he decided to go looking for the old council seat.

As he shuffled along the forest path, he spotted a rock with a familiar-looking design peeking out from behind a wall of ivy. He never would have realized it was anything more than interesting weather patterns on the stone if he hadn't seen them all over the tunnels.

He moved the ivy out of the way so he could see the design better. It led to an opening in the side of the hill. Surprise and excitement coursed through him. Maybe Cael was right. He followed the passageway a short distance, but it led abruptly to a dead end. Disappointment felt like a bucket of cold water. Maybe he had gotten excited for nothing. He chastised himself for overreacting before he found anything real.

Winded from his excitement and still recovering from his poisoning, he leaned heavily against the wall. Suddenly, a grinding sound filled the air and a stone slab slammed to the ground behind him, cutting him off from his exit. He pushed against it, but it didn't budge. Pink smoke creeped along the floor, slowly filling the chamber. His torch flickered but stayed lit.

His heart raced loudly in his ears, and it was difficult to breathe. He felt like something was squeezing his chest and he couldn't catch his breath. Alarmed, Mahkai studied the walls, desperately looking for another way out.

One wall was covered in concentric circles with odd but familiar patterns on them. Hesitantly, he touched one of the circles. It slid easily under his fingers. "Oh! It's a puzzle," he declared as two halves of a bird met between two of the circles. He rotated each circle, attempting to complete the picture. Some circles only turned one way. Others turned both ways, but moved a different circle as well. After a few minutes of frustration, he figured out the trick to it.

The door lifted, revealing another tunnel. With a cough, he stepped through just before the stone doorway slammed shut behind him. The stone was smooth on this side, with no levers or pulleys. Fortunately, the pink smoke stayed in the previous chamber. He couldn't go back the way he came, so he ventured ahead into the long tunnel.

Ideas and scenarios peppered his thoughts as he walked for what he thought was only an hour or so based on how little his torch burned down. Eventually, he reached the end of the tunnel. It opened up into the fresh air, but in his haste to reach it, he tripped and slid a short way before being deposited in a gully on the side of a mountain. That was strange. He didn't remember there being mountains near here.

Thunder boomed overhead and rain began to fall, gently at first, then in sheets. The storm grew in ferocity and his small gully was rapidly flooding. His head darted around, looking for cover. This reminded him a lot of the last time he was on a mountain. He spotted an opening in the stone not too far off, barely wide enough to squeeze through.

Mahkai shuffled into the cave opening and out of the rain. Outside, the branches and vines lashed aggressively in the storm. He removed his cloak and wrung out the worst of the water. Then he found a large boulder to drape the soaked cloak over to dry.

The cave was unusually warm. Warmer than it rightly should be. Were there hot springs in this cave? He followed the tunnel further in, intent on finding the hot springs, if there indeed were any. Might as well, while he waited out the storm.

The cave was conspicuously smooth. Normally, there were jagged bits hanging down to snag his horns on—or jutting up to trip over. By contrast, this cave was easy to explore. He rounded a corner and came face to face with an enormous obsidian-scaled mound resting in the large, open heart of the cavern.

Arcs of blue and white light played over the surface like lightning in the clouds before a summer storm. His fur stood on end as the air crackled and a rush of heat blew out of two large holes in its front. The mound shifted, and he found himself staring into a cerulean blue eye larger than he was tall.

"Oh, hello!" He stumbled backward. "Can it be...? It is!" Mahkai's energetic baritone voice broke the silence. Excitement surged through him and he could barely hold still with his elation.

"I can't believe I finally get to meet one! Oh, this is splendid, simply splendid!" he continued as he clasped his hands together in delight. "You are a dragon, yes?" Mahkai nodded to himself as he took notes. "Have you always lived here? How old are you? What are you called? Are you considered average for a dragon?" He paused as he sketched a rough outline of the dragon's form on the page, then looked up sheepishly.

"Do you mind my asking questions?" He felt a little silly asking this now. "Begging your pardon, of course."

He froze as the dragon tilted its head to observe him but relaxed fractionally when it made no other movement. It blinked.

Mahkai noted it had a third eyelid, translucent, like a lizard and some cats.

"You see, I have never actually met a dragon before, so, as you can imagine, I have many questions." He knew he was babbling, but he hoped his explanation would... He didn't actually know what he was hoping for, actually. It felt right though, so he continued.

"Ah, where are my manners? My name is Mahkai." He placed a hand over his heart and bowed his head in what he hoped would be taken as a sign of respect. Was bowing a sign of respect for a dragon? Or was it a sign of aggression like it was for the minotaur?

Mahkai held perfectly still as the glossy-black reptilian head swiveled toward him with its long graceful neck. Its nostrils flared, and the air inside the cave swirled, kicking up dust that sparkled in the dim light from the mouth of the cave. Was it smelling him? What could a dragon tell about him from his scent?

He resolved to ask it when it felt appropriate. The trouble was, he was never sure when the appropriate time to ask questions was exactly, so he tended to blurt them out as they came to him.

"*Proceed, young scholar,*" a deep, gravelly voice echoed in his mind.

Mahkai blinked in surprise. "Begging your pardon, but what is a scholar?"

The dragon made a sound that was somewhere between a chuff and a chuckle. "*A scholar dedicates themselves to the learning and exploration of things. Someone who asks questions of the world around them with an open mind with the intention of understanding.*

A long time ago, in another place, there were...places dedicated to developing young minds such as yours. They housed innumerable books, like those you carry with you, that contained the answers and knowledge the preceding scholars had discovered. Or sometimes simply more questions." Its words were unrushed and thoughtful.

Mahkai's whole body trembled, unnerved at hearing someone else's voice in his head. It wasn't unpleasant, though. He liked the sound…if you could call it a sound. He wondered if the dragon could hear his thoughts?

"I can only hear what you think toward me while we are talking. Your thoughts are still your own." He answered a question Mahkai had not yet arrived at asking, but he was relieved with the answer.

"You mean there were places with more people like me?"

The dragon simply nodded.

Mahkai's mind raced, imagining a wondrous place such as that. It must have been marvelous to have so many inquisitive minds in one place. "What was it like?"

The dragon did not answer immediately. It looked almost thoughtful. *"Azar Barak, but you may address me as Azar. And before you ask, no Az is not acceptable."*

"P-pardon?" Mahkai stammered.

"You requested my name?" the dragon replied.

"Oh—OH! It is a pleasure to make your acquaintance," Mahkai sputtered.

Azar hummed. The air crackled with energy as arcs of light sparked down his body. *"I appreciate your manners. It has been a long time since I have conversed with someone so young that is not my kin."*

Mahkai looked around. "Are there more of your kin here?" he asked excitedly, and somewhat apprehensively.

Azar chuckled. *"No. We are alone, as you perceive it."*

"What do you mean, 'As I perceive it'? Do you perceive

things differently? Are there things I'm not perceiving? What am I not perceiving? Do they come to visit often?"

"*In a manner of speaking. They are not too distant. Some of them, at least. Some are like you. Inquisitive. Others believe they have all the answers they need. Those do not seek me out. As I prefer it. They would not listen anyway. One of my grand-daughters prefers the company of dwarves. She asks a great many questions.*" Azar sounded pleased, or even proud.

"How old are you?"

"*I do not know. I do not know how you record time and I do not wish to any longer. I am old and have forgotten more than your historians will ever know. I remember when the titans still walked among the inhabitants. When the magic was wild and untamed and not divided, like it is now. When nymphs and dryads still roamed. When my kin were plentiful and had not relegated themselves to their islands. When they were unified, not divided.*" His voice boomed and echoed in Mahkai's head.

"Are you the oldest of the dragons?" he pressed on, curiosity winning out over caution.

"*Perhaps. Perhaps not.*"

"Are you considered average for a dragon?"

Azar snorted indignantly. "*You are a scholar, would you read something to me?*" he said, changing the subject.

Mahkai wondered briefly if he had offended the dragon. "I—I would be honored." He rummaged around in his bag until he found the two books he was looking for. One was a novel by his favorite author about strange, far-off lands. The other was a collection of poetry he quite adored. He never went anywhere without them, if he could help it.

He thumbed through the book of poetry until he found a page discolored and frayed on the edges with old tea stains from countless readings. This one was Aunti Lani's favorite.

Tears pricked his vision as he remembered her asking him

to read it to her for the last time before she died. Her eyes had failed her near the end, so he had read anything and everything he could get his hands on for her, but she kept coming back to this one. He didn't need to read the faded words on the page, having memorized them long ago.

"Out of the night that covers me,
 Black as the pit from stern to pole,
I thank whatever gods may be
 for my unconquerable soul.

In the fell clutch of circumstance
I have not winced nor cried aloud.
Under the bludgeonings of chance
My head is bloody, but unbowed.

Beyond this place of wrath and tears
 Looms but the horror of the shade,
And yet the menace of the years
 Finds and shall find me unafraid.

It matters not how strait the gate,
 How charged with punishments the scroll,
I am the master of my fate.
 I am the captain of my soul."

The echo of his voice in the cave faded until the only sound surrounding them was the pelting rain outside.

"Mmm…" Azar's hum rumbled through the cavern like thunder in the distance. *"Would you like to see the library?"*

"What is a library?" Mahkai slid his books back into his satchel. He had never heard of a library before.

"Come and see." The ground shook and rumbled as Azar

rose and ambled into the opening of a tunnel branching off the main cavern.

Mahkai snatched up his damp cloak off the rock and followed. He noted with surprise that the walls of this tunnel had markings similar to the ones he had sketched in Cinntire when he met Gwen. Most of these drawings didn't make sense, though. They seemed to depict floating mountains, boats that flew like dragons or birds through the air, and fairies or puka or in their fae form with great wings like a bird... They were familiar somehow, like something he couldn't quite remember.

"Come, young scholar. We do not have much time."

"What do you mean?" he asked. Azar remained silent.

Mahkai picked up his pace, following the dragon through a labyrinth of tunnels. Even the ceilings were covered in paintings and carvings. His mind raced as he tried to take in everything, loathe to forget even the smallest detail.

They crossed a narrow stone bridge across a cavern. Azar merely stepped across the great chasm like it was a shallow stream. Mahkai peered over the edge to see how far to the bottom, but it stretched beyond the dim light. Azar did not wait for him, so he hurried to catch up.

They entered a massive cavern that appeared to have no end, the walls disappearing into the darkness. Mahkai gasped, not only from the grandeur of the cavern, but from the piles of scrolls and books covering tables and stuffed into nooks cut in the walls of the cavern.

"What is this place?" he asked in breathless wonder.

"This, young scholar, is the Library. A place of shared knowledge passed down from those who have gone before."

Mahkai blinked rapidly as he took in the room. He stepped closer to the wall and reverently touched the binding of one. "This is incredible! May I read one?"

"On your left, the black scroll. You might find it helpful."

Mahkai's hooves clicked on the stone floor, echoing loudly as he located the scroll the dragon indicated. Dust billowed as he slid it from its home, tickling his throat and making him cough. Carefully, he unrolled it.

"Oh my!" He coughed again. At first, the words didn't make sense, but then he realized it was a list of titles. The scroll contained a list of other scrolls and books and papers contained in the cavern. He scanned the list. Many words were unfamiliar to him.

"Where are the keepers of this place? How old are these?"

"*They are gone.*"

"Gone where?"

"*Gone from this place. A long time ago, in your understanding. Before your mother's mother's mother took her first breaths.*"

Mahkai counted in his head, "More than nine hundred cycles?" he breathed. "But how are these so well preserved?"

"*Because of the magic in them, but that magic is fading.*"

"What do you mean?"

"*You will understand in time.*"

"But…"

"*The scroll called Teinte might be most insightful. Collect it. We must be leaving.*"

"What do you mean?"

"*Come, minotaur,*" Azar boomed. He turned to leave, moving quicker than Mahkai thought possible.

Mahkai located and snatched up the scroll, stuffed it as gently as he could into his bag, and raced after Azar. The ground rumbled and a deep humming sound thrummed distantly. "What is that?" he asked.

If Azar answered, Mahkai never heard him. The cave rumbled and the air around them vibrated and warmed.

Beads of sweat gathered in his fur. His clothing felt too

constricting and warm. The air hurt to breathe; it was too hot. Mahkai panted and stumbled against the wall of the cavern. It shocked his hand on contact. He jerked away. "Azar?" he rasped out. His tongue felt swollen in his mouth and his head felt fuzzy. Everything tingled like a thousand tiny thorns were pricking him.

Azar spread his wings and sucked in a large breath of air. Mahkai stumbled back, fear lancing through him.

This was it. This was the end.

Then, cool air enveloped him and the burning sensation abated. He filled his lungs with a deep breath of the cool, sweet air that smelled of rain and shivered. He was drenched in sweat, and now that sweat was cooling rapidly.

"Maybe it is best to depart. Quickly. These tunnels are fickle—unstable—and not suitable for one such as yourself."

"Why not? What is happening? Has it always been like this?"

"The Ardra didn't heed the stone's warning. They spread too far and the stone between the heart of the mountain and the cavern is too thin. You must go. Now. Or you will not survive."

"How do all the scrolls survive then?"

Azar's growl was like thunder, making everything quake.

Mahkai clutched his bag tightly to his chest and ran as fast as his hooves could take him over the rocky terrain of rubble and through the labyrinth of tunnels to get to the surface.

His breathing was labored and sweat soaked him as his body fought to keep him cool. Azar had disappeared through a different tunnel. Mahkai wondered if this affected the dragon at all. Was he causing it?

He knew he was getting closer to an exit when the air blowing toward him was significantly cooler than the air at his back. His breath came a little easier.

He emerged into the main cavern he'd originally met Azar

in and gasped. A wall of flame blocked his exit. He dashed down another tunnel and found stone stairs spiraling upward. They ended abruptly at an ornately carved stone ceiling.

A small divot in the stone reminded him of the one on the obelisk, shaped like his pendant. Sweat rolled down his hocks as the heat from below grew hotter. Smoke filled the staircase, making it hard to see, choking him. He pulled out the pendant and placed it in the divot.

A groaning sound surrounded him and the ceiling slid open, revealing the open air.

Not wasting a moment, he bolted up the remaining stone stairs. Emerging at the base of the obelisk atop the mountain, he skidded to a stop and fell to the cold ground. His chest heaved and he lay looking at the sky, gasping for breath. His body trembled but he wasn't sure if it was from the heat, exertion, or cold air and stone.

Slowly, he calmed down, forcing his breathing under control. He chuckled and shook his head, not completely sure what was funny exactly, but he couldn't seem to stop. Perhaps the stress of the escape had made him finally lose his sanity. Wiping the tears from his eyes, his stress-induced laughter finally abated.

The rain from earlier had stopped, but the ground was still damp, so Mahkai spread out his cloak before him. He unrolled the scroll on the cloak and set rocks on it to keep it open and still. It was written in a very old dialect, but he was confident—well, pretty sure—that with the aid of the diagrams and depictions alongside the text, he would be able to read it.

At first glance, it seemed the drawings meant to depict something about the flames he encountered, but he couldn't yet be sure. He could make out a few words, but many of them were unfamiliar. He rolled up the scroll, placed it gently in his satchel, and buckled both straps to ensure it would stay closed.

He headed home, excited to tell Gwen all about his day. He missed her.

Lethe Tea

Lemongrass

Peppermint

Green Sencha

Tulsi

Saffron

Fennel

Licorice

Star Anise

Orange Peel

Dearmad Root

Will help you forget... I have forgotten what I was
going to say to beware of.

-Lani

Chapter 16

Mahkai arrived home to his treehome and climbed the rope ladder. Hartley said she had an idea for how to make getting to the upper half easier, but he would have to wait until she was finished with her latest project.

"Gwen?" he called into the space. She reminded him of a cat sometimes with the interesting places she chose to sleep. Her favorite was still in one of his bags.

Her little hoot greeted him from outside the window. He leaned out and grinned. She was perched on a branch in the sun, preening her feathers.

"Gwen, you will never guess what happened!" He dropped his voice to a whisper. "I met a dragon. A real one. And I'm still alive! He was quite civilized and did not threaten to eat me. Everything we were taught as young bulls is all wrong. I wonder what else we were taught was wrong too? They were wrong about puka and fairies, and now dragons." Words poured out of his mouth in his excitement.

Gwen hooted at him in agreement and walked her way towards him on the branch, wings outstretched for balance. They looked fine. He wondered, not for the first time, why she did not just fly. He would need to ask Cael what she said next time he came by. He did so enjoy their conversations over tea, and he hoped they would continue once Cael returned from his trip.

He cleared his table, placing his other books, pages, and scrolls on the floor in the corner. He would clean and organize them later. He unrolled the scroll from the dragon's library on his table and hunched over it, squinting at the text and pictures. He lit several lanterns and even brought out the fairy light Hartley had gifted him. He felt the tingle of magic buzz under his fingers as he turned the knob to light it.

He took out several blank pages and a fresh stick of charcoal and began taking notes on the contents of the scroll.

He had figured out the different symbols were supposed to represent the different types of magic, but there were still a few symbols he could not decipher. There had to be a point to this scroll, but he was still baffled as to what it was. Why did Azar tell him to take this one over the thousands of others?

"You know what this needs?" he asked Gwen, rubbing his chin thoughtfully.

She hooted at him.

"Yes, quite right. What would you like?" He held out his hand and she hopped into his palm. He carried her over to their tea nook, a cabinet on top of three drawers. He opened the top doors and set her inside then pulled open the drawer and took out several clay jars he kept his tea blends in.

He found they kept longer in clay or stone than the wooden ones he'd tried before. He opened three he knew she was particularly fond of and set them before her. She approached each of them and then finally clicked her beak at one.

"Ah, ZippiTea. Good choice. I am rather fond of that one as well." He felt like drinking from his tea bowl today, so he pulled it out and righted it from the upside down position he stored it in to keep it clean. He retrieved her much smaller bowl as well, then put his kettle filled with water over the fire to heat.

While he waited, he stroked the top of her head. She made pleasant owl noises, like a cat purrs, only distinctly owl. When their tea was finally brewed, he sat on his cushion on the floor with his bowl, blowing on it to help it cool, while he thought. His mind wandered to the dragon and he wondered if Azar could hear him from anywhere. He concentrated his thoughts and asked, "What is this scroll depicting?" After a few moments, he came to the conclusion Azar could not hear him.

He had just finished his second cup when it hit him. The scroll was depicting the revealing ceremony. He recognized the bronze bowl with carvings on it, though it had more carvings on it now than it did on the scroll. Six individuals stood around the bowl with their hands stretched toward it. He could just make out different colors in the flames. That couldn't be right. Flames do not burn multi-colored, do they? He needed to test it out. Do different things burn different colors? What were they adding to the fire to make it burn like that?

He made notes on his notebook and shuffled over to one of his piles to look for his notes on rocks burning. He flipped through and found several that, once ground into a powder and cast into the fire, burned green, blue, and purple. He even found one that burned a brilliant white, but nothing that burned like the scroll depicted.

Mahkai considered how to go about investigating. Thoria was several days' journey from here, but Kamea should be returning soon from her latest patrol. She could get him permission to see the ceremony site. He wanted to test out his theory.

Excitedly, he made a few more notes, gathered several books and scrolls he thought he might need, and stuffed them into one of his bags. Next, he searched through his collection of rocks and selected the ones his notes had indicated. He also made a list of the ones he didn't have and potentially where to find them.

Would leaves burn different colors too? He made notes on what fresh plants he wanted to gather to try as well. He packed his best change of clothes and his cloak in his overnight pack as well as provisions, a selection of his favorite teas, his travel pot and mug, and his cold brewing horn. When he was satisfied he hadn't forgotten anything, he rolled up the dragon scroll. He debated leaving it here or taking it with him for a moment, unwilling to risk damaging it. Finally, he decided to bring it with him. He would endeavor to copy it to his notebook at some point.

    ☕   ☕   ☕

On the way to Thoria, Mahkai stopped by the Makanui camp to see his father, but he was told he had left for a meeting of the elders and wouldn't be back for a few days. He stopped by his designated hut and found it in the same state he had left it. Not bothering to rearrange or clean anything, he took everything he could carry and stuffed it in his satchels. He needed to hurry if he wanted to escape camp without someone dragging him into their nonsense. He had just about made it out of camp when Maleek hailed him.

"Hello, brother! Where have you been? Where are you off to? You can't leave now, you've only just arrived."

Mahkai tried to keep his shoulders from drooping. He'd been so close. He braced himself and turned to face his brother.

"Hello, Maleek." They clasped forearms. "I'm headed to test an idea I got from a scroll I was reading. It is very fascinating…"

Maleek's eyes glazed over, so Mahkai stopped talking. He was so used to this response that he didn't bother continuing. But it bothered him more than he remembered it bothering him before. He supposed it was because he had gotten used to Hartley and Gwen actively listening to him talk about things instead of talking over him or tuning out.

He sighed. "You probably don't want to hear about that, though. I am headed to Thoria; do you think Kamea is still there? I hope to ask her for something."

"You are going to Thoria?" Maleek perked up with interest, noticing Mahkai's overstuffed bags for the first time.

"Well, near there. Hartley is helping with the new council seat project and I want to see it too. She said all the council will be there, so I'm hoping she might introduce me to the Histories Master. I have quite a few things I would like to ask. If they will talk to me, that is."

Maleek looked thoughtful. "They will all be there, you say? Away from Thoria? Do you know whereabout?"

"I think she said it was near the lake. Why?"

"Oh, no reason," Maleek said nonchalantly, picking at something between his teeth with a fingernail. He turned away, but then turned back as if he remembered something. "On your return journey, I'll meet you with some of the cousins on our favorite training field and we can travel home together."

Mahkai blinked, surprised and more than a little delighted. Maleek had never offered to spend time with him willingly. "Oh. That would be...nice, actually." He hesitated to get his hopes up. Was this a prank? Did they really want him to meet them?

"Have a good trip." Maleek punched his shoulder lightly then lumbered toward the center of camp.

Mahkai froze in shock at the gesture Maleek usually reserved for his closest friends. Maybe things were changing. What had he done to elicit this response from his brother? Had he somehow heard about his budding friendship with Bree and Hartley and his work at the inn? Had his actions really helped to foster more peaceful relations between the minotaur and the rest of the fae? That had to be it. His chest warmed at the sign of affection as he trotted toward Thoria.

Waking Memory Tea

Green Sencha	Tulsi
Chrysanthemum Blossoms	Saffron
Marigold Petals	Green Cardamom
Hibiscus	Peppermint
Sarsaparilla	Raspberry Leaves
Citron Peach	Forget-me-not Blossoms

Will help you remember things you have forgotten. Be wary, do not consume more than a mouthful. It will bring on sudden and vivid memories. Side effects can cause confusion and delayed recovery of the present.

-Lani

DO NOT DRINK ALONE!
-Mahkai

Chapter 17

Two days later, Mahkai sat on a rock, sipping from the thermos of tea he had prepared earlier in the morning. It never crossed his mind that he would not be able to get into Thoria to see the revealing site. After trying everything he knew to do, including trying to sneak in, he finally gave up. He thought over his puzzling notes, going around and around in his head, as he watched a few fairy children learning to control their magic.

They were not technically children anymore at age thirty—the age of their magic awakening—but he enjoyed watching them learn to master it for the first time. He pushed down the bitter feelings of his own inadequacies and tried to be happy for them. He really did enjoy the look of glee on their faces when they finally got it.

"Hey, you!"

Mahkai looked around and spotted the magic instructor approaching him. "Who, me?"

"Yes. What are you?"

He looked down at himself. "A minotaur?"

Snorts and giggles erupted from the class. "No, I mean your magical class. Historian? Ardere? Aqualite?"

"Ah, Aerophyte, I have air magic." His face warmed with embarrassment.

"Oh, perfect. Can you demonstrate to my class how you access your magic?"

"Oh, I am not... I cannot, should not..."

"It will be fine. No need to be so modest. Show them what

you can do, but slowly, and then talk them through it. I want them to see that people access their magic differently."

"Oh really, no, I—"

"Hey, Mahkai!" Hartley's voice interrupted him.

Stars bless her. The tension building in his chest loosened.

"I needed to take a break, so I came to check on you. Didn't get in, huh? Corsen says to bring you by."

He had never been more grateful for her than he was in that moment. "Hartley!"

The teacher blinked at them both with wide eyes. "You have an audience with Master Corsen? You must not keep him waiting. Do not let me keep you," he sputtered then turned back to his class. "This is apprentice Hartley of the great Arboreal Archetectorialist, Arlo. Second only to Master Corsen himself." The class waved, more than a few of their faces awestruck.

Hartley beckoned him, and he hurried after her. "Much appreciated. Did you actually talk to Master Corsen?"

She grinned mischievously. "No. I just said that because you looked like you needed saving, but now that you mention it, I could probably cause an accident in such a way that he has to come supervise."

Mahkai gasped. "You wouldn't."

"Oh, I would. And for much less important reasons than whatever you want to talk to him about. I love the way his face scrunches up and all the others scurry around trying to fix it," she cackled, her eyes twinkled with mischief.

He shook his head, failing to hide his smile. "That's horrible."

"Yea, but you love me anyway."

"Indeed." He chuckled with her and bumped her shoulder with his.

They walked together toward Hartley's little apartment, where she lived adjacent to her family.

"So…do you want to help me grow mushroom circles to torment the fairylings with? We can tell them they are portals to other realms and if they step foot inside they will be trapped in the human world and become human."

"Hartley!"

"What? Why not?"

He snorted. "I'm not dignifying that with a response."

"Ah, but you just did." She grinned at him and nudged his shoulder with hers.

He huffed and pretended to be mad, but he couldn't stop himself from grinning back at her. Her energy and vibrancy were contagious, and soon he found himself relaxing.

"Wait 'til you hear about my adventure! I found a scroll and,"—he glanced around and dropped his voice to a whisper—"I met a dragon."

"Now who's telling tall tales?"

"No, I'm serious. His name is Azar Barak, and he said I could call him Azar."

"Now I know you are joking. Dragons don't talk to anyone."

"Hartley."

Her eyes met his and her grin faded. "You are serious."

He nodded.

"You have to tell me everything!" She grabbed his arm and shook it. "But not here. I need tea and scones for this!" She released his arm and zipped ahead. He hurried after her, trying not to trip as he attempted to catch up.

Once they were settled comfortably in her home—as comfortably as he could be in a home not meant for someone his size—she fixed him with her full attention. The intensity of her gaze was that of what she normally wore to tackle a particularly challenging project.

"Spill the tea. Well, don't, actually. Not the real tea, anyway. You know the saying..." She trailed off.

He smiled at her antics and filled her in on everything from start to finish. He pulled out the scroll and unrolled it on the floor for her to inspect the faded scrawling script.

"I am thinking this indicates a different kind of fire, but I have not worked out exactly what it is for or why it depicts the revealing bowl." He pulled out the rocks he brought and showed her his idea.

"What if it is more simple than that?" Hartley rested her chin on her open palm with her elbow propped on her folded legs. She tapped her cheek with her fingers as she thought.

"What do you mean?"

"Just thinking out loud here, but what if they are not feeding the fire with rocks but with magic?"

He looked at the scroll again and squinted.

"Oh, here. I was going to wait for the Autumn Solstice, but I think you should have it now." She handed him a small ornate wooden box.

He smiled as he tried to open it. "It's a puzzle." She just grinned and watched him as he worked it out.

Finally, he slid the last piece into place, and the lid sprung open. He dumped the contents into his hand. They were spectacles large enough to sit on his nose. He tried putting them on, but was unsure where they went.

"Here, let me." Hartley gently took his new spectacles from his hand and balanced them on his nose.

Mahkai was disoriented for a moment as his eyes adjusted, but now, when he looked at the unrolled scroll, he saw it with perfect clarity. He noticed details he had missed before. She took something out of her pocket and attached it to the side of the spectacles, then again to his tunic collar. He felt it. It was a delicate chain.

"So you won't lose them."

"Thank you so much." He fought the tears threatening to spill out of his eyes.

"You are welcome, bestie. Now, what do you see?" They turned their attention back to the scroll before them.

"What if they are all casting their magic together into the ceremonial fire bowl?"

"So you are saying what if that is meant to power the revealing ceremony? Might that be why everyone's magical abilities are diminished compared to history? What if the magic is not dying out, but we are simply not activating it properly?"

They looked at each other excitedly.

"We need to show the council!"

"I still need to copy the scroll. I don't feel comfortable showing it to them yet, in case they take it from me. I did not ask Azar if I am meant to keep it or if I am meant to return it to him."

"Oh, I learned a new trick. Wanna see?" She pulled out a fresh page and a jar of ink. "If the ink is made entirely from plants, I can... Well, just watch and see." She narrowed her eyes and held out her hand toward the page. She glowed with the silvery-green light of her magic. The ink from the jar floated in the air toward the scroll.

Mahkai sucked in a breath, but remained quiet. He trusted her, but he was still wary. He did not want anything to happen to the scroll.

The ink landed on the parchment, but did not soak in like he expected. It arranged itself over the pictures and writing on the scroll. Hartley set the blank page on top of it and the ink soaked into the page. When she removed it from the scroll, the page was an exact replica of the section of writing on the scroll. She proceeded to repeat the process a couple more times, so they had two perfect copies of the original.

Mahkai clapped his hands. "This is wonderful!"

She gave him a self-satisfied grin. "Alright, let's go meet Corsen. If he asks where we got this, just say some old records."

Mahkai nodded and followed her out the door.

🍵 🍵 🍵

Corsen thoroughly studied the pages in silence. His long, dark brown hair, parted by his pointed ears, fell like a curtain partially blocking his face from Mahkai. Mahkai attempted not to wring his hands while they waited for his assessment, but failed miserably. He gripped his hands together so tightly his fingernails dug into his palms, causing him to wince. Corsen had a lithe build and four translucent wings that looked like a dragonfly's not unlike Hartley's. Mahkai wondered if they were related.

"Hmmm… I suppose it could not hurt to try it. Master Althenaea, what do you think?"

Master Althenaea was tall for a fairy, but he found her fascinating. She had no wings to speak of. Were there multiple types of fairy? Most striking about her was her fiery, turquoise eyes and her regal grace that commanded the attention of every room she was in. Mahkai found it a little intimidating, not that he would ever admit that to her.

"Yes. Agreed. I'll gather the necessary individuals and meet you back here."

Mahkai vibrated with excitement. He was going to finally contribute something of value that didn't involve weapons! He moved to follow Master Althenaea, but Corsen held up a hand. "And where do you think you are going?" his voice was laced with disdain.

"I just thought…"

"Ah."

With one word, Mahkai knew he was no longer wanted on this project.

"Thank you for bringing this to our attention, Mahkai. We will take it from here," Althenaea said gently but firmly.

Dejectedly, Mahkai shuffled out of the interim council chambers, shoulders hunched and tail swishing, nearly dragging the ground. He didn't know what he expected, but to be completely dismissed from his discoveries was not it.

"Hey, Bree is trying out new pastry recipes tonight and invited us to come taste them for her. I'm headed there now, wanna come?" Hartley faced him as she flew backwards.

The first time she had done that he had been worried for her, thinking she couldn't see where she was going. But the more he learned about her magic, the more he realized she not only knew where she was at all times, but she was also aware of every growing thing in the immediate vicinity. His interaction with his treehome flashed through his mind.

He could only imagine what Master Corsen could do. Hartley snapped her finger in front of his face, bringing him back to the present. "Hmm, pardon?" He blinked at her.

"So, do you?"

Mahkai searched his mind for the last thing he'd heard. Oh yes, she'd asked him to come with her to taste-test at the inn. He smiled at her and nodded. That would most definitely make him feel better.

He couldn't stay too late though; he had promised to meet up with Kamea and Maleek tomorrow. A thrill shot up his spine as he remembered the way his brother had nudged him affectionately. Something akin to hope blossomed in his chest. His eldest brother was finally acknowledging him. It was still a far cry from acceptance, but this was a step, and he'd take it. Maybe Maleek would help him talk Father into accepting his new home and life.

He reined in his excitement before he got too ahead of himself. *One thing at a time, Mahkai,* he reminded himself as he followed Hartley down the path. It was lit with strings of tiny starlights, making her look like she was a living flame dancing down the path.

He glanced over his shoulder as they walked and caught sight of a shadowy pair of ears a little distance away. He felt a surge in his chest, wishing it were Cael. But that'd be silly. Cael was probably off doing something important. He'd enjoyed his chats with the dark-haired puka and even thought fondly of the time he'd come to his aid when he'd poisoned himself.

"Hartley?"

"Hmmm?" she glanced at him distractedly as her hands were making weaving motions. He'd noticed she did this when she was thinking about her next project.

"Do you think Cael would want to join us?" he managed to blurt out. He rushed on. "I'm sure he is too busy or probably has better things to do. I just thought… Nevermind. It was silly." His cheeks burned as he waited for her to tell him it was a terrible idea. Except she didn't.

"Mahkai, that is a great idea! I'm sure Bree wouldn't mind, and I have this game I have been dying to try, but it takes four players. We could probably convince Bree to play a hand, or one of the hive, or maybe even one of the other patrons. I should warn you, the hive might cheat." She grinned at him and flew to sit on his shoulder.

His smile faltered and he stopped in his tracks. "One problem. I don't suppose you know where he lives, do you?"

"Where who lives?" Out of the shadows stepped none other than Cael himself. His long hair was pulled neatly into a ball on the back of his head. His eyes reflected the light like a fox's, flashing momentarily, then gone in an instant. Mahkai's chest warmed at the sight of him.

"Oh, splendid! We were just about to come looking for you. Would you like to accompany us to the Winding Way Inn for a night of tasting Bree's new confections and perhaps a game?" Mahkai asked while he tried to work out if the shadow had indeed been Cael or not. In the end he decided it didn't matter. Cael was here now.

"That sounds interesting, to say the least. Lead on and tell me of this game." Cael stepped next to them and assumed an easy, relaxed gait next to them as Hartley began to explain the game in great detail.

As they drew close to the inn, delicious aromas of fresh pastries wafted out the open doors and windows. Mahkai inhaled deeply as his hooves seemed to move of their own volition toward the kitchen. Whatever it was that she was making, was making him forget the rules Hartley had just spent the better part of the walk explaining.

His companions seemed to be under the same spell, as their eyes were slightly glazed over as they wordlessly entered the inn. They found Bree humming to herself as she took a tray of tiny star-shaped pastries from one of the ovens and placed it on the cooling racks. Instantly, his mind went back to Aunti Lani's kitchen and how she sang while she baked. He could almost see her swaying to her tune, lost in the moment standing next to a steaming cup of freshly poured tea.

Surprisingly, it was the first time his heart didn't hurt thinking of her. He felt only fondness, and a sense that he had found something similar here with these three odd individuals. He watched Bree and Hartley tease each other and relax into their normal banter. Cael seemed at ease leaning against the wall with a cup in one hand and a pastry in the other.

His eyes lifted, meeting Mahkai's, and something warm twinkled in their depths. Mahkai couldn't even begin to sort out what he was feeling. Cael tipped his head and gestured for him to join them at the table Bree was filling with more and more things for them to try.

Mahkai smiled back and took a seat across from Hartley, who was mixing up a stack of thin wooden disks. She made four piles, handing each of them a small stack.

"Don't show us what you have. That is part of the fun, guessing what everyone else has. So, first you decide which three you don't want and pass them face down to the person on your left."

"Um," Mahkai interrupted.

"Yes, Mahkai?"

"How do I know which three I don't want?"

She sighed dramatically, then ruined it by winking at him. "You are trying not to take any points, meaning you don't want to have the highest number, so you don't take any tools… What?"

"Why are they called tools again?"

"Because they look like things that anyone who isn't an Arborealist uses to dig with."

It made sense to Mahkai, so he nodded along with her. He had tried to take notes initially, but after a few times of him requesting Hartley repeat the rules so he knew he'd taken them down right, Bree had banned all notes and note taking devices.

Mahkai thought he understood the gist of the game even without his notes. He looked again at his handful of wooden disks with little runes and one of the four marks on them— rocks, bushes, leaves, or tools. He picked three of the highest bushes and passed them to Bree, who shot him a dirty look when she saw them. When he looked alarmed at her reaction, her expression softened and she patted his hand. He relaxed; she was only being competitive.

He picked up the tree tiles Cael passed him. They were surprisingly low. He didn't have time to ponder it much though, because they started playing. Each of them placed one of their tiles in the center, each one trying not to be the highest. It was more difficult than he had originally thought, but after a half dozen rounds he was starting to get the hang of it. It was his turn to swap tiles with Hartley. He only had one tool and two rocks, so he gave them to her. When he saw she had given him the highest three tools, he knew he was done for. He swallowed hard and glanced up at her from his tiles. She gave him a look of pure innocence that didn't fool anyone at the table. Bree chuckled as she took a bite of a spiral cinnamon pastry she had dubbed a "cinnamon roll." Mahkai thought they were too soft to roll—not to mention it would be a waste of a perfectly delicious treat.

"What'd she do?" Cael looked at the three of them with playful suspicion before he leaned over and promptly looked at Mahkai's tiles. "I'll trade you if you want?" he said in a low voice.

Mahkai was too shocked to do more than just stare at him. Cael gazed back at him, the firelight glinting in his eyes, making them sparkle like the night sky. He gave Mahkai a small smirk, then reached over and gently took Mahkai's tiles and replaced them with his own. Mahkai looked at his new hand in disbelief. Cael had just traded him a winning hand for a losing one.

He looked at Bree, who shrugged, and Hartley, who had missed the exchange altogether while intensely studying her tiles. She played first, then Cael played his. Mahkai took a deep breath and played his tile. Cael lost and took points. The rest of the round went that way, with Cael ending up taking all the points. Mahkai felt more guilty as the round progressed. Before this one, Cael had been just behind Hartley for least amount of points. Now he was sure to lose. Cael took it like a champ, and his smile only grew as the round finished and he was left with all the points.

Mahkai felt terrible. Hartley surprised him when she swore. She counted, then recounted the points and swore again. Cael only grinned more. Confusion must have shown on Mahkai's face, because Bree pointed to the tally. Instead of Cael getting all the points, Hartley had increased all of their points by the total.

"He caught the moon."

"He did what?" Mahkai didn't think that sounded like a good thing. What an absurd thing to say!

They all chuckled and Bree explained, "It means he took all the points, so instead of him getting them all, everyone else gets them and he takes none. And since it puts both you and me over, it means he wins the game."

Cael looked quite pleased with himself. Mahkai didn't know whether to feel betrayed or impressed, so he settled for a bit of both.

"You knew and you let me feel bad for you?"

His grin dimmed and he looked at Mahkai with remorse. "At first it was out of pity, but then I realized I had a chance if I played it right. I really did want you to win."

"That is exactly what I would expect my brothers to pull." Mahkai sighed tiredly as he realized just how late it was. "Speaking of, I am supposed to meet them and some of my cousins tomorrow, so I think I'm going to call it a night." He turned to Bree. "All of your creations were delicious, but I think this one, the sticky one, is my favorite. Thank you for inviting me to be a taste tester."

He turned to Hartley and Cael. "Thank you for the pleasure of your company tonight." He smiled tiredly at them, pushing aside the uncomfortable feeling rising in his chest.

Cael rose also. "I, too, have pressing things to attend to to-morrow, so I will also take my leave."

Bree embraced him and bid him goodnight, telling him not to worry about cleaning up. The hive would handle it. Mahkai gathered his bag and left the inn toward his room without another word. He rubbed at his chest where a prickling feeling was eating away at the warm feelings he had before. Doubts about how they saw him and if they were only tolerating him began to creep into his thoughts. Did they see him like his clan saw him? Were they really no different? Had he deluded himself into thinking things could be different?

He reached the door to his unofficial room here at the inn, which Bree kept available to him whenever he needed it, before he heard the telltale flutter of wings. Cael's raven alighted on one of the branches by the door before shifting to stand before him. He reached toward Mahkai and paused. His hand hovered a hair's breadth away from actually touching him before he pulled it back.

"Mahkai, wait. I'm sorry. I wasn't thinking. I was caught up in the game and didn't think about how it would come across to you. Please, forgive me." His voice was pleading. His hair came loose from the knot and blew in the gentle breeze. His dark eyes begged Mahkai to listen.

Mahkai let out a sigh. This was Cael, the one who had dropped everything to come to his aid when he was ill, the one who had entertained his seemingly endless questions, who had treated him with respect and listened to him. The one who cared to ask about him and his life and what he thought. He nodded and felt the tightening in his chest begin to abate.

Cael's smile looked relieved. "I'll be gone for a while I expect, but when I get back, what do you say to trading questions over tea and scones?"

Mahkai stared into his dark eyes that caught the starlight

and lost himself. He was drawn to Cael, now more than ever. He wanted to spend more time with this strange but gentle puka. He realized after an extended silence and the increasingly expectant look on Cael's face that he hadn't answered the question.

"Yes, I'd like that." His baritone voice rumbled in his chest more than it normally did.

A ghost of a smile played on his lips as Cael bobbed his head in acknowledgment. "Alright, until then. Goodnight, Mahkai." Cael flourished his hand, and a fog rolled in across the gardens, covering the inn from view. He gave Mahkai one last dazzling smile and stepped backwards into the mist, disappearing from view.

Mahkai stared into the swirling white before him for a few more heartbeats, then went inside. He promptly collapsed into the waiting hammock, warmth spreading through his chest. He replayed the recent events in his head as he closed his eyes and allowed hope to take root for the first time he could remember. Things were going to be different, he was sure of it.

Reali-Tea

Spearmint

Nettle

Oatstraw

Raspberry Leaf

Red Clover

Forget-me-not Blossoms

Drink after you finish with Waking Memory Tea. It will help lessen the after effects.

-Lani

Chapter 18

Mahkai shuffled down the dirt path strewn with golden and crimson leaves, humming to himself. *"Baby, you're the one I love..."* The song was stuck on a loop in his head. He couldn't help it; it was so catchy. *"... But finally, you put my love on top."* He spun dramatically and swayed his shoulders, flinging his arms out to the sides of his large frame as he modulated to a higher key and began the chorus again.

He was not the largest minotaur by any means, but compared to fairies and puka, he was enormous. He prided himself on being fairly light on his feet—hooves, as it were—for his hulking size.

He hummed a few more bars as he trotted toward the edge of the forest, where he was supposed to be meeting Maleek to walk home together. *"...you make everything stop..."* He paused in his song. Silence wrapped around him almost tangibly. The next words died on his lips, all levity gone.

Something did not feel right. It was too quiet; not even crickets chirped. The deafening silence pressed in on him uncomfortably. Even the wind seemed to have stopped.

He hurried to the treeline and emerged into the field, eager to meet his brother. The long grass waved like millions of flags in the wind. A lone figure knelt a short distance away, head bowed and shoulders hunched. His long, black hair blew like the grass surrounding him.

Large brown and black boulders lay strewn around the field. That was new, Mahkai mused. Long gouges in the ground broke up the grasses. That didn't make sense either, unless they had altered the field for training. Had they finished training already? Where was everyone?

Mahkai took out his notebook to sketch the strange changes in the field he had traversed countless times.

This was his brothers' favorite field to play war games. It provided great strategic points for the opposing teams, or so they said. The team on the crest of the hill was actually at a disadvantage, contrary to what would normally make sense. Something about the way the sun set in the sky and the placement of the rocks. Mahkai usually stopped listening at this point, his attention on something much more interesting.

Now he wished he had paid better attention. He couldn't shake the unease settling in his chest. Where was Maleek? He should be here by now. Mahkai knew he had been running late, but he wasn't *that* late, was he? They wouldn't leave before he got here, would they? Mahkai shook his head. No, that was not it. They would have left a sign or something. His brother would never pass up an opportunity to chastise him.

Mahkai took a few steps toward the fae, not wanting to interrupt whatever they were doing, but needing to know if they had seen his brother and cousins. The wind shifted, and he caught a metallic tang mixed with the earthy scent of freshly turned dirt.

A small sparrow-like bird flew in ever-growing circles in the distance. Or, it looked like a bird, but he had the sneaking suspicion this was a puka. Sparrows did not fly like that. This flew more like a bird of prey.

Suspicion prickled at the back of his neck. He hid behind the closest boulder as best he could as he watched the sparrow land and slowly shift into a man. Mahkai was glad he hid because seconds later, a large group of heavily armed fae surrounded the kneeling figure. He finally looked up at the fae, anguish written all over his features.

What happened here? Was he ok? Did he need help? Mahkai was about to step out and ask when the phrase "Restrain the Bacia" drifted to him on the wind.

Bacia—death bringer. Mahkai shivered as cold air trailed down his back. Quietly and carefully, he crept backwards toward the trees as fast as he dared. When he reached cover, he looked up. The kneeling figure met his gaze, dark eyes full of a myriad of emotions Mahkai couldn't differentiate.

The ground rumbled and rolled. The rocks sank beneath the grass, like stones in mud. When the motion stopped, the field was covered in twisting vines with tiny buds growing amongst the grasses. *What is this?* It was over in a matter of minutes, like nothing had happened.

When everything stopped moving again, the figure rose without a fight, and they departed immediately. Mahkai huffed. He was confused and still no closer to finding his brother.

He checked his bags. He was low on provisions, but he didn't mind scavenging for berries and seeds to eat. He had his mug and a small pot to brew tea, so he might as well get comfortable and wait for them. Maybe they had gotten called away. Surely they would not have left without him.

He busied himself taking notes and sketching the leaf patterns and vine growth of this new flower. He tried to guess what the blossoms would look like when they opened. He hoped they smelled lovely. Would they make good tea?

He thought about picking the buds to try in his tea, but decided to wait to see the full blooms first. What if they were poisonous? He didn't think he could make it back to clansland on his own if he poisoned himself.

Again.

No one would know what became of him. Would Maleek let him stay long enough to see the flowers bloom? He hoped so. He shifted uncomfortably on the log he had chosen for a seat.

He was considering sitting on the damp ground instead, but didn't want to chance getting mud on his only clean clothes. He sighed as worry invaded more of his thoughts. He could not concentrate on anything anymore.

The setting sun bathed everything in brilliant fuchsia and amber for a few breathtaking moments before sinking below the far hills. "I suppose I could stay here for the night. It would be quite the adventure, I imagine," he said aloud to himself. It would give him a chance to see if the flowers bloomed in the morning. Then he could collect a few to take back with him.

He looked at the clouds and hoped it would not rain, but just in case, he wrapped all of his charcoal bits and papers and books in the oiled cloth and put them back in his bag. He built a small fire from dead twigs and grasses he gathered and began warming water in his tiny pot for tea. The cool harvest breeze blew out his fire a few times before he had the idea of digging a small pit to shield it from the wind. He grinned at his ingenuity and mentally patted himself on his back.

He glanced up at the sky, intent on gazing at the stars, but there were too many clouds to see more than a few. He sighed again and poured the hot water into his cup with the petals, leaves, and bark he had blended earlier. This was his favorite blend yet, but he suspected that would be how he felt about many of them.

He took a deep breath of the delicious aroma wafting out of his cup and began a countdown in his head for when he needed to take them out. Otherwise, it turned bitter. It had taken him countless times to get it right.

He had just finished sifting out the last leaves when the clouds parted. The full moon peeked through, bathing the surrounding trees and the fields beyond in moonlight almost as bright as day. A flash of silver shone from the field. Mahkai was immediately on alert. His skin prickled and his heart pounded loudly in ears. Was there someone out there? Could it be his brothers? What were they doing out there in the middle of the night?

He walked silently to the edge of the trees for the second time that day. Everywhere the moon shone, silvery blue and black flowers reflected the moonlight like the surface of a lake. The breeze caused the flowers to shift and move like gentle waves on water. It took his breath away.

Clouds passed across the moon. All at once, the flowers folded up, closing in on themselves. He wanted to cry, and he did not quite know why. He felt lost with how fast they were there and gone. A deep sadness he couldn't explain rolled through him. Tears streamed down his face as he dropped to his knees, overcome with this strange grief and wonder.

He was just drying his eyes and getting to his feet when the clouds parted, and again the entire field bloomed with moonlight. Careful not to crush any of them, he waded out into the sea of blooms. He loved the way they swayed with the twitch of his tail. On impulse, he plucked one of the blossoms and inhaled deeply.

He braced himself for the deep emotions he suspected might be brought about by these strange flowers. They were still present, but muted somehow. Instead, comfort warmed his chest, like the first time he sipped the perfect cup of tea, or sitting next to a fire at the end of a chilly day.

He picked one more and held them delicately in his hand. He hoped they would not close when the moon hid behind clouds, but he was curious, too. He rubbed the leaves between his fingers; they gave off a pleasant aroma as well, so he tried to pick one of them, but he might as well have been trying to pry a leaf made of stone. It stayed firmly attached to the vine. The edges felt sharp like they might cut him if he grasped it too tightly.

He made a mental note to write down his findings when he went back to his campsite, but he was hesitant to leave the field immediately. What if the moon didn't emerge again tonight? He might never see this again. He still didn't know what brought this about in the first place.

His thoughts turned to the kneeling figure. He must be an Arborealist, but Mahkai had never seen any of the clans do this. Not even Hartley or Arlo. Could Master Corsen? And why did they call him the death bringer?

The moon fled behind an especially thick bank of clouds, and like before, the flowers closed. He waited a long time in hopes the moon would peek out a third time, but the clouds rolling in were too thick. A storm was approaching. Disappointed, Mahkai shuffled back to his campsite to retrieve his books and charcoal.

His tea was cold, but he didn't care. He sipped it anyway, enjoying the subtle yet complex flavors swirling over his tongue. Nestled in his large palm, only a little bruised, the moon flowers remained open. He wondered if they had a name other than moon flower as he sketched them in as much detail as possible by the light of his little fire.

The breeze shifted, and again he felt the deep anguish from earlier. He'd never felt anything so powerfully before, negative or otherwise. Even his happy experiences felt muted and subdued compared to this. Sobs racked his body. Rather than fighting it, he gave himself to the feelings, knowing they would run their course and eventually abate. The breeze shifted again, and he felt released.

He wiped his eyes on the corner of his tunic and took a deep, steadying breath. On a hunch, he poured more water into his pot and placed it over the fire. He fished out the scrap of cloth Hartley had given him from his bag and blew his nose while the water heated up. When it began to steam, he placed one of the blossoms into his now empty cup and poured the water over it like he was brewing tea.

The cup did not give off a smell so much as a feeling. He inhaled the steam rising out of his cup in a deep breath. Its warm embrace enveloped his entire body, like being wrapped in a sun-warmed blanket on a cool harvest night. Like the hugs Aunti Lani had given him when he was little. Like the peace and stillness of the calmest night where everything is just as it should be. He took a sip, and the feelings continued, stronger even, until he had drained the whole cup and all that was left was a silvery residue coating the bottom.

Mis-Tea

Belinay (Moonflower) Petals

Made from the petals of the Belinay flowers that bloom only in the light of the full moon on the fields of Alinorr. Will let you grieve, then comfort you.

-Mahkai

Chapter 19

Mahkai awoke the next morning completely drained emotionally. At some point, he had fallen asleep, but his dreams were fraught with emotional turmoil. Something terrible had happened in his dream, but it eluded him now that he was awake.

Quickly, he searched the area, hoping his brother and cousins had arrived in the middle of the night. He sighed dejectedly. This wouldn't be the first time his brother had invited him somewhere then failed to show up. He dismissed his concerns for his brother. *It was fine, really,* he told himself. He refused to be disappointed. It was better this way. He preferred solitude anyway. His brother was probably too busy with clan responsibilities to make the trip.

Physically, Mahkai felt fine, well rested and ready to make the journey to the clan lands. He collected the rest of his belongings and drank the last dregs of tea he did not remember making last night. He looked around the field one last time. The grasses waved in the wind where they grew through the new tangle of vines. So that part wasn't a dream, then.

He took longer than he intended to reach the Makanui clan winter camp. His mind was still on the strange flowers from last night. He missed Gwen. He wished she had come along for this journey, but his reasoning for leaving her behind at their treehouse was still valid. He didn't trust she wouldn't get injured if things got rough, as they were prone to when family was involved.

He had barely crested the hill in view of the huts when he

saw several scouts patrolling. *That's odd. They don't normally patrol so openly, nor so close to home.* What had happened in the short time he was away? They would have told him if they were at war again. Surely he would have heard something while he was in Thoria. What was going on?

As the huts came into view, he was certain something was wrong. Everyone wore their armor and carried weapons, even in the middle of camp, and strode about like whatever they were doing was vitally important. No one smiled or lazed about chatting like they normally did.

Kamea burst from the main hut and charged toward him. "Mahkai! You're alive! Thank the stars you're alive!"

"Alive? What are you talking about? Why wouldn't I be? Tell me, cousin…what has happened?"

She hugged him so hard he felt his back and neck pop. He could hardly draw a breath, she was crushing him so tight. When she released him a little and looked into his face, tears streamed down her face. His strong, never-shows-emotions-so-she-won't-be-seen-as-weak cousin was openly sobbing. Confusion and dread dug their claws into his chest and made it even harder to breathe.

"Kamea, please. What happened?" He hugged her tightly and stroked her back and arms as her body gradually stopped shaking with sobs. She took deep gulping breaths and hiccuped once before she could speak again.

"Maleek…" Her voice broke. "…and some of the others we were supposed to meet…" she continued.

Chills ran down his back. No matter how her statement ended, it would not be good.

"… decided they were going to take Thoria. I was not there because I got held up with my reports with the Council, and when we received word of the battle, I came straight here. How are you not…" She broke off her question.

"Thoria? But I was just there… I waited at the training fields where we were supposed to meet, but no one was there except…" He paused.

"Except?" she prompted, fear shining in her eyes.

"There was someone there in the middle of the field, but he was alone. I was not close enough to see who it was, but then others came and took him away. But, oh, you won't believe this, someone turned the whole field into flowering vines that only bloom…"

"Mahkai!" she interrupted him sharply. Her bloodshot eyes glared at him under furrowed brows. She was angry, and he wasn't sure why.

"How could you talk about flowers and vines when I just told you many of our family are dead?" She ground out. "Maleek is dead. As in never coming back, dead. Real dead, not pretend like in the stupid war games. What is wrong with you?" She snarled at him and withdrew to a few steps away.

Mahkai recoiled from her words and tone as if she had actually hit him. "I… I…did not mean…that is, I did not intend to…" His face burned with embarrassment from her rebuke and the implication that he was not taking this seriously.

He didn't know how to process what she had just told him, so he focused on what he could—the vines and flowers. But she clearly did not understand and thought he did not care.

He blew out a breath of frustration. She didn't give him time to find the right words to help her understand. She stormed back toward the main hut and disappeared inside.

He felt raw, like he had been scraped out from the inside and there was nothing left but an empty, hollow shell. He did not feel like being around anyone. Questions flared in his mind in a jumble, but he could not sort them out. It didn't feel real, and yet it felt familiar. He had felt this way just last night with the vines.

He must have arrived not long after the battle ended. Why had there only been one person left? Where did everyone else go? Unless... Surely one person was not strong enough to slay or bury all of the warriors? All of them? Only the Masters on the Council were rumored to be that powerful. Powerful enough to turn an entire field into a tangled mass of vines in mere moments?

Mahkai wandered aimlessly as his mind worked through everything. His fingers picked at the hem of his rumpled vest like if he could just find the right thread, he could unravel the knot of thoughts in his mind also.

He found himself standing before Maleek's hut with a simple, unadorned door with more than its fair share of dents and chips in it that he knew almost as well as his own. He hesitated, then opened it and stepped inside.

His breath caught in his throat. A book lay open on the table. The book Mahkai had lent him. Though Maleek had claimed rather loudly he would never read it, he had taken it anyway. Mahkai remained in the entryway and took everything in. It looked like Maleek had momentarily stepped out and would return at any moment.

Mahkai sat down heavily at the table. His strong, brave, courageous brother, whom he had looked up to even if they did not always agree...was gone. He buried his head in his hands. He didn't know how long he'd sat there when he heard hoof-steps outside the hut.

For a moment, his heart leaped with the impossible hope that Maleek had somehow avoided the battle, that it had all been a misunderstanding and no one had died.

Mort burst in. And froze.

"You. I thought..." His shoulders sagged and his hopeful expression fell from his face.

"I thought the same when..." His voice was rough with

emotion. He cleared his throat. "…when I heard your approach." Mahkai felt his own desperate flame of hope flicker, then snuff out.

"I mean, I am glad you are alive." Mort rubbed the back of his neck. "I just hoped…"

"You heard someone in here and hoped I was him… That he had escaped…or…or…or not been there, like Kamea." Mahkai finished for him.

Mort nodded. The pained expression on his face relaxed slightly.

Unsure what else to say, Mahkai blurted out, "Would you like some tea?"

Mort blinked and started to shake his head, but then stopped. "Actually, yeah. That would be great." He sat down across from Mahkai by the cold fireplace and held out his hand toward it. After a moment, a small spark leapt from his hand toward the waiting firewood.

Mahkai pulled out his pot from his satchel and filled it with water from the rain barrel and placed it on the cooking grate Maleek kept over the fire for cooking late night snacks. They sat in silence, watching the fire dance to a silent tune.

Once the water was ready, he pulled out his cup and found one of Maleek's. He added mint, lavender, and a few other flowers he knew would be soothing, to the hot water and counted down in his head until it was ready.

Mort remained silent throughout all of it, but he pulled out another cup and placed it across from them in Maleek's favorite spot, as if he were running late and would be there shortly.

Mahkai pulled out one of his pouches with flowers he had gathered to make tea with later and selected a white chrysanthemum. He placed it in the mug and filled it with hot water, the same as he had his and Mort's cups. It floated to the top.

Gradually it opened, releasing its earthy aroma into the room. His throat constricted, and he fought a fresh wave of tears.

Mort nodded his thanks when Mahkai handed him his cup of warm, fragrant liquid. They sat staring into their respective cups; the air felt heavy with emotion and unspoken words. When Mort finished his tea, he set his cup upside down next to Maleek's and placed a hand on Mahkai's shoulder. Then, without another word, he exited, leaving Mahkai alone with his thoughts.

Mahkai finished the rest of the pot, cleaned the cups, and put them away. Except Maleek's. He left it where it was and tucked Maleek's book into his bag. He would never be able to look at it the same again, but it was something of his brother he could hold onto—as if reading the same words his brother had would keep him close.

The sun was just setting as he peeked out the door. Even the colors in the sky felt less brilliant, muted somehow, as if they too felt the loss. He still did not feel like speaking to anyone. He missed Gwen, Hartley, and his treehouse, acutely aware this was no longer his home.

Home. When had he started calling his treehouse home and not here with his clan? He'd never felt so alone before. He took one last look around the hut, then slipped out and shuffled quickly to the edge of the forest and headed home.

☕ ☕ ☕

Mahkai stood in the center of his tree home, surrounded by the familiar smells and items he had been amassing over his relatively short life. A feeling he had been trying to name throughout the night as he traveled back home rose to the surface.

Lost.

He felt lost, aimless, drifting in a void of thoughts and feelings threatening to overwhelm him.

His gaze found the tea cups and pot he used exclusively at home sitting on the ledge above his small fireplace. They were fragile and did not transport well. They looked a bit dirty and stained, so he removed them from their shelf. He cleared a place on his table and filled a small bucket with soap and water. Retrieving his cleaning rag, he began furiously scrubbing at the stains as he let his mind drift.

He did not know where to even begin to process the last day. Had it only been a day? It felt so much longer. He had stood before Maleek's killer and had not even known it. Who was this Bacia? This death-bringer, aptly named?

His brother, sisters, cousins, uncles and aunts, clan members…they were gone. Dead. Killed in battle. He snorted bitterly. All for the sake of glory? He hated that word. There was no glory to be found here. Only death and pain.

He scrubbed harder at the stubborn stains in his cup. *How could they do this? What were they thinking? Fighting was not the way to bring about change, not when negotiations were still possible. Why couldn't they see that?* He knew they had been taught, same as him, of the time when magic was stronger, when a great war tore apart the land to its foundations, forcing a truce lest it threaten everyone's survival.

Had history taught them nothing? What did they have to show for it other than a broken, hurting people in pain from the loss? Robbed of a potential future. Each of the lives, minotaur and fae alike, lost. They would never know what each of those individuals would have accomplished. They would never hear their brethren sing under the full moon or see their lopsided grin as they delivered the punchline to a terribly-not-funny pun or joke.

The cup in Mahkai's hands blurred as tears tracked unbidden

down his face and dripped, mixing with the soapy water. He was so lost in his thoughts, he didn't hear Hartley come in until she placed a hand on his arm.

"Mahkai, I heard what happened. We came as soon as we could." Gwen hooted at him sadly in agreement.

He looked into her eyes. "Hartley, they are…gone." It was all he could manage to get out.

Gently, she took the teacup from his hands and set it down in the bucket of water, then pulled him down onto the cushions on the floor. She draped a soft blanket around his shoulders and set a cup of water within his reach, but not close enough he would knock it over should he get up. Then she brought another cushion and sat with her legs crossed in front of him.

"What do you need?" she asked quietly after she got settled.

"I…don't know." He stared at the smooth floor in the small space between their cushions like it had all the answers.

"Then we will figure it out together," she said in her matter-of-fact way and nodded sharply.

He felt like crying, but the tears refused to fall anymore. After a few minutes of silence, Hartley shifted, stretching out one of her legs. She must have lost the feeling in them.

She drummed her fingers on her knee for a moment, then looked at him thoughtfully. "Tell me about something. Teach me something."

"Like what?" he asked dejectedly.

"What goes into a soothing tea?"

Mahkai didn't need to think. The ingredients flooded his mind and were on his tongue before he even realized he was listing them. "Mint, lavender, chamomile, jasmine…"

"What happens if I mix citrus, cream, and honey in my tea?" she interrupted before he finished.

He looked up at her abruptly. "Don't do that? No, no, that would not be good at all. Why, the cream would—" he paused.

Her eyes sparkled as it dawned on him what she was doing. His heart warmed, chasing some of the sorrow threatening to drown him away. He tried to smile, but failed miserably.

"Ah. Thank you. You are…most kind." He exhaled deeply. "I appreciate you more than I say. I hope you know that. You mean the world to me." He said it quickly, before he lost his nerve. He was not used to expressing his feelings because his tribe did not do sentimentalities. This was yet another way he was different from them, he supposed bitterly.

Hartley blushed a little, then grinned. "Yeah, well, you listen to me and entertain my crazy ideas. Oh, that reminds me, I had an idea for getting heavy objects, like furniture, into the tree."

She chattered about a string of things, not expecting him to answer and letting him engage when he wanted to. She organized some of her sketches on her tiny drawing table she used to draft designs when she visited, which was more often than not. She set a stack of books next to him without a word. He picked them up to find a random assortment of his notebooks and books from his favorite storyteller. Slipped in the middle of the stack was a new one he had not read before.

He opened the book and inhaled deeply the smells of leather, parchment, and ink. It smelled like magic, if magic had a smell. Gwen stirred from her sleep, ruffling her wings and preening her feathers. She climbed down and hopped over to sit on his shoulder, looking expectantly at the book in his hands.

The smell of tea permeated the room as Hartley added tea leaves and flower petals to the hot water. She brought him his favorite tea bowl filled with steaming, amber liquid that smelled of honeysuckle and honey. She had even added a little alfalfa sprig. His eyes welled again, threatening to spill over as he sipped on his tea.

She brought one of her drafting books and charcoal over

and sat with her back against his side. She tucked her knees up close to her chest, balancing her book on her knees, and wordlessly began to draw, sipping occasionally from her own mug.

He turned to the first page and allowed himself to be pulled in, immersed in the imaginary world of the tale contained within the pages of this gift from his best friend. Gratitude and comfort seeped into him like hot tea warming him from the inside out—surrounded by good company, delicious tea, and his books.

🍵 🍵 🍵

Mahkai hefted his double-headed battle axe and swung it repeatedly through the practice forms and patterns he had been doing since he was a small calf. His back and arms burned with exhaustion and his legs trembled from the effort of keeping his footing in the muddy pit that had developed from his daily training for the last few weeks. He had traded his normal attire for simple pants, now splattered with mud and drenched with sweat, but he didn't care. With a last swing, he finished the form and trudged over to the lean-to he had constructed against a tree on the edge of the training field they were now calling Alinorr.

He dropped his weapon with a huff and sat down next to the little campfire he'd lit to keep the mid autumn cold at bay. If Hartley saw him like this, she would scold him.

He took a long drink from his canteen and dumped a little on his head. Muddy water trickled down his face and he shook, sending mud flying everywhere.

The fire hissed and popped from the droplets. His skin shivered from the cold, but he didn't care. He deserved this. He didn't deserve to be clean. Minotaur didn't need to bathe. They didn't sleep in trees and they definitely didn't drink tea.

Mahkai was trying to be as minotaurly as possible. He had been wearing muddy clothes, sleeping on the ground, and not bathing. He'd stopped carrying around his satchel and notebooks, and he couldn't even remember when his last cup of tea was. All he spent his time doing was practicing his weapons forms like a good minotaur.

He had spent the last few weeks here, forcing himself to feel the pain and sorrow every time the wind blew. No one else dared to come near this field now.

If his father could see him now... Only, he couldn't face his father. Guilt and anguish burned anew in his chest. Instead of pushing those feelings away, he embraced it and channeled it into his anger, forcing his tired body through another set of fighting poses and forms.

"Mahkai! What are you doing?" Bree's voice barked harshly at him.

He didn't stop. He'd show her how strong and capable he could be. He swung harder and faster, his axe no more than a dark blur until his grip slipped, slick with mud and sweat. His axe went flying. Unbalanced by the sudden loss of weight, he tumbled to the ground in a heap.

"Oh, honey." Her voice had lost its reproach. She laid her small hand on his matted and muddy shoulder and patted him soothingly. Gwen hooted at him mournfully from her shoulder.

"What are you doing here?" Mahkai muttered sullenly.

"Hartley said you were in a bad way, so I came to check on you. I think she understated it a bit. We haven't seen you for quite a while and we are all worried about you."

"I killed them," Mahkai whispered, not daring to look at her. "It's all my fault."

"It is not your fault. Mahkai, sweetheart, come home."

"I can't face anyone, especially not..." He had intentionally avoided thinking about Cael. There was no way he would look at Mahkai the same ever again, not with what he had done.

"Can't face who? Me? I am here now," Bree soothed.

"Cael." The name felt wrenched from his chest. There, he'd said it. "I can't face Cael. I know he is, at minimum, angry with me. How could he ever forgive me? I know he must be…or… or…or he would've come here already."

Silence stretched between them for so long Mahkai finally looked up at Bree. He expected to see irritation, surprise, anger even, but that was not what was written on her face. Tears welled in her eyes, and she fought them fiercely until they spilled over and dripped down her chin. Her shoulders shook. Deep sorrow shone out of her eyes as she held his gaze. And then he knew.

No. Not Cael.

He didn't know he could feel worse than he already did. The world spun and blackened on the edges of his vision as dread and horror shuddered through him. He felt like he'd been kicked in the chest. If he hadn't already been on the ground, his legs would have given out.

The only thought running through his mind was that this was all his fault. Cael was…was… He couldn't even think it. If he hadn't said anything to his brother about Hartley's project that day at camp, they wouldn't have tried to take Thoria… This was all his fault.

He didn't know how long he lay there, but at some point, Bree sat down next to him. Occasionally, Gwen ruffled her feathers but was otherwise quiet as well. The sun had begun to set before Bree moved again. Wordlessly, she rose and took his hand. He let her tug him to his knees, then stood. She tugged gently on his hand, so he followed, his body on autopilot. His mind taunted him with images of the last time he had spoken with Cael and their planned conversation over tea they would now never get.

What had he done? He'd heard from Hartley that the Fae Council had banished the figure he'd met here—a captain and the son of the newest member of the council as it turned out. The Bacia. *They should call me Bacia too, for my part in it. The Council should banish me too. This was as much my fault as the captain they exiled,* he thought bitterly.

He resolved to turn himself in. Maybe Bree would help him get there. But maybe they would think she shared in the blame too. *No.* He shook his head. He couldn't do that. Everyone probably would be relieved when he was gone, anyway.

She led him to the edge of the field and stared out at the twisting mass of tangled vines and grasses. The fading light painted everything in golden hues as it slipped unceremoniously below the horizon, like it did every night. She sat on her knees and folded her hands in her lap. A bee landed on her hand and crawled unhurriedly over the back of it. She raised her hand to watch its silent golden dance to music only it could hear.

It was mesmerizing, and he found the longer he watched, the more he felt the pull of exhaustion tugging him down to the ground next to her.

He didn't remember falling asleep, but he awoke to the scent of flowers he had only smelled once before. Tonight must be the full moon. Sitting up, he rubbed sleep from his eyes and was greeted by the familiar field of moonlit flowers he'd named Belinay after the reflection of the moon on the lake.

Bree handed him a smooth wooden bowl of warm, sweet-smelling floral tea. She sipped on her own cup while she watched the flowers nod in the night breeze. He stared down into the liquid like it held all the answers, but didn't drink. He didn't deserve this.

"I am going to tell you something someone wise once told me," Bree said. "I know you are not ok. And you don't have to be—nor do you have to be ok anytime soon. But I promise you that you will be eventually. It will take time and that is ok. Let it take as long as you need it to. The world might feel like it has ended, but one day, you will wake up and things will feel a little less terrible. And you will find you are ready to be a part of it once again." She tipped her cup back and finished the last of her tea, then took his chin in her hands, forcing him to look her in the eye.

"Drink your tea, Mahkai. We will be here for you when you are ready. Always." She patted his cheek once more and gave him a gentle smile, then shuffled back into the forest.

He sat unmoving long after his tea had grown cold, letting her words sink in. A bee buzzed around him, then landed on his shoulder. A few moments later, Gwen hopped over to him and nestled in the leaves beside him. She bumped him with her beak once and gazed at him like she had the first time they met. He took a deep breath and let it out slowly, feeling something loosen in his chest, then drank his tea.

Honeysuckle Tea

Honeysuckle Blossoms
Jasmine
Alfalfa Sprig for garnish

It's the simple comforts...
                    -Mahkai

Chapter 20

A month later, Mahkai stood in the middle of the main room in his treehouse surrounded by puddles of water, bits of soggy wood pulp, and thistle fluff.

"Uh, hey, Mahkai." Hartley's voice shattered the silence of the treehouse. "Whatcha doing? What is all this?"

"Hartley, my apologies for the state of things. It seems to have, erm…gotten a bit out of hand. You see, I was attempting to follow my aunt's recipe to make my own paper, so I wouldn't need to buy or trade for it anymore. But, well…you see how it is going." He gave her a sheepish, lopsided smile.

"You know, there are fairies who have spent their entire lives perfecting the art of making paper and parchment. What is wrong with getting it from them?" Hartley laughed at the exasperated look he gave her.

"I was curious to see if I could."

"And can you?"

"Yes." He nodded affirmatively.

She raised an eyebrow at him.

"Yes, I can make it, but it is very time consuming without the aid of the appropriate magics…and very messy." His shoulders slumped as he surveyed the mess around him. "But you are also correct. I will be acquiring paper and binding materials from someone else for the foreseeable future."

Hartley's expression softened. "I didn't mean to imply you could not do it. You are capable of so very many things. It just looked like a tree had an outburst in here."

Mahkai spun to face her again. "Wait, you mean they do that?"

Hartley laughed again. "Of course. Some of them are quite feisty and opinionated. Most don't know to listen and those that do, don't." She shrugged. "Do you want some help cleaning up?"

"Oh yes, if you would be so kind."

He watched in awe as she held her arms out and a silvery green light shimmered in her tiny, upturned palms. It never got old seeing her connection to her magic and the plants and trees. The bits of bark and wood pulp strewn around the room floated toward her and piled themselves at her feet. She reached down and stroked the pile gently, then looked back up at him with a mischievous glint in her eyes.

"What does the look mean? What are you planning, Hartley?"

"Mmm, nothing much." She tried and failed to suppress a grin.

Mahkai pursed his lips in thought and chewed on the end of the brush he was still holding. He still needed to clean up the water spilled all over the floor and work table.

"What? Don't give me that look."

"What look?"

"The look that you give me sometimes when you question my sanity."

Mahkai sputtered, "I do *not* question your sanity. I believe you to be quite sane." He paused. "Well, for the most part, anyway. You do choose to spend the better part of your free time with me, so you must be at least a little insane. But other than that…" He waved his hand.

She grinned and reached for his hand, giving it a squeeze. "I think you will like it. I just need to sort some things out, and I don't want to get your hopes up if I can't manage it."

"Manage what?"

She winked at him. "Now that would be telling."

Mahkai huffed, then chuckled. "Alright. Any ideas on how to clean up all the water?"

"Way ahead of you." Hartley's hands glowed silvery green again and the bits of bark swirled around the floor, soaking up the water, then flowed to the open door.

When they had finished cleaning up Mahkai's colossal mess, he put the kettle full of fresh water on the grate above the fire for tea. He was mulling over what kind of tea he wanted.

"I know that look. What are you thinking?" Hartley fluttered over to him and landed on his shoulders, her legs dangling on either side of his neck.

"Well, I was just thinking about what one of the shopkeepers said to me about naming my teas the day we met in the market. What do you think?" He tilted his head slightly to nudge her leg with his ear.

"What do I think about what?"

"Naming my teas. Will you help me? I have a few ideas, but I would be open to your suggestions."

"I think naming them is a great idea and all, but where is this coming from?" The kettle whistled, so she launched herself backwards off his shoulders and zipped over to remove it from the fire.

He fiddled with the jar in his hands nervously. "Well, I was thinking of asking Bree if she would stock some of my teas or serve them to her patrons at the inn." Hartley was silent for a few moments. When he summoned the courage to look at her, she was grinning from ear to ear.

"Mahkai, I think that's a great idea! I know Bree will love it! Your teas are amazing, and I'm not just saying that because I am your friend. You have so many, and you haven't even worked out half the teas in your Aunt's journal."

Mahkai sighed and gave her a pained look. "Don't remind me."

"No, silly. That is a good thing. It gives you something to work on. You'll never be bored." She smirked at him. Her eyes again held that mischievous look she got sometimes. She brought over the steaming kettle and set it down next to him.

"What would you like today? I can't decide."

"Let's try a new one while we start coming up with names. Maybe something with vanilla."

Mahkai flipped open his aunt's journal and one of his own and flipped through the pages until he found one he hadn't tried yet. He ran his finger down the list of ingredients: blood orange, blue cornflower, ginger, hibiscus petals, orange peel, rooibos, rosehips, turmeric, vanilla.

Perfect. This one sounded nice from the ingredients. He rummaged around his nook until he found the various jars and bowls he needed. Looking again at the recipe, he grumbled in dismay. His aunt had not written down measurements. How was he supposed to know how much of something to add? She used words like a "pinch" of this and a "smidge" of that.

"What is it?" Hartley asked in concern.

"Oh, just that my aunt apparently didn't believe in writing down specific amounts of each element," he huffed and pointed to the page. "See? How am I supposed to know how much a dash of turmeric is?!"

She giggled at his antics until tears escaped the corners of her eyes and she wiped them away.

"What? It's not that funny, is it?" he huffed.

"It is a little. Trust your instincts, Mahkai. You've used all these ingredients before. You will figure it out, and if you get it wrong, then we'll keep trying 'til you get it right." She placed his spectacles on the bridge of his nose and hummed. "I guess I'll just have to drink all your experiments… Whatever will I do?" she said dramatically and winked at him.

206 | ADRIENNE HIATT

Feeling better, he turned back to the jars set out before him. She was right—it was kind of funny. One by one, he added the ingredients into a bowl. Some, like ginger root and tumeric, he knew were rather potent, so he only added a small amount. Others, like the blue corn and hibiscus, he knew from previous blends to add a little more.

He carefully wrote down how much he used of each ingredient in his notes. Once he was fairly happy with it, he gently mixed it together. It was very colorful and aromatic already. He couldn't wait to try it.

"That looks very pretty," Hartley said as she watched him pour it into the teakettle.

He nodded and bit his lip. His aunt's notes only said "steep." He let out a frustrated huff. "You would think she could have written down how long to steep it for. Longer? Shorter?"

Hartley laughed and shook her head. "That would be too easy. Can't have that," she said dryly. "Oh, c'mon. Where is your sense of adventure? If she gave you all the answers, it would be no fun." She wagged her eyebrows at him when he frowned at her, which made him laugh.

"I suppose you are right," he said, grinning back at her. She nudged his shoulder with her own tiny one.

"So, any thoughts on what to call this one?" She retrieved a pair of tiny cups decorated with twisting vines and delicate leaves and set them next to him.

"What are those?" he asked, confused. "What is wrong with our normal cups?"

"These are tasting cups. They are much smaller than your normal gargantuan bowl. So you can try it plain or with honey or cream or lemon without having to drink half the lake in the process." She looked quite proud of herself.

"You're brilliant, absolutely brilliant." He kissed the air next to her cheek dramatically.

"Brilliant enough to let me name it?" She gave him a sly look.

He had walked right into that one. He chuckled. "Yes, but I reserve the right of 'last say.' I can reject something too crazy or embarrassing." He strained out the tea mixture.

She gasped and dramatically held a hand to her chest. "Would I do that?"

He raised his eyebrow at her as he poured the first round of tea for them to taste. She giggled and reached for a cup. They sipped the new brew. The flavors exploded on his tongue, mirroring the beautiful colors of the mixture before him. If colors had taste, he imagined it would taste like this.

"You know, I don't think it needs anything. Maybe a dollop of honey, but that would be it," she said thoughtfully after finishing her cup and retrieving her normal mug. "I would like a full cup of that, please. I had every intention of giving you the craziest names, but a tea this lovely deserves a name just as inspired." She tapped her chin thoughtfully with one hand as she cradled her newly filled mug in the other. Her wings quivered and buzzed like they usually did when she was deep in thought.

While she thought of a name, Mahkai filled his own regular mug and stirred in a spoon of honey. He wrote down his own thoughts in his journal, commenting on what he knew the benefits of the individual ingredients were and his guesses as to what they would do together.

He reached for his mug for another sip, but found it empty. Had he finished it already? He didn't remember finishing it. He blinked and realized his charcoal was almost used up, too. Hadn't he just started a new one? He had written half a journal full of notes and thoughts, half of which had nothing to do with tea. He didn't remember doing that.

"Hartley, I…" He looked up at her. She was sitting at her sketching table surrounded by a stack of papers and sketches on one side and a pile of miniature trees, houses, bridges, and numerous other things Mahkai didn't recognize on the other side. "Hartley?"

She blinked at him as if just now remembering he was there. She had smudges of charcoal on her face and hands. "What's up? Oh! When did I do all this?" She surveyed the piles around her.

"I was going to say the same thing," Mahkai said, still baffled.

"I thought of a name!" She waved a piece of paper in the air at him. "I was going to say we should call it Artsi-Tea because of how pretty it is, but now I'm wondering if we should call it Productivi-Tea."

"Did you do anything to the tea?"

"What do you mean?"

"Perhaps when you were drinking it or even as I was mixing it. Did you use your magic, by any chance?"

She frowned and thought about it a moment, then nodded. "I think I did, when you were mixing the ingredients before pouring the water into it. I was thinking about how much I needed to finish for Arlo and how I seem to always run out of time or get distracted by things easily. I think it kinda slipped out." She looked at him sheepishly, then with dawning horror.

"You don't think... Oh." Her crestfallen features at having potentially ruined their experiment pierced straight to his heart. She thought she had done something wrong. He knew that feeling well.

"No, no, Hartley. This is wonderful. Do you know what this means?"

She shook her head, downcast.

"Well, I don't actually know yet either, but this is wonderful. A happy accident, if you will."

She smiled up at him, gratitude written on her face. "I wonder what else we can do."

"I aim to find out. Just maybe not tonight. My mind is tired, and I think we both need rest."

She nodded in agreement and gathered her papers and miniatures together. "I need to take these to Arlo anyway. I think he will be interested to see them. Do you need help cleaning up here?"

"No. I'll just put these few things away and deal with the rest of it tomorrow, I think." He yawned and wrote down a note about the possible after-effects of Productivi-tea.

☕ ☕ ☕

The next day Hartley took him to meet her family. It was an awkward affair, to say the least. Given Hartley's disposition, he figured her family would be very much the same. What it was in reality was rather jarring. They were very formal and nice, but warmth was not a word he would ever associate with them.

Hartley's parents were the picture of perfect hosts. Nothing was out of place and everything was pristine and perfect. Mahkai was impressed and intimidated, which was quite the feat given that her family, like her, were tiny. But that was where the similarities ended. Where Hartley was witty and clever with a penchant towards friendly banter, her family was straight-laced and serious. Where she was amiable, a smile never far from her face, their smiles never reached their eyes. They didn't joke around, and their interactions were clipped and strained at best. Her siblings barely even acknowledged their existence, zipping in to eat in silence and zipping back out again after giving a brief report of their achievements or projects.

Mahkai found himself missing the loud and raucous antics

of his extended family, fighting over food and trading affectionate barbs and laughter. He barely held in his sighs until dinner was over and Hartley whisked him off to her wing of the sprawling home…if you can call it that. Estate might be a better word. Each family member had their own wing, complete with cooking area and living space. They never had to interact if they didn't want to.

Hartley led him through what she explained were her receiving rooms—the rooms where she received her parents if they came to check on her. They were just as pristine and orderly as the rest of the estate. It was a stark contrast to her personal rooms and her workstation in his treehouse. She closed the door with a flick of her hands and slumped into the nearest open space to sit. Vines and branches weaved together to cover the opening they had just passed through, which vanished like it had never been there.

He took in the intricate designs that flowed into each of the walls and ceiling. It was clear she had been practicing in her room to perfect her craft. He marveled at her creativity yet again, daunted by her mind and what she was capable of. He wasn't jealous of her magic, not exactly. He just wished he could do useful or pretty things with his own magic rather than destroying everything.

He cleared his throat, not sure what to say. "Your family seems…erm…nice," he said lamely.

She gave him a pained expression. "That's a word for it." She snorted and slid around in her chair, letting her legs dangle over the arms. "Judgmental, strict, lifeless drones, constricting, restricting, cold, heartless… I could go on and on. Others have, actually. It's fine," she said bitterly.

"Oh, I didn't mean that. I just…" He trailed off. Everything he thought to say would only make it worse. "You know my family is the same, but just...different. They are still judgmental and not accepting of me and my...differences."

They sighed at the same time. The corner of her mouth quirked in a wry smile. "I think that's the hardest part, you know? Family is supposed to be that loving support system, the place you feel safest to be yourself. But it isn't. Not for me—or you, apparently." She waved her hand at him.

He nodded, a strange feeling settling in his chest—wistfulness mixed with relief that someone else understood what he was going through. "Having to constantly hide parts of yourself and mold yourself into what they deem 'appropriate' or 'normal' is so...draining."

Hartley nodded seriously, her brows pinched in a frown. "Every time I feel like I'm making ground with my parents and they might actually be starting to accept me, I get a rude awakening that hurts every bit as much as it did the first time."

"And you never feel good enough for your family, but still find yourself wanting that acceptance and affirmation, knowing they will probably never give it to you."

She laughed humorlessly. "You'd think we'd have learned by now that even if we become what they want us to, change everything about ourselves to become someone else, it'll never be enough. All we'll have done is lose ourselves in the process and have nothing to show for it."

They sat in reflective silence for a while before Hartley straightened in her chair and turned to him, her eyes sparkling with a look he knew well. She was scheming something. "Let's go talk to Bree about tea."

Productivi-Tea:

Ginger
Hibiscus
Turmeric
Rooibos
Orange Peel
Rosehips
Blue Cornflower
Blood Orange
Vanilla

Will make you hyper-productive for a short time, but you will lose sense of time and all else until the effects wear off.
DO NOT EXCEED 2 CUPS IN A DAY! Will make you lethargic and induce sleep for extended periods of time afterward.
                    -Mahkai

Chapter 21

Mahkai intended to revisit Azar much sooner than now, but Hartley had gone with him to talk to Bree about stocking his tea blends at the inn for her patrons. The last week had flown by with gathering herbs and trying out blends, as well as determining the logistics of selling them. Would they sell just the prepared teas? Would he offer small jars for patrons to take with them and brew the tea at home?

He shook his head to clear the never-ending thoughts swirling in his mind. He needed a break, which was why he was going to see Azar again. That, and to return the scroll he had borrowed last time. He wondered what had come of the copy they gave Master Corsen and Master Althenaea. Did they figure out what it meant? Would it work, whatever it was meant to do?

He sighed and paused under the shade of a large maple tree. Its leaves were a brilliant orange that reminded him of the way the light caught Hartley's hair. He plucked a leaf the size of his palm and tucked it between the pages of his journal. He wished she could have come with him, but he wanted Azar's permission first. Gwen hooted sleepily at him from her spot in his other satchel. He stroked her head affectionately before continuing onward.

The trail was much steeper here. He watched his footing, his tail swishing behind him to help him keep his balance. He wondered what it was like not to have a tail to balance with. How did fairies and humans not fall over all the time?

He consulted his map one more time to make sure he knew

214 | ADRIENNE HIATT

the rest of the way to the peak. He'd sketched it after his last visit. He hadn't felt like visiting the clan, or more specifically his father, since...

He swallowed around the lump that formed in his throat and shoved all thoughts of Alinorr aside. He wouldn't think of that now.

He climbed the final steps to the top, where the obelisk stood. He stopped to rest a hand on it as he caught his breath. He wiped the sweat beading on his brow with the back of his forearm. Other Aerophyte could use their magic to maintain perfect temperatures for all situations, but he didn't have that luxury. And what a luxury that would be.

Huffing, he pulled out his pendant and placed it in the divot. It clicked into place as he rotated it slightly. The hidden alcove slid open like the last time. This time, he knew to press the top of the alcove to release the doorway and steps leading to Azar's labyrinth.

He found Azar in the records halls—the library, he had called it. Azar was staring at a scroll, unmoving except the tip of his black tail that twitched and flicked, not unlike a cat. Mahkai grinned at the thought of comparing this behemoth of an ancient dragon to a pet.

"But your pets cannot level this mountain with a single thought, young scholar." Azar's amused voice feigning irritation broke into his thoughts and mental images. He must have been thinking it fairly loudly.

"My apologies. I meant no disrespect—"

Azar's snort cut off the rest of what he was going to say. "You did well with your first task. I have another if you are so inclined."

Mahkai felt his mind empty from shock. "I...erm... What?"

"I need you to retrieve something for me. It is of great personal significance. Are you willing?"

Gwen chose that moment to poke her head out of his satchel and blink sleepily at the dragon before her. She tooted her customary hello trills and climbed up the strap of the satchel until she was sitting on his shoulder. Her head tilted and bobbed as she surveyed their surroundings.

"In human culture, owls are considered wise. A fitting companion for a scholar and budding librarian," Azar quipped, his deep voice resonating with approval.

Mahkai blushed, unable to speak. Azar continued, "There are archives in the old temples, not much more that ruins now, I expect."

"What are the temples?" Mahkai interrupted.

"Don't concern yourself with them. What they are is not important, for now." He leveled a meaningful look at Mahkai before continuing. "You will find a map in this scroll before you, but there is a very good chance it is incorrect, so tread carefully. You will come to a room of reflection. Pass the test and proceed quickly. Or, if you can, avoid that chamber altogether. Sometimes it lets you. Sometimes not."

"What is the room of reflection?"

"You will see. A word of caution: some things are meant to happen whether we like them or not. Do not meddle in things you do not understand."

Mahkai blinked in confusion. What did that mean? What things? How was he meddling?

"Retrieve but a single item for me. No more, no less. You will find the archives of artifacts, and in them you will find a feather of the purest white, the length of your forearm. It has a blue tip and a silver quill. Bring it to me. And you may have your pick of this collection."

Mahkai sputtered as he tried to process the information. His head hurt and his mind spun with all the possibilities and questions, which led to more questions.

🍵 🍵 🍵

Mahkai found Hartley sitting in the middle of her floor, surrounded by a score of half-finished projects, muttering to herself. She reached for an empty teacup without looking at it then raised it to her lips. Realizing there was no more tea in her cup, she glared at it like it had greatly offended her. She reached for another sitting a little further away. It was also empty. She scowled in turn at the other half dozen empty cups and bowls scattered around her.

"Ah, erm… Hartley, how many cups of tea have you had?"

She startled at his words. "Oh, hey. Not many, just a dozen—"

"A dozen?!"

"—in the last couple hours." Her words tumbled out of her mouth at an alarming rate. She spoke faster than he'd ever heard her speak before.

"Hartley!" He knew he shouldn't chastise her because he was guilty of doing the same on occasion, but that was a lot of tea for anyone. Maybe it was one of the hydrating and soothing blends, he thought. But given the way her eyes were darting everywhere and she was tapping her hands rapidly on her chin, he had a sinking feeling he knew which tea was the culprit. "What blend of tea did you have?"

"Productivi-Tea, of course. This is the best! I get so much done. Mahkai, you can't even imagine what I can accomplish if I drink a steady amount of it. I don't even need to sleep, my mind is doing *all the things*. Here, look. I cleaned the cups, mugs, and teapot, but then I got to thinking about how I could make it better, so I not only cleaned it but I built a better one and reorganized..." She spoke faster and faster, and Mahkai was having trouble keeping up.

"And then I started thinking about this other thing and how I could improve this and then I started working on this other thing…" She gestured to the pile of partially finished odds and ends around her. The wash station was dismantled; her pantry was in pieces scattered across her table and chairs. Her hammock was halfway unraveled and looked like she was in the middle of weaving a different pattern in it.

"Your bed is a mess, where did you sleep?" Mahkai asked, concerned.

"Oh, I didn't. Haven't needed to. I thought you were going to be gone a few days. How was your trip? Can I go with you next time? What did he say?" Her words tumbled out at the speed of hummingbird wings

"Erm…I was gone a few days. Have you not…slept since then?" His concern was rising.

"Days? Oh. Nope." She shook her head and continued to work on the sketch in front of her. "Haven't needed to."

Mahkai smirked and ran his hand down his face to hide his smile. They had been in this position before. The tables could very easily be the other way around and she'd be the one admonishing him for forgetting to eat or sleep. "I have something I need to get for Az and, well, would you want to…" He paused. She looked really busy and he didn't want to take her away from her projects.

"Well, I don't know how long we'll be gone, so, erm…." He shifted with uncertainty. He really wanted her to come, but he was at war with himself. Would she come because she felt obligated to? He shook his head. No. Of all people, Hartley was the least likely to do something out of obligation or just because it was expected.

He let out a strangled breath and decided to ask anyway. He could trust her to make her own decisions. If she wanted to come, then she would. If not, then she wouldn't. He rubbed his chest at the feeling of disappointment and rejection bubbling up in anticipation of her response. Shaking his head, he tried to dislodge the assumption that she wouldn't want to come on his errand for Azar. He hadn't even asked her yet.

She stared at him, waiting for him to finish his question. "W-would you want to come with me?" he stammered before he lost his nerve.

A slow smile grew on her face until she was beaming at him. "You want me to go on an adventure with you? Heck YES!" She leapt into the air and launched herself at him for a hug. When she released him, she zipped around her home, collecting things into a pile before stuffing them into her pack: jars and pouches, both empty and full of seeds and random objects. He helped straighten and organize things while she gathered.

When she was all packed and her rooms more or less put back in order, they began their journey. Hartley fluttered up to sit on his shoulder but couldn't sit still. She flitted from shoulder to shoulder for a while until finally sitting with a leg on either side of his neck and resting her forearms on top of his head. He had been telling her about some of his ideas for new tea blends when he realized she hadn't responded in a while. "Hartley? Hartley." No response. He smiled affectionately at Gwen, who was watching everything with rapt attention from her normal place in his satchel. "I think her tea finally caught up to her." Gwen hooted softly in agreement.

Mahkai continued telling Gwen his ideas for teas and anything else that came to mind. Hartley slept the rest of the day and through the night, not even rousing when he placed her in a makeshift hammock by the fire when he made camp.

Hartley was out cold, still sleeping away when he found the hole to the tunnels he had climbed out of with Gwen a few moons ago. Autumn leaves covered the rim of the hole, and the last of the season's flowers speckled the area. At first, he doubted it was still there and that this was the right place, but just as he was about to leave, steam rose from the opening, curling into the chilly afternoon air.

He debated waiting on Hartley to wake up before entering the tunnels, but just then the wind picked up, reminding him it was at the very least warmer in the tunnels than up here. The sky threatened snow. Come nightfall, they would be grateful for any shelter and warmth they could get.

He marveled at how much the temperature and weather varied over such a short distance. He sighed thinking of the most powerful Aerophytes who could alter the weather to suit their needs. Pushing away those unproductive thoughts, he tied a vine around the straps of his bags and began lowering them into the tunnel. Gwen used her beak to free them by the time Mahkai had climbed down, careful not to drop his sleeping best friend still draped over his shoulders and head. Her quiet snores punctuated the silence every once in a while.

It was quite a bit warmer in the tunnels. The balmy air currents curled around him like a caress, gently tugging at the tasseled end of the sash tied at his waist. He lit the oil lantern and held it aloft, grateful he had thought to bring with him at the last moment.

"Well, shall we?" he asked Gwen after having situated his and Hartley's packs over his shoulder. He appreciated the buckles Hartley insisted were necessary on the straps. It meant he could remove it even when wearing a cloak overtop—or in this case, carrying her sleeping form. Gwen trilled her agreement.

Mahkai followed the map Azar had given him through the tunnels, taking notes as he went until he realized, rather abruptly, that the carvings were a repeating pattern. Were they sigils meant to represent something? Sometimes they just seemed to be decorative swirls, while others almost looked like a blurry scene he couldn't quite make out. What were they? What did they mean? Who put them here? Why?

He stopped to run his hands along the stone for the millionth time, but Gwen tooted at him, urging him onward. He smiled affectionately at her. "Thank you, my friend. I'm glad you are here to keep me on track." She hooted back at him with the sound he learned meant she was happy.

A little while later, the tunnel opened into a cavern larger than the light from his torch reached. A large crevasse cut through the middle of the cavern. The tunnel continued on the other side. The only way Mahkai could see to cross it was a rope bridge that seemed to be rather in disrepair, rickety at best. If Hartley were awake, he assumed it would be fairly simple for her to reinforce the bridge for him to cross, but she was snoring lightly with her cheek pressed to the top of his head. He was fairly sure she was drooling slightly.

Gwen climbed out of the satchel and down his leg 'til she was standing on the cavern floor. She chirruped once, then hopped easily across. Mahkai sighed and tried not to look down as he stepped onto the first board. The going was slow as he tested each hoof step before putting his full weight on the rotting boards. The ropes creaked and groaned under his weight.

He looked up at the other side. He was halfway across. He wondered if crawling would be faster than this. Would the weight distribution be better or worse? He stepped on the next board, forgetting to test it first, distracted by his thoughts on alternate ways to cross the crevasse. With a loud crack, the board gave out. Mahkai's leg plunged downward but he caught himself on the guide ropes. They groaned with his sudden weight, but held fast.

He hauled himself up and continued, redoubling his cautious movements while also trying to move faster. He was not fond of a repeat experience and wasn't sure how long the aged ropes would hold him. As he neared the other side, a strong wind kicked up from below and sent the bridge swaying. The fraying ropes snapped and he was flung into the side of the cliff face. He managed to hold on, his heart beating wildly in his chest, but the rope cut into his palms.

Hartley shifted and began to slip backwards. The only thing keeping her from tumbling into the abyss below was her arm slung around his horn and the strap of his satchel her leg was tucked under. His arms burned. He was barely holding on. He begged his air magic to do something, but nothing happened. Panic seized him. It was all he could do to just breathe. He should have been able to haul himself up, but his body locked up and wasn't responding. He kept imagining them falling to their death. Of all the ways he had thought of, *this* wasn't the way he thought he would go.

Gwen's distressed trills echoed through the cavern. Hartley shifted again, slipping further off his shoulders. He was losing her. Then he heard her take in a sharp breath.

"What the…?" She woke up with a start and launched herself from his shoulders. Her little wings buzzed as she flew above him and stopped near Gwen. "Hold on, Mahkai. I've got you," she called as ropes and vines wound around his arms and chest. He took a shaky breath. Hartley was safe. Gwen was safe. He willed himself to move. Hand over hand, he pulled himself up with the assistance of the vines wrapped around him.

With a mighty huff, he heaved himself over the lip onto the floor of the cavern. The vines held on for a moment longer, then retracted from him. They sat on the edge of the cavern and just breathed.

"What a way to wake up from a nap. How long was I out?" Hartley commented finally. "Maybe we shouldn't drink that much Productivi-tea at a time." She grinned cheekily and nudged his shoulder.

Wordlessly, he wrapped her in a hug and just held her, shaken by how close he had come to losing her, too. She hugged him back and let him take as long as he needed to stop trembling. When he drew back, she met his eyes, and a look of understanding passed between them. She held out her hand and he took it, letting her pull him to his feet.

They continued through the tunnels, Mahkai calling out directions as Hartley flew ahead to scout. She had produced tiny globes filled with bioluminescent moss out of one of her bags. They cast a blue-green light over her, sometimes making her look like a living flame, not unlike the picture from the scroll. The words had barely formed on his lips when he turned a corner to see Hartley floating before a dead end. Or what looked to be a dead end.

Mahkai double checked the map, but it gave no indication of a wall here. The room they were looking for should be right on the other side. He also wondered about the room of reflection, but they must have bypassed it somehow. Admittedly, he was a little disappointed. He would like to have gotten to see and experience it.

Something caught his eye. There was a difference in the pattern on this wall. Some symbols were out of order. He stepped closer and noticed the shapes were on sliding disks rotated around a central point.

He didn't know what they meant, so it felt impossible to know what the right pattern was supposed to be. Still, he had to try. He rotated the first disk around and tried to put it where it felt right. He couldn't explain it.

The other disks seemed to be missing one symbol or another. He pulled out his notes and handed Hartley the torch. Referencing his notes, he found symbols he thought represented the types of magic. He pressed one at random, one that looked like a windswept mountain with a flame at the center, but nothing happened. He pressed another one that looked like water and the disks reverted to their original position. He groaned and blew out a breath of frustration at having to rework the puzzle and try again.

"You've got this," Hartly encouraged softly.

He closed his eyes and tried to relax before opening them and trying again. His next guess was a triangular-ish symbol. After a moment, the door ground down to reveal an opening. Through the doorway, they saw a room full of artifacts and scrolls and drawings piled everywhere.

From what he could initially see, it looked like a jumbled mess, but as they tentatively traversed further in, Mahkai recognized a general organization to things. "Oh! It is categorized loosely by magical affinity." He clapped his hands in delight as he spun in a circle, seeing everything in a new light.

The door behind them ground back up, closing them in. Hartley inspected the stone door. "That's great, but how are we going to get out?" She looked over her shoulder at him.

He frowned in thought. "Let's get the item Azar asked us to, then figure that out?"

"Or you find the item and I'll work on getting us out." She smirked at him. "Whoever finishes first will help the other, though I suspect it might take you a while given the state of this room. What are you looking for, anyway?" She braced her hands on her hips and cocked her head to the side as she studied the mosaic on the back of the stone door.

"Azar described it as a white feather with a blue tip and silver quill. Have you ever seen something that has feathers like that?" he asked thoughtfully.

She shook her head, not taking her attention from the door. Mahkai gently scooped up Gwen and placed her on the nearest table so she could help search.

"Don't touch anything you don't have to," he warned her as

she peered at her reflection in a shiny bronze lamp with strange etchings on it. It sat next to a tiny, clear glass cup that wouldn't hold more than a mouthful. "Azar said to only take the feather." Gwen hopped across the table, nudging things with her beak to look underneath them. Mahkai held his breath, but when nothing happened, he left her to look across the room at a different pile.

If he were to categorize the feather, where would he put it? He wished Cael was here to ask. He would know—would have known. Mahkai felt a familiar stab of pain in his chest before he shoved it down. He needed to concentrate. He couldn't allow his grief to cloud his focus right now; he would deal with it later.

He figured he could rule out water and fire artifacts, even though he was incredibly curious about them. *Focus, Mahkai. Get the feather first, peruse everything else after,* he reminded himself. A feather made most sense to be in the Aerophyte collection. He'd check there first. Except where were the air magic relics? He looked around. There weren't any that he could see. A few scrolls and pages lay on a table between a lava rock, still faintly glowing red, and what looked like a pile of plain black rocks.

He unrolled one of the scrolls and used the rocks to hold it open. It depicted a series of pyramids made from various materials, but no mention of a feather. He removed the stones and let the scroll roll back up. His eyes wandered around the room; his attention landed on an ornate box with the Aerophyte symbol on it. Boxes and other items lay stacked precariously on top of it. At the apex of this pile was a half-full cup of tea. Or was it half empty? He shook his head and chuckled as he set it down on an empty space on one of the tables and continued removing the other items on top of his desired box.

Carefully, he slid it out and opened the simple latch holding it closed. A slight breeze wafted out of the box, smelling of sunshine, lilacs, and the air right after a spring shower. He inhaled deeply, letting his eyes close for a moment as he savored the sweet air. It was a stark contrast to the close, slightly musty air of the chamber.

He peered into the box and, resting in the satin lining, was a pile of multicolored feathers varying in length. They ranged from the length of his fingers to the breadth of his entire hand, their colors spanning from rich browns and bright yellows to deep reds and the blackest of blacks.

He stroked one of them gently, barely even touching it. A tiny arc of blue lightning shocked his finger. He jerked back and lost hold of the box. It crashed to the floor, splintering into pieces. The feathers went skittering in all directions.

One of the feathers ignited and caught the carpet on fire. Several drifted up into the air. The one that had shocked him, causing this incident to begin with, shot bright blue arcs at random objects throughout the room. It was breathtakingly beautiful, in a deadly sort of way, as it drifted lazily on the air currents.

Mahkai was mesmerized. He noticed a pattern in what objects were hit by the deadly blue light. Hastily, he sketched the arcs as best he could and noted what they struck and what they didn't.

"Mahkai, watch out!" Hartley cried, ramming into him.

He didn't move, but her contact had its intended effect. The spell holding his attention broke, and he realized the fire was spreading. Hartley stamped on the carpet embers, trying to put it out.

He found a feather floating in an ever-growing puddle. On a hunch, he picked it up and held it over the flames licking hungrily at the legs of a table laden with very flammable scrolls and papers. They went out at once. The flames seemed to retreat back to their original feather. Mahkai gathered it and the others he could reach, placing them in the satin lining from the destroyed box. He still hadn't found the feather Az described, though.

Hartley stared around the room. "Maybe don't touch anything else." She turned her intense amber gaze at him. "On the bright side, I figured out how to open the door. You just press here on this rectangle with these four runes on them." She demonstrated and the door ground down again like it had when they first arrived.

Some of the lingering smoke in the room cleared, but there seemed to be a concentration of it in the far corner. Mahkai went to investigate and found another feather he had missed. It emitted smoke in little tendrils. He noticed a space oddly absent of the smoke directly next to it. He reached out to touch the space and felt the silky soft edges of another feather. He grasped it, attempting to pick it up along with the smoke feather. Where did these feathers come from? What animals had these kinds of abilities? He'd never seen anything like this before.

He replaced the feathers in the satin with the others and was about to say something to Hartley about it when Gwen hooted in triumph from behind a stack of books and papers.

Careful not to bump into anything, Mahkai made his way around the various piles and artifacts scattered across the room to see what Gwen was so excited about.

Peeking out from under a pile of folded cloth and papers, an ethereal white feather sparkled at him. Gwen nudged the cloth to the side, revealing more of the feather.

Gently so as not to hurt it, he slid the feather out from under the pile and held it up. It was the length of his forearm and almost as long as Hartley was tall. There was something about this feather that was different from the others, like there was more to it, but Mahkai had no idea what that was. He would inspect it more later. Still, the questions nagged at him. What had it come from? Why did Azar need it? Why was it here? How did it get here?

All that mattered now was that they had found it. Reverently, he placed it in his largest satchel. It stuck out a bit, but that couldn't be helped. He desperately wanted nothing more than to catalog everything in the room and learn their secrets. But, afraid of setting something else on fire, he made his way slowly toward the door. He hoped he could come back sometime and explore more. The other feathers alone were intriguing.

His gaze longingly swept the room one last time, taking in things he'd missed on first glance. A single earring with a red stone set above a green teardrop rested on a set of shelves. Next to it was a golden ring with delicate flowing script encircling the band, which glowed with a ruddy hue. A shimmery cloak hung on a hook next to an ancient-looking set of armor from before the great war. No one had used armor like that since then. He hadn't realized there were still any in existence. Leaning up against the wall was a set of weapons, most notably a great sword with a blackened burnish handle and two wolf heads for the pommel. It looked like something Maleek would have really liked.

Mahkai sighed and held out his hand for Gwen to hop on. She was back on the table next to the oil lamp, admiring her distorted reflection. He turned toward the door, accidentally brushing the tiny glass on the edge of the table. Mahkai watched as it tumbled to the floor, as if in slow motion. It missed the carpet and hit the stone. It exploded with tiny projectiles in every direction. He dove back to get away from the blast, but still felt several stings in his fur. Hartley cried out from behind him and zipped toward the closest cover. Projectiles bounced and ricocheted off objects around the room.

When everything settled, Hartley peeked out from behind

a large stack of books, now with a smattering of tiny holes in them. No sooner had he released a breath than he saw another object teetering on the edge of a shelf high above her head. A solid diamond bracelet sparkled in the light as it tipped off the shelf and fell to the table below.

It bounced off a stack of books and, rather than shattering like he expected, it duplicated itself, sending a second bracelet careening away in a different direction. He watched in horror as every time it ricocheted off of something, it duplicated again.

"Time to go!" he shouted, grabbing Hartley and sprinting toward the door. He punched the tile Hartley had shown them earlier as the room filled with the clinking sound of duplicating jewelry.

The door ground open and he didn't look back to see if it closed behind them as he sprinted down the corridor. After a few minutes, he slowed his pace to catch his breath. His chest heaved and his legs shook with the exertion. He'd released Hartley at some point in their flight from the room—the "Room of Doom," as he called it in his head. He leaned against the wall and slid down to sit.

"Buried in a secret tomb of artifacts isn't the worst way to go, I suppose," Hartley huffed next to him, attempting to catch her own breath.

He nodded and chuckled with her as Gwen ruffled her feathers indignantly and began preening. "Better than falling into the abyss, though I don't think Gwen agrees with you." She glared at him with her giant goldenrod eyes and ruffled her feathers indignantly. He nudged her gently, then stroked the feathers along her back to soothe her.

"Can I see it?" Hartley asked, bringing the lantern closer.

Mahkai held the feather up in the light. The quill looked like liquid silver rather than something solid. It shimmered and sparked in the light, seeming lit from within, the blue tips casting a bluish tint on the white.

Hartley touched the edge of it. "It's not a feather, not exactly. What is it?" she asked reverently.

He shook his head. He had no idea. It was unlike anything he knew of. He couldn't put it into words, but something about it called to him. He felt drawn to it like nothing he had experienced before.

A cool breeze swirled around them, tugging at their clothing and the feather. Afraid he would drop it, he placed it back into his bag. They continued down the corridor with Hartley in the lead while he attempted to take notes in the dim light. He didn't want to forget anything.

Mahkai stumbled on a loose stone, sending him sprawling on the tunnel floor. Papers, books, charcoal sticks, and tiny jars and vials scattered in every direction. The side of his satchel finally gave out from the stress put on it; his previous attempts at mending it unable to withstand his tumble.

Gwen voiced her indignation at being unceremoniously dumped out as well, chittering at him and fluffing her feathers. Mahkai's palms stung from scraping them on the rough floor. Even his spectacles had gone flying, but thanks to Hartley's ingenuity and foresight of his penchant for falling, they dangled from his collar by their chain.

Hartley zipped over to him and grasped his hand with her two tiny ones. She tugged, trying to help him up. "Mahkai, are you ok?"

He brushed himself off and began gathering the closest of his belongings into a pile, huffing in frustration at the state of his ruined bag. He nodded wordlessly, trying to ignore his mounting list of aches.

"Here, let me." She took his ruined satchel from him and sat with it in her lap with her legs crossed. A look of deep concentration settled on her face. Silvery-green light glowed around her as she coaxed a seed to sprout and thread its tiny shoots and roots through the ragged edges of the material of his bag, knitting them together. When she finished, she leaned back and let out a satisfied "hmph."

"It is exquisite," he breathed as he inspected her work. The tiny vines had threaded themselves through the material of the entire satchel and become a part of it.

Hartley looked quite pleased with herself. "I've instructed it to feed from the air around you, so you don't need to worry about it getting enough food or moisture unless you leave it in the dark for too many days, but I don't see that being an issue." She smirked. "It should also leave the things you place in it alone, but it wouldn't hurt to check on it every once in a while."

Gwendolin hopped over and inspected it, then climbed in with a happy series of hoots as she nestled into it. Mahkai filled the rest of it with his pile of things. Slowly, he tested it to make sure it wouldn't give way under the weight of it all. It held easily. He grinned at Gwen and then at Hartley.

"I love it. You are brilliant." He kissed the air by her cheek.

She grinned at his praise and blushed a little. "I figured if we can make houses out of trees, why not smaller things?" She touched it again, her fingers flashing green, and tiny flowers with five white petals bloomed across the bag.

"It's perfect," he breathed.

They continued along through the corridors chatting about everything and anything, but after a little while, Mahkai hummed in thought.

"What is it?" Hartley asked.

"We should have reached the chasm by now." He didn't see anything he recognized, but he hadn't exactly been paying attention all the time either.

Hartley looked around them. "I don't see any other tunnels though. Did we miss a turn-off?"

Mahkai furrowed his brow and shook his head. "I don't think so, but maybe. I wasn't completely paying attention." He blushed in embarrassment.

They continued on, not knowing what else to do. He touched the wall to his left, letting his fingers drag along the smooth stone. A warm breeze smelling of jasmine and minerals greeted him, caressing his face. He inhaled deeply, enjoying the change of air as they continued on unhurriedly. It was peaceful down here. He felt more at peace than he could remember, like the weight he'd been carrying was lifted off his shoulders. It reminded him of the strange moonflower, the Belinay, that now grew across Alinorr. He almost wished he could stay here longer, but then thoughts of Azar and his caverns of books came to mind. If he stayed here, he would miss the sun and its warmth, and the bees, and of course, Bree.

He would finish this.

With that thought, as if on cue, a light appeared in the tunnel before them. Gwen trilled and Hartley let out an excited *whoop* and raced ahead. He shuffled along, curious where they were. He was not expecting the tunnel to open out into a mountain ledge not far from the obelisk.

How was that possible?

It took them two and a half days to get to the room of doom. The corners of his mouth twitched into a smile. That name made him smile. No one would believe them, except maybe Bree, but he needed to ask Azar if it was ok to share the existence of such a room, even with Bree.

"Where are we?" Hartley gasped.

Mahkai had forgotten she had never been here before. "That is the obelisk."

"The obelisk, as in *THE* obelisk? As in secret alcove and

secret entrance to an ancient dragon's lair? *That* obelisk?" Hartley babbled.

"I don't know how this is possible." He pulled out one of his smaller maps to show her. "My best guess as to where the room of doom lies is here." He pointed near Ere Vasan in the Cinntire forest.

"Doom room? Nice!" She grinned at him.

"I thought so too." He grinned back, then pointed to a blank space on his map on the other side of Osrealach. We are here."

"Where is the obelisk?" she asked

He shrugged. "I never actually drew it on the map. It isn't on any others I've seen either. I don't know why exactly, but it never felt right."

Hartley seemed to accept it. "So how did we make a two-day journey in a few hours?" Her brows pinched together.

He didn't have an answer because he simply didn't know. "Wanna meet a dragon?" he asked, excitement growing in his chest.

"Do I ever! Do you think it is alright?" she asked, uncertainty lacing her voice.

"Let's go find out." He took her hand, and they made their way up to the passage below the obelisk.

Sereni-Tea

Lemon Verbena
Chamomile
Linden
Anise
Orange Peel

Rooibos
Lemon Balm
Passion Flower
Cinnamon

Calming and comforting when everything around you is less so. Like the eye of a storm.
-Mahkai

Also named for the ship in one of my favorite stories

Hartley!?

What? You said I could name this one, so I did 😏

Chapter 22

A few days later, Mahkai ground cinnamon bark into a fine powder and added it to one of his teas for Bree to test out. Hartley was away, working with other Arborealists to carve out the space adjacent to the Winding Way Inn for their tea nook.

Even though rock and dirt were not her specialty, she was overseeing the whole project. She said she wanted it to be perfect. Mahkai was overwhelmed by it all and was grateful for her help. This was a lot more than he had ever dreamed of doing, and it was a bit intimidating if he were being honest with himself.

"Mahkai!" His father's voice boomed outside his home. "Mahkai, are you in there?"

Mahkai looked out to see his father, his brother Mort, and some of the other Makanui clan warriors gathered around the base of his treehouse. He sighed and set down his measuring spoon. *They could have at least rung the bell rather than shouting, but that would be too logical,* he thought bitterly.

He smiled affectionately at Gwendolin snuggled in her favorite spot in one of his satchels. She didn't stir as he gently stroked the soft feathers on top of her head. "I will be right back," he whispered, not wanting to wake her.

Closing his door softly, he climbed down the rope ladder to the ground. He took a deep breath and squared his shoulders, bracing for another altercation. "What do they want now?" he muttered under his breath.

He was hopefully optimistic they were here for a friendly

visit, but since they called him out rather than climb up to him, he was not setting his expectations very high.

"Father." Mahkai greeted them all with his fist to his chest and a nod. Tension built in his chest and shoulders as he surveyed the grim faces and rigid stances around him. *Definitely not a social call, then.*

"Mahkai. It has come to my attention that it has been a while since you've come home. The clan misses you. Molly asked about you too," his father started.

Mahkai nodded and waited for the rest of what he knew would soon follow.

"It isn't good for you to be out here alone. Especially since…" Father trailed off.

Mahkai resisted the urge to sigh. Father meant in the wake of Alinorr. "I thought there was a peace treaty. Why wouldn't it be safe for me here? And you know very well I prefer solitude." Mahkai tried to soften his tone, but it still came out clipped and irritated.

"It just isn't done. You should be home with us, your clan. It's not proper." He loomed over Mahkai, trying to intimidate him.

"*This* is my home now. I'm not going back with you," Mahkai spat back, refusing to be intimidated.

His father let out a long sigh, his face grave. "*This* isn't your home. You belong with your family."

"Tell me this, Father." He practically snarled the words. "When you look at me, do you see anything except failure?" The weeks of suppressed grief and pain finally burst free of his hold on them and came flooding out. He couldn't stop the words if he wanted to, but he found he didn't want to.

"I'm not like you. I'm not strong or have great battle prowess. I don't enjoy competition or even like to spar or show off.

Like... like..." He found—even now—he couldn't even say his brother's name.

"I am a burden to you and the whole clan. You treat me no differently than an outcast, so you might as well let me become one. I am so very different. No one understands me, not even you, my own father."

"Come along, son. It is time to go home." His father said firmly with an air of finality like he had just concluded a meeting of the elders, ignoring Mahkai's words.

"I'm not going." How could his father still expect him to come with him? What was this entire conversation about? *"This is my home,"* he said resolutely.

"I was afraid you would say that." His father sighed and rubbed a hand down his face. He nodded to the other minotaur.

What does that mean? What are they going to do? Cold dread flooded his veins, effectively dousing the heat of his anger.

Two of them grabbed Mahkai by the arms, pulling him further away from his treehouse.

"What are you doing?" Confusion mixed with fear ran down his back like icy water.

"I didn't want to do this, but you leave me no choice," Father practically growled as fire bloomed in his hands. "You will come home and be with your family. It is only right."

Mahkai struggled against the two holding him. He watched in horror as his father launched two fiery orbs at the base of his home. "No!" The word burned in his throat as if it too were on fire.

His tree exploded with the impact. Dead leaves littering the base of his home caught easily and the flames spread hungrily, licking up the trunk toward the higher branches.

"No. No, no, no." Everything he had been working on was up there. His notes, books, maps, and...Gwen! Mahkai combed the surrounding trees and ground with his eyes, peering into the shadows to see if she had made it out. Panic grew the longer he watched. Still no sign of her. He struggled harder against the bulls holding him, but he was no match for them. They were unyielding as stone. The fire crackled and popped as it spread. Was she trapped? He could not bear to lose her.

He would not.

Thinking quickly, he forced himself to stop struggling and allowed his body to slump, feigning defeat. After a moment, just as he hoped, they relaxed their hold on him. He grabbed the great axe from the one on the right and kicked out at the same time at the other. They cried out in surprise and let go.

He swung the flat of the blade against their temple. It connected with a dull thud and they dropped to the ground, unconscious. The other had just picked himself up off the ground and was charging him as his father turned around to intervene, but Mahkai was not looking to fight them, only to free himself.

He dodged the attack and chucked the great axe at his father to slow him down. Desperation clawed at his chest as he raced up the burning ladder toward his home. He didn't care if he got burned. He had to rescue Gwendolin.

Suddenly, he swayed wildly as one of the ropes snapped. The other caught fire a moment later. Mahkai had moments before he would plummet back down to the ground. Panic spurred him into motion as he climbed faster than he thought possible.

"Mahkai!" His father's cries rang out over the roaring fire, begging him to come down. He ignored him and managed to hook his fingers over the top as the remaining rope snapped.

His arms burned as he hauled himself up. He had no way down, but he would worry about that after he found Gwen. He had to find her.

Not stopping to open his door, he charged through the ornate wooden barrier between him and his companion. Thick smoke roiled around him, making his eyes water and his lungs burn. Where was she?

There. Her frantic hoots came from under one of his shelves. It had collapsed on top of his satchel, trapping her. He yanked it up and shoved it away. She poked her head out of his satchel. He scooped her up, satchel and all, and raced for the door, then tripped. Gwen went tumbling with a squeak and his satchel slid through the remains of the shattered door. She blinked at him through the smoke. He scrambled to regain his footing, but his tunic was snagged on something.

"Go. Fly away. Get out." He shooed her with his hands. He turned, twisted, and yanked on his clothes, desperately trying to free himself. Rather than fly away, Gwen hopped closer and pecked at the hem of his tunic.

The tree groaned and shifted. The overwhelming heat and smoke made his eyes water too much to see how to free himself. All he could think of was getting Gwen out. "Go, Gwen. Please," he cried desperately, his voice choked and hoarse. Why wouldn't she save herself?

He felt the fabric start to give from Gwen's sharp beak. With one last yank, he was free. He scrambled to his knees, scooping up his little owl and cuddling her to his chest protectively.

He crawled to the door with his other hand. His chest heaved as he coughed on the thick smoke. Desperately, he searched for a way down. The nearest trees hadn't caught fire yet, but there was no way he could jump that far.

He could throw Gwendolin, though. If he used his magic to cushion her, she should make it unscathed. Uncertainty warred in his chest. His magic was unpredictable at best. For once, he hoped it would cooperate.

He needed it, too, for Gwen's sake.

Introducing more wind in this fire would be disastrous, but he did not care about himself. He had to get her to safety. He begged his magic with every fiber in his being as he thrust her toward the tree.

His stomach lurched as she arced through the air and began to plummet like a stone toward the ground. Then a gust of wind buffeted her, and her wings opened. She sailed gently over the tree he'd aimed for and kept gliding out of view.

She got away. She was away from the worst of it at least and had a fighting chance.

The air around him swirled in a vortex of hot and cold. The flames raged higher and hotter as the tree groaned beneath him. On impulse, he ran to the edge and jumped, reaching toward the closest tree.

His hand brushed the outer edges of the tree as he plummeted toward the ground. He desperately wished his magic would come to his rescue like he had watched others do all his life. He grabbed onto anything he could, but they didn't hold his weight. At most, they slowed his descent fractionally, but not by much.

The ground rushed to meet him and he clenched his eyes shut and braced for the pain he knew would accompany his impact. Instead, he was met with a face full of soft sand and dirt as a funnel of earth rose to meet him and cushion his fall. He sank deeply into it and sputtered as he clawed his way out. Disoriented, he felt like he was drowning for a moment before a tiny hand grabbed his horn.

He dug upward and emerged into the smoky air. Taking deep, gulping breaths, he brushed the grit from his eyes.

"Mahkai! I'm here." Small, familiar hands held his face. He opened his eyes to Hartley's worried frown. The red and orange light from the fire made her amber skin appear like she was lit from the inside.

"Gwen, is she alright?" he croaked out, his voice hoarse and gravelly.

"Yes, she is fine. A little singed, but fine. I didn't know she could fly. I'm relieved she did, though. Are you ok?" Her eyes searched him for injuries.

He nodded. His throat hurt too much to speak any more. His entire body ached, and he was pretty sure he had burned most of his fur off.

Half submerged in a mound of dirt, he watched as several Aqualite and Arboreal fairies wielded water and dirt to subdue the wild flames. Mahkai freed himself from the rest of the mound of dirt with Hartley's assistance and sat resting with his forearms braced on his knees.

When the fires finally died down, the fairies retreated to the edge of the clearing to observe. Hartley grasped his shoulder. Soot streaked her grim features, dulling her normally bright skin. Her eyes glowed, reflecting the dying embers as she stood quietly next to him.

He sat unmoving for a long time, numbly looking at the smoldering remains of his home. The life he had built—they had built.

Feelings he did not have the energy to detangle fluttered through him like a flock of birds, swirling and chasing one another. What would he do now? Everything he had was in that tree. It was all gone.

His father and the other minotaur trotted toward him. He climbed to his feet slowly, coughing on the smoke still in his lungs. He could not look at his father, so he found a half charred leaf on the ground and stared at it like it was the most fascinating leaf he had ever seen.

Mahkai rocked back and forth. Should he just give up and go back to the clan? To what? Pretending to be someone he wasn't?

No. If his father thought he would go back now, he was mistaken. Did they think they could bully him into submission?

Did they think he would return to the halflife he'd been living, miserable and lonely, just to make everyone else happy? That wasn't living. No. If anything, he was further resolved to follow this path he had started.

"Father." He cut off whatever the chief was about to say. He drew himself up as tall as he could, squared his shoulders, and lifted his chin. "I know you came here thinking to convince me that my place is with the clan, but your endeavors were in vain. In fact, if I had any thoughts of returning, they went up in smoke with all of my belongings."

His father gaped at him and stepped forward. Mahkai held up his hands. They were shaking, but he didn't care. Anger and grief burned through him. He almost lost Gwen, and he had lost his home—the first place he had felt he well and truly belonged.

"You need to leave. Now." He said it with strength he didn't feel. He wrapped his arms around his stomach and turned away so he wouldn't have to see his father's reaction.

Behind him, his father sighed and whispered, "Mahkai."

"Just go." Mahkai didn't look at him. Couldn't.

"Mahkai…I'm…sorry."

Hoofsteps retreated, and Mahkai was alone. His shoulders sagged as he turned to gaze forlornly at his former home.

"Are you ok?" Hartley's gentle voice broke into his numbness. "Actually, don't answer that. I know you are not. Would it be weird of me to say I am proud of you?"

He looked at her sharply. She held Gwen in her arms, stroking her head. Her eyes were full of sympathy and care. If he allowed himself, he would dissolve into a puddle and lose what little resolve was keeping him standing. "Why would you say that?" he whispered.

"You stood up to your father, and I know that wasn't easy to do." She paused. "C'mon, Tiny, let's go get you cleaned up and see what Bree has cooking. I know she will want to fret over you. We can come back to sift through everything tomorrow." She held out her hand and waited.

He sighed a deep shuddering sigh and clasped her tiny hand gently with his giant one and walked with her back to the Winding Way Inn.

Quarrel-Tea

Oatstraw
Skullcap
Gingko Leaf
Ashwagandha
Clove

Not completely sure what this one does yet,
besides taste nice.
-Mahkai

oh that's easy. It helps calm raging hot tempers.

no, it doesn't.

I'm pretty sure it does.

and I say it doesn't!

Mahkai?

yes?

I know what it does...

oh... yes... quite right...

Chapter 23

Over the next moon cycles, Mahkai spent his time making more tea, reading books and scrolls with Azar in the caves, and discussing doodles of a new tree with Hartley. Most mornings, he had breakfast in the garden with Bree and Gwen, then ran errands for Bree at the market or explored whatever caught his attention.

"Ah, here we are." Hartley pulled out a small black velvet pouch and dumped the contents in her hand. She held up a handful of seeds and acorns and picked through them until she found five she was looking for, then returned the rest to her pouch.

"What are these?" Mahkai asked hesitantly as she handed him the seeds. What was he supposed to do with them? He rolled them around in his hand and ran a finger over their unique surfaces.

"They are seeds. Soon to be trees, to be exact. I've been experimenting with growing several trees together, so they meld their individual traits into a completely different tree with the strengths of all and reduced weaknesses or drawbacks." She grinned shyly.

"Take, for instance, this one." She picked one up and held it up for a moment before putting it back into his hand. "The redwood. It grows really tall and strong, but on its own has a very weak root system. It needs to be a part of a forest to survive." She grinned at him.

"Or this one, the Japanese maple. It doesn't get very large

and isn't strong enough to hold anything, but it is beautiful and turns a radiant red in the fall."

She picked up another seed. This one looked like it was attached to a little green wing.

"Or this one, the cedar. It smells amazing, but has sticky sap and resin that tastes nasty but is good for sticking stuff together. I'm sure you'd have a bunch of other uses for it, too."

"They all sound lovely," Mahkai said in wonder. "It's so fascinating."

"My idea, if you are open to it, is to grow them together for your new house. I took some liberties on your drawings, if I may show you." She pulled out the large scroll she had tucked under her arm and unrolled it across the large rock Mahkai had been using as a table.

He gasped. She had taken his rough sketch and made it much more detailed, even adding whole other sections.

"Here and here, I think we could make windows." Her small fingers pointed to various places on the tree drawing. "If we use some of the reflecting glass, you could have natural light all day long without needing to light candles and torches or bother anyone for Fae fire."

"And then here, I think you should have a path that wraps all the way around at the top so you can enjoy your view. I think this tree will end up fairly tall. Maybe taller than the rest of the forest. Which brings me to another point." She pulled out a map and spread it out over the treehouse drawings.

"Originally, your first tree was here." She pointed to Cinntire forest on the edge of the Clan lands. "But I think you should consider further south. Here." She pointed to a place on the map where the foothills of Thoria meet the river running to the lake. "The trees are older there and have better root systems to connect with, and you would only be a morning's walk from The Council and a day or so journey to Thoria."

She returned to the treehouse drawing and continued excitedly, noting other features and ideas she had for it.

Tears welled in his eyes, threatening to spill over. He was touched. Not only had she not laughed at his idea, but she embraced it and made it even better.

"It's... I..." Mahkai sputtered, then cleared his throat. "It seems I am at a loss for words. This is splendid, simply splendid."

Hartley's amber skin turned fiery red as she blushed at the compliment. "You think so?" She looked up at him, her large golden eyes wide in question.

Mahkai nodded enthusiastically. Gwendolin poked her head out of her new favorite satchel and made a little whistle-hoot.

Hartley grinned back at him and pulled out her piece of writing charcoal. "I just had an idea. What if we made little cubbies to store your scrolls and books in the ceiling as well as the walls? Gwen could retrieve them for you. Or I could rig a ladder attached to the wall that would glide around where you needed it to reach things when we aren't there to help."

☕ ☕ ☕

Mahkai sat with Hartley leaning against the base of his tree, sketching the area around his home while letting his mind wander. The steam from his tea bowl mixed with the curling vapors of his own breath in the crisp morning air. Bright leaves covered the ground as the weather turned colder. The sun was warm on his fur despite the chilly air, and he knew it would warm up later. This was his favorite season. He loved the cooler air after the hot seasons, loved the harvest of the previous seasons' efforts, loved the crunch of leaves under his hooves. Even the sky seemed vibrant and full of color.

Out of nowhere, the leaves began swirling in a violent

cyclone. Mahkai scrambled to catch stray loose pages before they blew away. A dark shape blocked out the sunlight, casting everything in shadow. Thunder rumbled in the distance.

A pile of boxes, crates, and large cloth sacks dropped to the ground beside him. Startled, he looked up. The dark shape drew closer until Mahkai could see black scales with blue light arcing between them along the reptilian body and enormous wingspan. Azar landed in the clearing, his head snaking left and right, surveying the area.

"Azar, it is good to see you." Mahkai smiled at his friend. It made his heart happy that he could call Azar a friend. Or as close to a friend as anyone could be with an ancient dragon.

"It is good to see you didn't burn." Azar's voice rumbled like thunder. "This new one suits you." He nodded his head slightly at Mahkai's new tree home.

"How did you—"

"Dragons know many things, young scholar." His cerulean blue gaze made Mahkai feel like the dragon could see straight through him.

"What was the not-a-normal-feather for anyway?" Hartley blurted out, looking up at Azar. She was acting like it was no big deal, but Mahkai knew Hartley. This question had her bursting at the seams to know. It was all she had talked about for days. She had spent countless hours laying on the floor in their new treehouse staring up at branches above, guessing at what it was and what Azar needed it for and who the room and all the artifacts belonged to.

Mahkai didn't want to know the answer to the last one. The Room of Doom—they'd nearly not made it out. Someone who had powerful magic enough to protect that room in the tunnels was not someone he would like to know. And if it turned out to be someone he already knew, he'd rather not have to look them in the face and pretend he didn't break in and steal something from their super secret room filled with super secret magical and wondrous items in the super secret tunnels no one even knew existed outside of campfire tales.

Azar didn't seem to notice Hartley was practically vibrating with curiosity and anticipation. He huffed out a breath of warm air. "It belongs to a friend." He went on without pausing, as if he knew both Mahkai and Hartley would pepper him with questions. "I brought some things for you for safekeeping. You have proven yourself worthy, and I am needed elsewhere." He brought his head down level with Mahkai's, his eyes intense as they bore into Mahkai's very soul. "Guard them with your life."

"What—" Mahkai's voice faltered and he cleared his throat. "What are they?" he asked as he peered at the pile of boxes, crates, and sacks beside him.

"They are the only written record of the history of these lands. They are now in your care. I trust you to continue what those who have gone before you have begun."

"Why here?" Mahkai blinked several times, trying to wrap his mind around this.

"The tunnels are no longer stable, and I cannot sustain them for you while I am gone."

"Gone? Where are you going?"

"To visit an old friend." The dragon replied cryptically.

"The same friend the not-really-a-feather belongs to?" Hartley interjected.

"Perhaps."

Mahkai started to ask more, but the sky darkened and black clouds rolled in faster than was normally possible, blotting out the sun. Wind whipped through the trees, tugging at his clothes.

"Wait!" Mahkai cried, afraid that this was goodbye. His chest burned, tears pricked his eyes. "Will we see you again?"

"Perhaps." Azar inclined his head to him then raised it to look at the clouds above him. Mahkai stepped back as Azar's enormous black wings spread as wide as the clearing would allow.

Mahkai prepared to watch Azar spring into the air like a bird or a cat before he took flight. Azar glanced down at him, meeting his eyes, and winked. All of Mahkai's fur stood on end. His heart raced and his hands shook. The air crackled and there was a faint buzzing in his ears.

Azar's body turned into brilliant blue, white, and purple arcs of blinding lightning, then streaked upward into the clouds with a loud crack and rumble. The clouds flashed again.

Mahkai could have sworn he saw the shadow of a massive dragon spreading from horizon to horizon as one last rumble of thunder shook him to his very bones. The storm dissipated as quickly as it had appeared. Mahkai's new home was now lit with the full strength of the harvest sun. His attention was drawn to the pile of things Azar left with him.

What did the inscription say? Mahkai wondered as he retrieved one of his translation books for reference. Painstakingly, he translated the inscriptions on the side of the crates.

"Oh." He let out his breath all at once and sat down right on the ground in surprise.

"What do they say?" Hartley asked, running a hand along the script on the nearest crate.

"It says, 'The Osrealach Chronicles'."

Fru-Tea

Apple
Hibiscus
Carrot
Sea Buckthorn Berries
Goji Berries
Raspberries
Rose Petals
Citron Peel
Pomegranate Petals

This one's for you and the bees, Bree. Sweet and refreshing.

-Mahkai

Chapter 24

Mahkai closed his eyes and reached out his hand, visualizing what he wanted just like he had been instructed all his life. He reached inside himself, feeling for the "something" within that would let him access his magic. He waited. And waited. He blew out a breath of frustration some time later. It did not matter how many times he did this exercise, he simply could not summon his air magic.

He grumbled a very un-bull-like sound and gave up. He would have to do this the long way. Hefting a large crate onto his shoulder, he paused to look up at his newly-grown tree. When Hartley had the brilliant idea to regrow his new home in a tree, he hadn't thought about how he would get all of his belongings up there.

He began the arduous climb up the walkway that spiraled around the trunk all the way to the top. Any other individual graced with air magic would have simply coaxed the wind to transport their load where they needed it. On the bright side, any visitors, wanted or otherwise, would also have to make this trek in order to call on him.

He huffed and puffed when he reached the top balcony and set down the crate. He leaned against the rail—a twisting branch that ran the entire way around his balcony—as he took in the beautiful view. The smooth wood spiraled and twisted in an ornate pattern Hartley had grown it into.

Not for the first time, and certainly not the last, he appreciated the splendor that was his home in Osrealach and the attention to detail his dear friend had given to every piece of it. The sunset drew his gaze. The clouds were painted with bright colors, melding from purple to fuchsia, to amber and gold. He'd never been privy to these brilliant colors when he lived in the clansland. He vowed never to get used to this or take it for granted.

Sighing, Mahkai tore his eyes from the horizon, picked up his crate, and hauled it into his new room. One down, forty-seven more to go.

On his twenty-somethingth trip, he stopped to catch his breath for the not-enough-breath-to-counth time. It occurred to him suddenly that he might be able to use a vine or a rope to raise the crates rather than have to carry each of them by hoof.

Crate forgotten on his ramp, he hurried to his room to retrieve his sketching charcoal and notebook. He was still working on his designs when he heard a yelp.

"What is a crate doing here of all places?" Hartley sounded annoyed. "Mahkai! Are you up there?"

Her round face peeked into view from the hatch to the balcony. "There you are. What are you working on?" she asked as she hefted his abandoned crate beside the opening. She shoved a second one next to it.

"Oh, Hartley! I had a brilliant idea. I think you will like it." He held his breath as he showed her his drawings.

She blinked and was quiet for a few moments as she surveyed the charcoal-covered pieces of paper spread around him on the crates he was using as a table.

He let out his breath when she finally grinned up at him.

"Mahkai, this is brilliant!" Her large golden eyes sparkled up at him in the flickering firelight.

"Rather than place it here on the outside like you've drawn

though, what if we attached it down the middle of the tree? That would solve our other problem as well."

He grinned back at her. "Let's do it."

Tea-riffic

Ginger
Cardamom
Turmeric
Orange Peel
Hibiscus
Clove
Rose Petals
Stevia Leaf
Lavender

That's it! Hartley, you do not get to name any more teas!

You know you love it.

Chapter 25

"Hey, c'mon." Hartley beckoned him from the door.

"What?" He looked up, blinking at her over the top of his spectacles.

She fluttered over to him and gently removed them from his face and placed them in his front chest pocket. Taking his hand in hers, she tugged gently as she moved toward the door. "We are getting out of here and taking a break. You've been at this nonstop for the last few days."

"I took breaks," he protested.

She gave him a look like she knew better. "When was the last time you ate something?"

He thought for a moment. "I had a scone."

"Uh-huh. When?"

"Erm…"

"You mean the scone I brought you yesterday? That scone?"

He blushed. Had it been yesterday? Maybe she was right. "But I need to finish for Bree…" he protested weakly, not really putting up a fight.

"She will understand. Actually, she would be appalled to know you hadn't been taking breaks and getting proper rest. Everything will be fine." She tugged harder at his hand and he let her lead him to the door.

"But what if I need…" he started.

She shoved his satchel into his arms from its hook by the door. Gwen fluttered to his shoulder and hooted her assent.

"What ab—"

"Already in there."

"Bu—"

"In there. Let's go!" She released his hand, flew behind him, and pushed on his shoulder blades toward the door.

He laughed at her antics. She knew he wouldn't budge if he didn't want to, but it made her happy when he let her push him around. "Fine, fine. Where are we going?"

"I'll tell you when we get there." With the flick of her wrist, she closed the door behind them with a decisive click.

He trotted down the ramp, around and around to the ground, and flipped over the sign that indicated whether he was home or not. No one wanted to climb all the way to the top just to find out he wasn't there. They had installed a little bell attached to a string, but Mort had been a little overenthusiastic with it on his last visit and Mahkai kept forgetting to tell Hartley so she could fix it. Actually, he mused, this would be a good time to tell her.

"Ah, Hartley…"

"Mahkai, we have everything we need."

"I was just going to say…"

"If it has to do with anything in that tree, it can wait 'til we get back."

"But wha—"

"Nope, it can wait."

He huffed and conceded to enjoy her presence and whatever this surprise was she was taking him to, letting everything else in his mind rest.

Her eyes sparkled in the evening light as they walked down the familiar mossy path. The stream gurgled in its bed next to the path. Gwen took off to catch moths and whatever else she could find.

Hartley led them to a small clearing overlooking the water of Lake Iria just as the sun was setting. They sat in the soft, lush grass in silent wonder, watching the sun sink into the water's embrace in a splendorous display of colors.

As the light faded, the fireflies flitted about over the grassy bank, blinking their calls to one another like tiny stars in the night sky. He liked to believe they were communicating with each other and wondered what they were saying.

He would need to ask Ca— His chest tightened, and he swallowed around the lump in his throat. He pushed away the overwhelming feelings he had been refusing to acknowledge for weeks. Forcing himself to focus on something else, he wondered if the stars communicated like fireflies in twinkles and flashes.

Hartley lay back in the grass next to him and gazed up at the stars emerging in the sky. He took a slow, deep breath and lay back next to her. She squeezed his hand once and released it.

She pointed a finger lit with her silvery green magic at the stars and traced patterns between them, her magic trailing behind her finger for a breath before it dissolved. It was entrancing. Then he noticed she repeated the same pattern with the same stars. And it hit him. It was a bird with a thick, curved beak.

A raven.

Cael.

And a bright new star where the eye would be. Mahkai's eyes leaked, and for once, he let them. For the short time he had known Cael, he'd made a lasting impact on him. He could almost hear his voice now.

I spent a long time just listening to me, the inner me. My true self...

Block out all the voices and expectations...just listen until you know yourself.

Just listen.

He took a shaky breath as his tears abated. Gwen perched

on a nearby branch, watching over them with her luminescent eyes.

Mint-Tea

Mountain Mint
Spearmint
Peppermint

Hartley!?

It wasn't me. This was Bree's idea. This one is rather tame, actually. You should have heard some of the other ideas the hive came up with. 🐝

Chapter 26

Mahkai stood at the base of his new treehome, feeling like history was repeating itself. He could see his father's glossy black horns swaying back and forth as he ambled toward them. Shoulders hunched, Mahkai froze, waiting for the reprimand he was sure was coming.

"Do you want me to stay?" Hartley's words were quiet, intended only for him.

He shook his head and lifted his gaze to meet hers. Concern clouded her eyes. "Ok. I will be just over there with Gwen if you need us." She inclined her head and turned to go, but turned back to squeeze his hand briefly. "Do not let him bully you. I'm proud of you." Her wings shimmered as she rose into the air and retreated from the approaching bull.

A soft smile played on his lips. He couldn't imagine life without Hartley and Gwen. He didn't want to. He wasn't the same minotaur that had left home at the beginning of harvest so many moons ago. He could not go back, even if he wanted to. The minotaur who sacrificed who he was, his identity, to make others happy had died in that fire, had been dying a little every day since he left home, actually. Every time he learned something new and made a new discovery, every time he made a mistake and tried something else, he became more and more himself. And he liked who he was.

His father stood before him and took a deep breath, letting it out slowly.

Mahkai took a deep breath himself and reached for the

words he had been thinking since the day his father burned down his first tree.

"Hear me out," he started before his father could say the first word. If he didn't get this out, he was afraid he would lose his nerve, and he owed it to himself to tell his father how he truly felt.

"I know I am not who you want me to be. I know you want me to be a warrior, a protector, strong, noble, and tough. But that simply isn't me. Not in the way you want, anyway.

"Tell me this. When you look at me, do you see anything except weakness? I'm not like you. I'm not aggressive, nor do I have great battle prowess. I don't enjoy competition, sparring, or showing off. I am a burden to you and the entire clan.

"Son, that's not... You can't..."

"No? Tell me I am wrong. Tell me that every time you look at me, you aren't counting how much I cost you. How much shame I bring you because I am different."

"Maleek—I mean Mahkai..." he trailed off.

Mahkai looked up sharply as pain lanced through his chest. "You can't even get my name right, you want so badly for me to be him and not me. I know you wish I had been the one lost, not him."

"I want no such thing! What he did was reckless and stupid and it got him killed," Father spat. His hands balled into fists at his sides. His bare, muscled forearms flexed.

"And you blame me."

"No!"

"You should, though. If I hadn't told him..."

"Why would I blame you? I don't blame you, I blame my-self," his father thundered. Anguish and misery twisted his face as he slumped down to sit on a fallen log and buried his head in his hands.

"If-if I had only been here. If I had only spent more time with him and the others, maybe they wouldn't have—"

"You mean if only I hadn't told him where I was going? If only I had kept my mouth shut for once and not said too much? If only I hadn't told him about the council project? If only I hadn't given him reckless ideas?" Mahkai spat bitterly.

"Mahkai, stop! You didn't do this. You didn't make him do any of this… And as much as I want to blame myself, I can only take partial blame. Neither of us made him do anything. I knew he looked up to me. I knew he just wanted to make me proud of him…

"That's the thing, I was proud of him. Very proud. And I am proud of you, too." He looked deep into Mahkai's eyes and gave a slight, pleading smile. "I can't pretend to even begin to understand how your mind works, my brilliant, bewildering boy. My sister, Lani, did. And maybe your mother would have too, but we'll never know."

"I never felt good enough for you. Strong enough, smart enough, good looking enough, successful enough. But…"

Mahkai's eyes found Hartley standing a ways off holding Gwen and stroking her feathers, watching them. The memories of every genuine laugh and smile Mahkai shared with them warmed his heart. His heart ached as he thought of his conversations with Cael about knowing himself. He smiled at Hartley, then straightened his shoulders and lifted his head, looking his father in the eye. Mahkai took a deep breath and continued.

"But I don't have to be. The only one I have to be good enough for is me. And I believe I am good enough. I don't need to wear certain clothes based on the shifting whims of others. I don't have to pretend to be anything I am not. Even if I don't know what that is. I get to be me even when I am not sure who that is some days. And that's ok. I would like to enjoy it. To embrace the journey—no, the adventure—of discovering who I want to be…or don't."

The words kept tumbling out, and he didn't stop them. "And you cannot tell me it is wrong, because I am happy. Genuinely happy, Father. And happiness can't be wrong. I refuse to believe it just because it looks different from your happiness. Playing war games and sparring and challenging each other to see who can best whom with your different weapons makes you happy. Being surrounded by the clan all the time with their lively music and loud antics makes you happy. And that is ok."

His father looked startled, but for once did not interrupt. Emboldened, Mahkai kept going. "Tea and books make me happy. Strolling in the fields or forests, thinking about and drawing whatever I happen upon makes me happy. I love asking questions. I love meeting new people, hearing their stories, and sharing those stories with others.

"I enjoy my days spent in quiet solitude or with just my closest companions. I spent my whole life chasing what everyone else wanted me to be and feeling entirely insufficient. But a friend helped me see, I am good enough for me. I am proud of me. And most of all, I am happy, and I can only hope future me is too." He fidgeted with the tassels on the sash around his waist. He was rambling and beginning to repeat himself.

"What I'm saying is… I've found the love and belonging I think I have always been searching for, here in my treehouse with my books, my tea, and my best friends. I'm not cut out to be a warrior. I'm not cut out to be you. Because I'm not you—and that is ok. Because you are you and I am me, and I can only be the best me I can be…" He trailed off, feeling silly and a bit lightheaded from voicing his thoughts.

He had started pacing at some point, but his father stopped him by wrapping his arms around him. He squeezed him like when he was a tiny calf. "I was going to say, I'm happy you are alive. I thought I'd lost you too…" His voice caught, and he cleared his throat. The sound rumbled through Mahkai.

He pulled back but kept his hands on Mahkai's shoulders, looking him in the eye. "I am so proud of you."

Mahkai blinked in surprise, and tingles ran down his spine, settling as warmth in his chest.

"You were brave that day. You stood up to me. Twice now. You climbed into a burning tree to save your companion. You are pursuing your passions, even if I don't understand them. I won't pretend I understand any of this." He gestured to Mahkai's clothing and his new tree.

"But I do know I cannot ask for more than who you've become. You have taught me many things, Mahkai. And you've reminded me of others I had forgotten. Like the value of keeping an open mind and asking questions. Of compassion and generosity. Seeing the best in someone. Of strength that can only come from gentleness…" He trailed off awkwardly and smiled sheepishly.

Mahkai marveled. He'd never seen his father this vulnerable.

"Oh, I brought you something." His father reached into the pouch on his belt and pulled out a pair of familiar bull statues. "I think she intended for you to have these." He offered them to Mahkai.

Mahkai took them. Shaking his head and chuckling, he glanced over at Hartley. It occurred to him that without these little statues, none of the wonderful adventures he'd had these last few moons would have happened. Thank the stars he let his curiosity get the better of him that day in his father's tent. Without it—and Aunti Lani—he may never have met Hartley and Bree at all.

Hartley smiled warmly back at him and gestured with her

head toward his new tree home. Gwen flapped her wings and hooted at them.

"Would you like some tea?" he asked hesitantly, directing his gaze back to his father.

His father blinked in surprise for a moment, then smiled affectionately.

"Yes, actually. I would."

Warrior's Tea

Yerba Mate	Green Rooibos
Cinnamon	Ginger
Orange	Lemon Grass
Aniseed	Almond
Pineapple	Mango
Papaya	

A tea to steady the mind and invigorate the body before battle or play. Steep for the duration of your meditation.

Is better when shared with loved ones, both old and new.

Add honey, an alfalfa sprig, and a splash of milk for a sweet alternative.

                    -Mahkai

Epilogue

⚔ 15 SolarCycles Later ⚔
(humans call them years)

Mahkai hummed a song stuck in his head as he trotted toward the Winding Way Inn, where he was meeting Hartley to restock their tea blends. He was running late, but then again, when was he not? He chuckled to himself and stroked Gwen's head peeking out of her little nest in his satchel. She hooted softly at him.

The sound of cascading sand and a dull thump caught his attention as a breeze of hot, dry air blasted his face. That was most definitely odd. Approaching the grassy bank of the stream, he spied a dark form rising to their feet. A vortex of sand swirled behind the figure for a moment before disappearing. They were dressed in strange clothes, smelling of what he always imagined a desert to smell like based on the descriptions from Azar's books.

The light caught the color of their eyes as the wind ruffled their hair, revealing rounded ears, and then he knew for certain. "OH! Hello! My, my, my! Can it be...? It is!" His whole body vibrated with excitement and he clapped his hands together. "I can't believe I get to finally meet one! Oh, this is splendid, simply splendid!

"You are human, yes?" Mahkai nodded to himself as he opened the notebook tucked under his arm. "How did you get here? Are you considered average for your race?" He took out a stick of charcoal and began taking notes.

"You see, I have never actually met a human, so as you can imagine, I have lots of questions. I was about to put on some tea. Would you like to come have tea with me? Do humans

268 | ADRIENNE HIATT

drink tea?" He scribbled furiously before closing the book and tucking it back under his arm. "Come, let us have tea, and we can discuss everything."

The End

Bonus Chapter

Howling winds alerted the imprisoned fae that he had a visitor to the black void of his cell. Had it been a whole solarcycle already? Time was a fluid thing when there was no light to tell you when to wake or sleep. He was fed by way of nutrition bricks and a small stream that trickled into a shallow pool in the corner of his cell.

The darkness had driven him mad at first. He used to yell and scream to be let out, desperately hoping someone would hear him, but with time, he accepted that no one could hear him. He was alone in this inky place except for once a solar cycle when his food was replenished.

There had been another, a long time ago, in the place he had been kept before this. They had conspired to escape together, but when the time came, something had gone wrong and only one of them could escape. He chose to stay, and after that they moved him here.

He hoped she had gotten out and made a life for herself. He often wondered what had become of her. He imagined different scenarios to help pass the time and to keep the loneliness at bay.

Sometimes he told stories to the void. He liked to pretend it listened. He told it about a sweet, gentle, brilliant, minotaur who was pure-hearted and too good for this world, even for him. That didn't stop him from wanting him anyway. Did he even remember him?

The wind howled again. Whomever was coming sure was taking their sweet time in doing it. They must be new. Suddenly, the ground bucked and convulsed, heaving under him like waves on the sea. He curled up as small as he could and covered his head with his arm as he listened to rocks crumbling around him, pinging and ringing off something metallic. To his surprise, nothing hit him. What was going on?

The room glowed red as he saw for the first time that he was in a box made of iron. That explained things. The air heated up around him and the metal grew hotter and brighter, changing to amber, then gold, then white. He covered his nose and mouth with what was left of his tunic.

A horrid, wrenching sound made him cover his ears. He squeezed his sensitive eyes closed against the bright light when suddenly, everything stopped. A cool breeze that smelled of saltwater and jasmine caressed him gently, like a long-lost lover. His skin pricked with the sensation. He had long ago given up ever feeling again.

He cracked his eyes open and found himself blinking against a brilliant shaft of light coming from above. As his eyes adjusted, he saw a set of stairs cut into the rocks leading up and out. To freedom. He scrambled away from the twisted, melted remnant of his cage, pausing long enough to grab two bricks of nourishment, enough for a couple of weeks if he rationed them.

Slowly, he climbed his way out of the pit toward the sky above. He rested often, his body unused to prolonged rigorous exercise. He reached the top and lay face up, staring at the wide open sky above him. He had never seen something so beautiful.

And then he wept. After sixteen long solar cycles, Cael was finally free.

Acknowledgements

This book would not be possible without a number of people who poured their soul, sweat, and tears into making Mahkai's story what it is today.

Travis Baldree, thank you for paving the way for the entire cozy fantasy genre with Viv and the rest of the crew in Legends and Lattes. It is truly a special book that touched people's hearts, in just the right way, when we needed it most. My hope is that my story can carry on the same light and comfort for those who need it.

Rebecca Thorne, thank you for letting me participate in your writing class and patiently guiding me through laying the framework that brought Mahkai to the page. And for advocating and supporting the indie author community in the way that you do.

My editor, Sarah Sanders, thank you for taking the raw mess I gave you and painstakingly turning it into the gem it is now. I value your insight and expertise beyond any words I could express here.

My alphas and betas: Kailin, Alex, Missy, Lauren, Brandon, Xander, and Mo. Without you, I would still be lost in the dark, wandering around in the bushes having forgotten what I was supposed to be doing or where I was going. You will always have my deepest love and appreciation. From the bottom of my heart, Thank you.

My artist, Kaylee, thank you for bringing Mahkai to life beyond the page. From the moment I saw the very first sketch of Mahkai, I fell in love with him all over again. You have a special way of making characters so much more than words on a page.

Mom and Dad, thanks for putting up with my sometimes delirious rants while I worked out what story needed to be told.

Gabby, Crab, Addy, and Jeremy, for every late night unhinged conversation, every tear we shed, and laugh we shared, thank you! You mean the world to me, and I'm grateful and honored to get to do this thing we call life together.

Bree, you know what you did.

And to you, dear reader, I wouldn't be here without you. Thank you for taking a chance on a little story about a neurodivergent, bookish minotaur and his friends. I hope you know you are always accepted and welcome here.

Thank you for joining me for tea with a minotaur.

Author Bio

Adrienne is a shield maiden and a scholar whose pen is sharper than her sword. When not writing, she enjoys frolicking in the woods with dragons and fairies, fighting trolls with magic, logic, and witty one-liners. She also enjoys the simpler things in life: a hot cup of tea or coffee and a good book next to the fire.

Made in the USA
Middletown, DE
23 October 2024